WORDHUNTER

WORDHUNTER

A Novel

STELLA SANDS

HARPER

NEW YORK · LONDON · TORONTO · SYDNEY

HARPER

WORDHUNTER. Copyright © 2024 by Stella Sands. All rights reserved. Printed in the United States of America. No part of this book may be used or reproduced in any manner whatsoever without written permission except in the case of brief quotations embodied in critical articles and reviews. For information, address HarperCollins Publishers, 195 Broadway, New York, NY 10007.

HarperCollins books may be purchased for educational, business, or sales promotional use. For information, please email the Special Markets Department at SPsales@harpercollins.com.

FIRST EDITION

Designed by Jen Overstreet and Jamie Lynn Kerner
Hand icon © vladwel/Adobe Stock
Face icon © Gopal/Adobe Stock

Library of Congress Cataloging-in-Publication Data

Names: Sands, Stella, author.
Title: Wordhunter : a novel / Stella Sands.
Description: First edition. | New York, NY: Harper Paperbacks, 2024.
Identifiers: LCCN 2023036408 | ISBN 9780063345300 (trade paperback) | ISBN 9780063345317 (ebook)
Subjects: LCGFT: Detective and mystery fiction. | Novels.
Classification: LCC PS3619.A56557 W67 2024 | DDC 813/.6— dc23/eng/20231103
LC record available at https://lccn.loc.gov/2023036408

ISBN 978-0-06-334530-0 (pbk.)

24 25 26 27 28 LBC 5 4 3 2 1

For Ula Jane and Yabby

WORDHUNTER

PROLOGUE

"Encrypted," Maggie sang syllable by syllable as she skipped past the bald tires strewn across the Tidwells' yard. "Knackered," she exclaimed to the rusted hubcaps dotting the patches of weeds in front of the Martinez home. "Pneumatic," she trilled to oranges hanging heavy on the branches as she bounded to Lucy's house.

Maggie had devised this new word challenge while her mother was droning on and on about grounding her for . . . who knew what this time? She had challenged herself to come up with three nine-letter words with "n" as the second letter. The day before, she had rearranged as many six-letter words as she could into new ones. The day before that, she'd focused on coming up with a five-syllable word for each letter of the alphabet. Word games, tried-and-true escapes.

When Lucy's trailer came into view, Maggie picked up the pace. Every morning, the two best friends strolled together to Jefferson Junior High School, located at the end of a potholed dead-end street in Nowheresville Cypress Havens, Florida, where, the girls agreed, all roads were dead ends. Moseying along with Lucy—giggling, gawking, gossiping—was Maggie's favorite time of day. No one bullied her. No one picked a fight. No one made her feel less than—sneering as they called her "Brainiac Bitch."

As Maggie giant-stepped closer to Lucy's, she slowed, looked all around, then stopped. Lucy wasn't waiting at the curb. Lucy wasn't anywhere. Not a day went by when Lucy wasn't sitting there. Not one. Ever.

Maggie's eyes darted across the weedy patch of front yard. Maybe Lucy was hiding behind the frangipani and would leap out to scare her.

She didn't.

Maggie walked up to the screen door and knocked. Maybe Lucy would pop her head out and yell, "Boo!"

Maggie stood on tiptoes and peered in. The big comfy chair was pushed off to one side. Broken glass littered the floor. The TV screen was smashed. Heel marks trailed across the room.

Maggie banged on the door. "Lucy?" She waited. "Lucy!"

No answer.

She turned the handle and stepped inside. A jagged line of blood stretched from her feet to Lucy's room. Lucy's necklace with the three charms—a cowboy boot with rhinestones, a cowboy hat, and the letter L—lay next to the overturned chair, its silver chain broken. Maggie wore the exact same one, only her charm was engraved with an M. They had exchanged these gifts and sworn BFF status when they turned fourteen in January. Neither had taken hers off since.

"Lucy!" Maggie screamed. She crept her way down the hall toward her best friend's room. "Lucy?" She put her hand on the closed door and gave it a push.

ONE

Maggie was mentally diagramming each sentence Professor Ditmire spoke. She couldn't help herself.

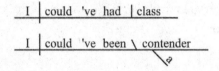

He imitated Brando perfectly.

The Language of Film was Maggie's favorite grad school class at Rosedale, located in the piddling town of Hyacinth, Florida, some forty miles up CR 187 from her home in the even more inconsequential boondocks of Cypress Havens, population 3,598 and dwindling. Ditmire's seamlessly sprinkled cinematic allusions from Kubrick to Kaufman to the Coens never failed to remind her how words can surprise and inspire, inflict and wound. Plus, the professor's course was a much-needed respite from all the rape-bind-torture-kill of forensics. And it didn't hurt that he was easy on the eyes:

tall, buff
casually disheveled
strong jaw
light stubble
piercing blue eyes

Maggie had to smile whenever she saw the gaggle of girls fidgeting and fussing as they hung out after class to ask him a question—messing with their hair, wriggling in their jeans, reapplying lip gloss. See me! Choose me!

Not her. No fucking way.

"Terry Malloy's philosophy," Ditmire continued, "is expressed in one exquisitely formed sentence. 'Do it to him before he does it to you.'"

Maggie automatically diagrammed the words Brando's character spoke, using her favored Reed-Kellogg system:

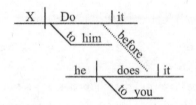

Placing words in precise positions on the horizontal, diagonal, dotted, and pedestaled lines took laser focus as well as expertise—and Maggie was a master. Ms. Barker, her seventh-grade teacher and a throwback to the age of the Stegosaurus, told the students that they would go nowhere and be no one if they couldn't take sentences apart, analyze them, and put them back together again. Eager to be someone and go somewhere, Maggie embraced this visualization technique like a treasured lover—word patterns hopscotching across the mental screen of her mind.

And now, almost a decade later, she was still at it, despite having learned the more sophisticated parse tree, the system studied in most linguistics classes. Today's diagramming served a different purpose than it did back then. Today, it was her version of om. No friggin' way she'd ever do yoga.

"We've seen how Malloy's word choices and syntax reveal key details about dock workers and organized crime in the fifties," the professor continued. "His sentences are *that* evocative. Keeping that in mind, jot down as many common greetings as you can that reveal something specific about a speaker's demographics. Emphasis on *specific*. Hey you!" he yelled. Everyone looked up. "That's a freebie." Ditmire's eyes twinkled as he scanned the room. "Email me your lists before you leave."

Maggie had already typed "Yo!" "Wassup" and "Pardon me, ma'am" before he'd even finished speaking. She kept going: "Howdy." "Sup." "Hi y'all." "How's your mom'n'em." "Namas . . ."

"Miss Moore?"

Maggie jerked.

"Sorry. Sorry to spook you," the professor said as he sat down next to her in the last row. "Great concentration you've got there."

Maggie looked around. The class had emptied. She quickly dropped her head, hoping to hide the hot flush she felt crawling up her neck and spreading across her cheeks. She nervously twisted a jet-black corkscrew curl.

"Something's come up that I need to discuss with you," he began. "Can you meet me in my office in a few?"

Maggie's head nodded bobble-like.

"It's in Fanworth. You know, last building at the end of the quad. Fourth floor, 401."

As she watched the professor walk away, Maggie realized she hadn't uttered a word. In fact, she'd never spoken to the professor since she'd started at Rosedale a year and a half ago. This was the first class she'd taken with the esteemed man, whose accomplishments were legendary: archivist at the Museum of Motion Pictures; film critic both in print and on radio; author of the acclaimed *From Here to Infinity: A Brief History of Film*.

But why did he want to speak to her? Had someone reported her for . . . smoking in the stairwell? Scoring weed in the parking lot? Passing answers to some dude during midterms? She bit her lower lip until it hurt.

After cramming her books and computer in her backpack, Maggie raced across campus to Fanworth. Breathing heavily from having bounded up the four flights, she plunked down on the top step and took out her sentence diagramming notebook. A moment of calm—before the storm. She concentrated on finishing the first line of Zora Neale Hurston's *Their Eyes Were Watching God*. Once completed, it would be her fiftieth first line, bringing her halfway to her goal.

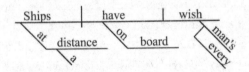

Although entire theses had been written on the analysis of that one sentence alone, Maggie chose to interpret it literally. She imagined a fully rigged ship with three tall masts sailing far out on the horizon carrying tiny scraps of paper detailing every person's greatest wish, including her own. However, as lovely as that image was, she feared that hers, in spite of it having been written succinctly, precisely, and from her heart, would be "mocked to death by Time," as Hurston had suggested some were.

After placing the adverbial prepositional phrase, *on board,* below the verb, *have,* she put her book away and calmly strolled down the long, deserted hall to Room 401. She knocked.

"Come in, please."

Seeing the professor standing next to his desk, Maggie automatically added new details to the ones she'd already made:

fixed, serious gaze
knitted brow
arms across chest

By now, cataloging physical and emotional details of everyone was automatic. "By observing quickly and astutely," her forensics professors had drilled into the students' heads, "you'll be able to make key deductions and educated guesses about the person in question." Of course, this technique was crucial in crime-solving, not so much in everyday encounters, but Maggie couldn't always separate the two. She'd finally understood what it meant to see the world through the lens of one's profession. "If all you've got is a hammer, everything looks like a nail."

Ditmire pointed to one of the two chairs in front of his desk. A poster of *Pulp Fiction* was on the wall. Of course, Maggie thought. That movie had arguably the best dialogue of any film. "Does he look like a bitch?" Maggie quoted to herself. "No! Then why're you trying to fuck him like a bitch?" and "English, motherfucker. Do you speak it?" and "Because you are a character doesn't mean you have character" and—

"Sit, please," he said lowering himself into a large chair behind his desk.

Other than the poster, the walls were bare.

"Your midterm paper," he began, "was outstanding. The best I've seen in all the years I've been here."

"Oh!" Maggie hadn't expected that, but then quickly figured it was a warm-up for what was to come, something like, "I noticed you were handing answers to someone sitting . . . I saw you pass . . ." Her palms were sweating.

"Specifically, the section on accents and dialect in *Fargo*."

Maggie rubbed her hands along her jeans. Niceties out of the way, here it comes.

"Okay, I'll get right to it." Ditmire folded his hands on his desk and leaned forward. "Last evening, a detective Silas Jackson called. He's from up by Olemeda."

Maggie's leg started bouncing.

"The call was directed to me since, as you may know, I'm the Academic Affairs Coordinator. Calls to any graduate department come to me first."

Maggie ripped some skin off her cuticle.

"Seems they've got a cyberstalker on their hands. The person's been texting threats to a twenty-three-year-old woman. She'd been ignoring them, but they got so disturbing she finally contacted her local precinct. That's when Detective Jackson got in touch and asked for our help."

"And you think I might—" Maggie managed.

"Yes. I'm thinking you might be able to help the detective solve this."

Maggie stared at him, speechless—and let out a huge sigh. She continued looking at him, saying nothing.

"You with me here?" he asked.

Nodding furiously, Maggie finally said, "You betcha."

The professor chuckled in recognition of the Fargoism. Then, checking his notes, he added, "Jackson's boss asked him to call us. Seems Chief Josiah Murray had seen a show on the Unabomber and learned that word analysis helped bring the guy down. He asked Jackson to follow up at Rosedale, hoping someone here might do the same. Guess our forensics department garners some attention in this neck of the woods."

"Kaczynski's manifesto gave him away," Maggie blurted.

"I did follow the case some, but I'm not recalling the specifics."

"It was his word choice, but also his incorrect use of an idiom that—"

Maggie stopped. It was either feast or famine. Verbal diarrhea, or as she preferred to label it, furor loquendi—or mum. The latter in response to her mandate never to toot her own horn, to know when to hold 'em, to know when to shut the fuck up. Echoes of *Brainiac Bitch* were never far away.

"Which idiom?" the professor asked.

Maggie scrutinized his face. His eyes were wide open. He was looking directly at her. His chin was tucked slightly. His eyebrows were raised. All that? Interested. Curious.

"Eat your cake and have it too," Maggie said. "It was the reversal of the verbs in the idiom." She heard her voice rise at the end of the sentence, a reaction to not wanting to look too brainy. However, she swallowed hard and decided to go on. "It probably sealed his fate."

"How's that?"

"Well, that exact faulty phrasing showed up several times in Kaczynski's other writings." Maggie looked down. Her left thumb cuticle was bleeding. She wrapped her other hand tightly around it. A thumbiquet. Her very own neologism.

"Fascinating. Go on. Go on."

Furor loquendi be damned. "Plus, his use of the terms 'negro' and 'broad' helped linguists estimate his age. On top of all that, the person who had written the manifesto *and* Kaczynski both had used several uncommon words in their writings, like 'chimerical,' 'cool-headed logicians,' and 'anomic.' I mean, how many times have you used any of them? Chimerical? I mean, come on. I don't even know if I'm pronouncing it right."

Ditmire chuckled. "Clearly, you're up on all this."

"There's more," Maggie said. "The Unabomber also consistently used certain unusual spellings, way-out ones, that rabid researchers discovered were taught *only* in the Chicago schools for a brief period in the sixties. Wild, right? Words like *analyse,* spelled with an *s. Licence,* wrongly ending in *ce. Skilful,* with only one *l. Filfilment,* totally wrong." Maggie stopped long enough to catch her breath. "Kaczynski was born and raised in the Chicago area. Bingo." She looked at the professor for the first time during her soliloquy. "It's my passion," she said. "Sorry if I went on too long."

"Sorry? Not at all."

By now, hot and sticky blood from her thumb had seeped into her fist. She pressed her thumb into her jeans.

"You're exactly who the doctor ordered," Ditmire said. "Now listen to this. At the end of the conversation, the detective said things had gone all catawampus. Catawampus!"

"So he's a country boy from the South," Maggie said, finally relaxing. "A perfect word for the situation. Things have gone haywire. Totally out of control."

The professor grinned. "I knew that if anyone could help, it'd be someone studying forensic linguistics. So I asked around. All the profs begged off—overwhelmed with record keeping, grading, under too much pressure, whatever. 'Who would you recommend for a project of this kind?' I asked."

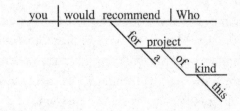

Maggie diagrammed his sentence across her inner eyelids . . .

. . . and wondered if she should point out that *whom* not *who* would have been a more grammatical choice. She firmly believed in maintaining the distinction between the subjective and objective forms of *who* and *whom*. But she knew only too well that *whom*, in this instance, was falling away. It seemed that descriptivism often trumped prescriptivism. Ms. Barker would be crestfallen.

"And your response is?" he asked.

"Hell yeah!"

The professor laughed, tore a sheet from his notebook, and gave it to Maggie. "Here's his info. Give him a call ASAP."

Maggie quickly turned away so the professor wouldn't see her ear-to-ear grin. The truth? A simple word challenge—an anagram, a ditloid, a timed pangram—would've been enough to send her over the moon. But this? Cock-a-hoop.

She slung her backpack over her shoulder, ready to find a quiet place to make the call. "Thank you," she said as she reached the door.

Don't forget your manners, her addled mother would scream at her from time to time over some imagined insult from her daughter. "Don't forget yours," Maggie always wanted to reply—but didn't. A heart filled with pity restrained her.

"Before you go," Ditmire said, "I'm wondering if I could throw something else out there. I'm looking for a research assistant. Based on your stellar record—I checked it out, perfect 4.0—might you be interested?"

Maggie held her breath and counted to five before answering in a restrained and measured way. "I would indeed. I really would."

"Perfect. So I'm working on second-dialect acquisition. Is that something you're familiar with?" He walked to the door where Maggie was standing, poised to exit.

"Yes. I think so."

"Can you tell me, in general, what you know?"

Maggie knew this was *not* the time *not* to toot her own horn. Double negative. Positively positive it *was* the time. "It's when dialect features are, or are not as the case may be, picked up by people new to a community. It shows to what extent integration is taking place. And that usually indicates a person's chance of success. In jobs and schools, you know?"

"Exactly," Ditmire said. "Mostly you'll be working with the techniques laid out in *Dialogue in Films of the Nineties*. Are you familiar with it?"

"Sorry, I've never read it."

"No problem. It's in the library. I teach it in my other film class. I'll email you a syllabus I'm working on so you can get familiar with—" Ditmire's cell chimed. It was the theme song from *Psycho*. "Sorry, gotta go. More academic stuff. To be continued?"

Maggie nodded as she silently recited her favorite *Psycho* lines: "A boy's best friend is his mother. It's not like my mother is a maniac or a raving thing." Maggie's mother had been dead for some five years, but Hazel's raving still haunted her.

"Hope you get your guy," Ditmire said.

Maggie looked confused. She was in the middle of mentally diagramming a quote from *Pulp Fiction*:

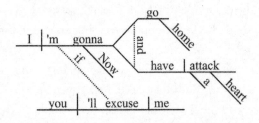

Ditmire pointed to the sheet of paper in Maggie's hand. "The creep," he said. "The stalker. Hope you catch him."

"Right," Maggie said hesitatingly. "Right. Me too."

TWO

Maggie flew out of Fanworth, across the campus, and into the parking lot where Annabelle, her Kawasaki Vulcan 900, was parked. "God-fucking-damn, Anna girl," she said lighting a Camel, inhaling deeply, and blowing several smoke rings. "Get this. I'm going to speak to a detective about a bona fide case, as in real life, ya hear! And I've been asked to be an RA. I mean, who would've thunk waking up this morning that this would be my day?"

Maggie crushed the butt, zipped up her leather jacket, and put on her helmet—the only biker in all of Florida to wear one.

"First thing we're gonna do with the stipend," she said to Anna-belle, throwing her leg over the seat, "is replace the brake pads and deal with alignment issues. Next, help with this semester's tuition." Maggie started up her bike and peeled out. "Plus," she screamed to the wind, "being an RA could land me a sick forensics job after grad-uation. Plus, plus, plus!"

Once away from buildings and strip malls, she hammered down—fifty, sixty, seventy, eighty—and passed miles of sawgrass, wetlands, abandoned farmland, billboards for Jesus, billboards for gator meat, billboards for free vasectomies. She passed single-wides flying the stars and bars, an occasional junkyard-slash-gas station, possibly even some dead bodies.

Slowing down, she meandered along a winding stretch of County Road 80A—her favorite. Maggie had to admit that Florida did have a few things going for it. Like the intoxicating aroma of orange blossoms and Lakeview jasmine. Like the blazing orange-reds of Mexican flame vines and tillandsia. Like the soft yellows of bush zinnias and the regal purples of bougainvillea. Like the sometimes tropical breezes.

As she inched down Royal Palm Court, where not one palm, royal or otherwise, grew, she passed her neighbors' yards, each overrun with detritus of every sort: rusted air conditioners, warped bike frames, cracked toilets, bald tires.

Three doors down from Maggie, a relative newcomer had moved in, attracting revving engines all night. A deep dubby repetition of manic techno-loops blasted from his crumbling one-story. What was *he* dealing? And why did he always come out to greet her with a shit-eating grin plastered across his face? "Name's Lee. Lee Buddy Walker. Why not come on over and let's make us some smooooooth music."

"Fuck off," she'd reply and head straight into her house. Anyone whose middle name is part of his identity is either a serial killer or planning to become one. For sure, that included most of the men in Florida.

Maggie pulled into the sagging carport of her dilapidated pink stucco. Would she ever get used to living in the godforsaken south-central Florida town of Cypress Havens? Why hadn't she left it in all her twenty-one years? Maybe she was suffering from a form of Stockholm syndrome. If it wasn't the crawling bugs, fluttering bugs, swarming bugs, stink bugs, no-see-ums, and kamikazes, it was the in-your-face, ever-present assortment of hustlers, rednecks, pedophiles, and mass murderers—all of whom, she was certain, lived on her block—not to mention the strung-out dropouts high on meth or heroin. Not to mention the dealers. The pimps. The . . .

Once inside, she put her helmet on a hook by the door, dropped her backpack next to the rickety end table she'd picked up at the dump, and plopped herself down on the couch that had been there since the day she was born, evidenced by spit-ups, throw-ups, and food spills of all sorts. She lit up, exhaled her customary large-then-small smoke rings, something she'd mastered in high school in the mistaken belief that they'd impress somebody, then rummaged in the cupboard for a Moon Pie. After taking a huge bite, she washed it down with a slug of Bud.

Maybe—and now she was heading straight into la-la land—this detective would offer up a new angle on Lucy. Maggie'd run into so many dead-ends over the years. Nearly seven years was a long time to stay determined, to pass by the same trailer every day—and sit on the curb and cry. To hang out by the lake every evening—and pray. To do nothing for days on end but mope and research, research and mope—only to come up empty.

She downed the rest of the beer, braced herself, and called the detective.

"Jackson here."

"Hello. Um, this is Maggie Moore. From Rosedale University. Professor Ditmire gave me your—"

"Yeah, hi. Hello. Gonna say this right up front. No talking to no one 'bout this, okay? Boss is real clear on that."

"No talking to no one," she repeated as she jotted down his words. The table had so many crevices in it that her pencil got stuck three times writing those five words. "No problem," she said.

"And we can't pay you."

"I don't expect any money." She wrote, *can't pay*. "I'm not doing this for—"

"If we had extra cash, we'd hire a legit firm that deals with this kind of thing. But we don't. We got all that straight?"

"Straight," Maggie repeated and wondered why the dig. *He's* the one needing help. He ought to—

"No money, no yammering," he said.

"Got it. I'm not planning to put a down payment on—"

"You know what we're working on?"

Maggie jotted down: *no sense of humor.* "My professor told me a little." Maggie pictured him pacing around some parking lot, spitting tobacco, adjusting his balls. Silence. She thought he would take it from there, but it seemed he was waiting for her. "Okay," she said, "this is what I know. You're dealing with a cyberstalker who's been harassing a woman and you thought someone at Rosedale might help because of a documentary your boss saw on the Unabomber."

"He saw it a while back," Jackson said. "Remembered that someone analyzed the wacko's writings. And that somehow led them to Kaczynski."

"In the Unabomber's case," Maggie asserted, "it was a bonus that he'd written so much. That made it easier for forensic linguists to compare his threats with his other writings."

"Our guy wrote four texts. Period."

"You never know. It could be enough. When did he write them?"

"First one about six weeks ago. Fourth one finally brought her in here. Going on a month."

For an entire month, Maggie thought, that shit was stagnating in the lap of the PD? Thirty fucking days with stalking threats hanging over this woman's head?

"If you don't mind me asking," Maggie said, "if this is over a month old, why are you getting in touch with me now?"

"This is a police matter, Ms. Moore," he said firmly. "We have our ways." He stopped talking and Maggie decided not to fill in the silence. "But I will say this," Jackson finally said. "Chief had a uniform on her for the past couple weeks. Lady felt the guy was spying on her.

Chief figured that'd be enough. Seems it wasn't. Now it's landed in my court."

Maggie thought about how the police had handled Lucy's case and all of a sudden, a month of doing nothing seemed like lightning speed. How about a year? Five?

"Chief told me to explore all available resources," Jackson continued. "He said go after the Unabomber angle."

"Can you email me the texts?" Maggie asked.

"We never spoke, okay?" Jackson stressed.

"Right," Maggie confirmed. "Ready? It's *misplaced modifier*, all one word, *underscore, at Maggie dot com.* Got it?"

"Misplaced what?" he asked.

Maggie spelled it out. "That's m-o-d-i-f-i-e-r."

"Got it. Chief's freaking out," Jackson said.

"Gone all *catawampus*," Maggie said emphasizing the very word he used with Professor Ditmire.

The line went quiet.

Jesus. Either he's a total fool or, on the positive side, he's got no interest in chitchat because he's laser focused on solving the crime. Maggie felt the jury was still out on that.

"Find something." Jackson hung up.

"Bye to you, too." Maggie stared at the phone. "And you're very welcome."

After polishing off the Moon Pie, Maggie heard her email alert, the tune from Kenny Rogers's "The Gambler": "You got to know when to hold 'em, know when to fold 'em." Those words had been Maggie's mantra ever since Lucy'd been suspended from school for calling her teacher a jackass. "Guess I ought to know when to hold 'em," Lucy had said to Maggie, smirking.

Maggie sent the email to the printer, then gathered her colored pencils to highlight key words and phrases. Grabbing the four pages, one text per page, she labeled them: *Q-doc #1, 2, 3, 4*—the *Q*uestioned ones, the words written by the unknown author, i.e., the stalker.

Maggie had learned to label Q-docs in Forensic Authorship Identification class, along with labeling K-docs—those written by *K*nown writers. Forensic linguists compare word choices, syntax, spelling, punctuation, and even unconscious stylistic decisions between the Ks and the Qs to help authenticate authorship.

Authorship identification was no simple task. In class, Professor Alcott had told the students, "Perps like to misdirect: purposely misspell, use grammar that's not considered *correct* according to the schoolbooks, choose words that suggest a different ethnicity or education level than their own. But," she added, "sometimes they're not as clever as they think."

Professor Alcott gave the example of a kidnapping that took place in a western state. The kidnapper's ransom note demanded that the money be left on the devil strip at the corner of 18th and Carlson. Renowned, astute forensic linguist Roger Shuy knew that the patch of grass between the street and the sidewalk is called various things in different American dialect areas, including "sidewalk buffer," "tree lawn," and "green belt." But it's called "devil strip" only in one regionally restricted area—Akron, Ohio. Fortunately for the investigators in the case, and unfortunately for the kidnapper, the suspect pool included only one gentleman from Akron. When confronted with the linguistics evidence, he confessed.

Maggie looked over the texts Jackson had emailed:

Q #1: Spread it wide for daddy.

Q #2: It's gunna be my will.

Q #3: Gunna lik and smell yr pussy.

Q #4: You do what I say, cunt.

"Goddamn pervert!" Maggie screamed. But she quickly stopped, forcing herself to pay attention to Professor Alcott's words: "The rabbit hole of becoming emotionally involved is a surefire road to failure," she'd say. "Keep your eyes on the words and the words alone in order to do your job."

Maggie still had fifteen minutes before she had to leave for work, so she began her analysis. First, she underlined key words in each text in the colors she'd ascribed—red for idioms, blue for nonstandard grammar, yellow for incorrect spellings, green for regionalisms, and so on. Then she looked for overall themes and tendencies. After a few minutes, she began making a list of what she'd found.

> *short words, six letters max*
> *simple sentences: noun, verb, direct object*

She pushed the tip of a fresh cigarette into the dying embers of the one she'd just finished.

> *perfect punctuation—even contractions*
> *perfect spelling, except several obvious mistakes: "gunna" "yr" "lik"*
> *no emojis*
> *no acronyms*
> *no fragments*

After looking over her work, she came up with several hunches:

> *educated*
> *wily/sly*
> *male—by sheer odds*
> *probably not a millennial or Gen Z*

Not a whole lot to go on, but it was a start. She cracked open another Bud, then punched in Jackson's number.

"This is Maggie," she said. "Thanks, I got them. I'm wondering if you have any suspects."

"Yup."

She waited for him to ask her why. He didn't.

"Do you happen to have any texts or emails from them? You know, everyday ones so I can—"

"Yup."

That's it? "Okay, then," she said. "Those'll help me compare the taunter's writings, the unknown-authored ones, with those from your suspects, the known-authored ones, to see if we can narrow down the pool."

"Okay."

"Could you send them to me?"

"Yup."

"When might that be?" This guy was a lot of work. "You know, so I'm not sitting around twiddling my—"

"Before midnight."

"Good."

"Wait a sec. On second thought," he said, "better not use email. Don't want to compromise the case."

"I work at Big Eats," Maggie said. "Maybe you could drop them off?"

"Where's that at?"

"On the corner of Cypress and 405."

"Got it." He hung up.

"Bye to you. Again," Maggie said to the dead line.

Maggie lay back on the couch and kicked up her legs. She hadn't felt this good for a long time. Soon, she found herself creating elaborate fantasies about exactly how she'd helped nab the guy. "You see," she was explaining to yet another awestruck newscaster, "by finding key syntactical patterns, I was able to point to a possible—"

Her phone alarm rang. Five minutes till she had to leave for work.

She began her routine in the bathroom, corralling her untamable hair into something that resembled a ponytail. She outlined her lips in Orgasm Red and applied Wild Dragon lipstick.

Just as she was tucking her black T-shirt into black jeans, her phone rang.

"Jackson here."

Shit. He'd changed his mind. She'd been too show-offy, too loquacious, too much of a Brainiac Bitch, too—

"Maggie?"

"Here." She sat down on the couch.

"We need to accelerate our timeline. There's been a development in the case." His words came out even more hesitatingly than before.

"Another text?"

"No." His voice dropped. "Our victim was found. In a sugar cane field. Out near one-eighteen."

"Is she alive?"

"I'll be at Big Eats in an hour."

THREE

When Maggie pulled into her usual spot in the rutted strip mall parking lot of Big Eats, the dinner crowd hadn't filed in yet. Only three customers were devouring the cook's special of fried catfish, spicy curly fries, and a basketful of biscuits. The local hangout offered piled-high plates at dirt-cheap prices twenty-four seven. Reliable, cheap, uncomplicated, like the flashing neon sign out front: BIGGER IS BETTER.

Maggie punched in, grabbed her apron, hugged BJ, who worked the earlier shift, and nodded to her regulars. No one was flagging her down in need of a utensil or coffee top-off, so she took her customary seat at the counter on the least slashed of the red vinyl swivel stools and opened her notebook to the sentence diagram she'd been working on for the past three days. It was by Proust and was proving nearly impossible. Come on, Marcel, a hundred and forty-one words? Really? The average sentence length in the English language was around fifteen. His longest, Maggie had researched, was nine-hundred fifty-eight.

"Hey!" came the booming voice of Forrest Walker. Maggie hadn't seen him come in and take a seat in his usual booth, but she knew what was about to follow. "Y'all know I'm 'bout to have a dying duck fit." Forrest yelled the same damn shit whenever he felt slighted—which was at least once a night. For sure, he'd never pitch a hissy fit. But a dying duck

one? Now that was something a real man could get behind. All he had
to do was exaggerate the snub with a thunderous wail, which, when
successfully carried out, included notes of feigned agony, aggrievement,
and inconsolable heartache.

He and Maggie had been sleeping together on and off since soon
after her mother died, five years ago. Forrest had been Maggie's first
foray into turning her sorry-ass life around, although in retrospect, he
probably wasn't the best choice. In fact, he wasn't even a good choice.

When Forrest had first asked Maggie to meet him in the cab of his
semi after her shift, she refused. At sixteen, she'd never had sex. She'd
never even gone on a date. But as the weeks passed and he kept at it, she
finally gave in. Why not? Why the *fuck* not? After all, Hazel and Lucy
were gone and Maggie was all alone, so why the fuck not?

Fuck had been Lucy's favorite word since they were nine. Maggie's
had been *please*.

Forrest had laid out the particulars before he showed her the rig's
single bed, TV, and kitchenette. He was married, had a bunch of kids,
and the two of them would be in it only for "carnal knowledge." That's
actually what he said—carnal knowledge—and Maggie had started
laughing. She and Lucy had watched that movie a million times and always ended up in fits after Lucy would scream, "Is this an ultimatum?
Answer me, you ball-busting, castrating, son of a cunt bitch."

"Hold your horses, cowboy!" Maggie yelled before extending a diagonal line from Proust's subordinating conjunction to the predicate
of the clause. Slowly and deliberately, she stood up, patted down her
apron, and strolled to his booth while silently quoting Gertrude Stein
and mentally diagramming her words: "I really do not know that anything has ever been more exciting than diagramming sentences."

<pre>
      Gertrude
  _____

   I | love | you
  _____
</pre>

By now, several other regulars had filed in. In no time, they were act-ing in their customary Neanderthal manner. "Got a good one for you," Buford, the night janitor at Haddem Elementary, said. "What's the difference between your wife and your job? You know, if you was a guy."

"Just tell me," Maggie said, hands on hips. "Can't stand the suspense."

"After ten years, the job still sucks."

Maggie shook her head. "And you're expecting coffee?" She did a one-eighty.

"What's with her?" Buford asked his buddies.

A few others—wolf-whistlers all—started demanding her attention. Maggie stood in the middle of the diner and spoke so everyone could hear her: "The louder you hoot, the smaller your dick. It's a fact."

No one said a word. Maggie could always count on her potty mouth, perfected over years of living on Royal Palm Court, to garner respect.

"Mag, oh Maggie, Maggie, Maggie. Go on and admit it. You love…"

Just then, Maggie noticed a "commanding presence" in the door-way. Those were the exact words that popped into her head.

six-three/four
two-fifty pounds or so
broad shoulders
huge neck
Cattleman crease black Stetson

The commanding presence strode over to a stool and sat down.

"Back atcha later," she said going behind the counter.

"Damn straight," Forrest yelled after her.

Standing in front of the commanding presence, Maggie asked, "What can I get you?"

"Maggie?" he asked.

"That'd be me." She wiped her hands on her apron.

"Jackson," the man said.

God-fucking-damn! She'd stowed away the meeting in a kind of mental storage locker tucked deep within her cerebellum by employing her advanced skill at compartmentalization. It was an invaluable tool she'd perfected growing up in a house that she needed to obliterate from consciousness. Compartmentalization was also a skill possessed by serial killers, a fact that didn't escape her. Had she been thinking clearly when she'd spoken to Jackson, she would've suggested they set up a drop-off spot and thus avoid what was sure to be an awkward face-to-face.

"Come this way," Maggie said showing him to a corner booth in the back. "Easier to talk here." Why the hell hadn't she made an effort to look bookish, brainy, and competent? She knew how important first impressions were in evaluating people—you never get a second chance to make a first impression—and this guy needed to see her as valuable.

Jackson maneuvered himself into the tight space, facing the door. Naturally.

Black
early forties
Wrangler boot-cut pressed jeans
rattlesnake belt
black cowboy shirt, white trim pockets, pearl buttons
black alligator boots
bulge on his hip: Glock no doubt

"Okay, let's get to it," he said, opening a notebook. "Patrol found victim at 2:06 p.m. Combed the field. Collected hairs, fibers, clothes. All bagged. Rape kit done at Mercy Hospital. Victim reported, and I quote: 'Someone came up from behind while I was taking my usual route home. He put a cloth over my mouth. I blacked out. Next thing I knew, I was lying in a field. No idea how much time had passed or who did it.'"

"I thought you said she'd been given police protection."

Jackson's eyes immediately narrowed. One didn't need a nerdy researcher on eye signals to interpret his squint, although Maggie qualified as one after having spent hundreds of hours studying what eyes reveal based on the size of the pupil, whether or not the eyes darted, stared straight ahead, blinked quickly or not at all, looked down, up, or off to the side, and so on. She'd even read about algorithms that revealed such things as openness, neuroticism, extroversion, agreeableness, and conscientiousness—all by examining eyes. Jackson's eyes were dead giveaways. They signaled disdain, disgust, and contempt.

"Guy was called away on a domestic disturbance," Jackson snapped.

"Florida's one big goddamn domestic disturbance if you ask me," Maggie said.

"Didn't." Jackson began to crack his knuckles. "Think you're gonna point us somewhere or what?"

"I'll sure try."

"For what that's worth."

Now it was Maggie's turn to squint, squeeze her lips, and shake her head. "Thanks for the vote of confidence, detective. Ever hear of encouragement and how far that can go? I'll answer that for you. No."

Ignoring her remark, Jackson began placing pages on the table. Five in all. "These're what you wanted. Everyday texts from our five suspects." He pushed them toward her, leaned in, and drummed his thick fingers on the cracked Formica table. Maggie could hear his boot tapping.

"These are called K-docs," Maggie explained as she glanced at them. "The *K* comes from the word *Known* because—"

"So whattaya see?"

"Oh, for Chrissake! Might a little education be valuable?"

"No. Not really."

Sadly, Jackson seemed far too familiar. Maggie remembered going to the Cypress Havens cop shop after Lucy disappeared. She'd check in every day, then every week, finally every month to see if any leads had come in. Three guys worked there, if you could call it *work*. Mostly, they told one another third-grade potty jokes that they made sure she heard before looking up to ask if there was anything they could do for her. Several times, just to show they were "serious" in finding Lucy, they'd all go into what was called the conference room. By its stench, Maggie figured it had once been a bathroom. Sitting around a small round table with five chairs, they acted as if they were listening when Maggie spoke. Sometimes, however, one or another would nod off. Most of the time, they simply doodled or stared into space. She knew damn well they'd assembled their useless butts just to appease her, hoping she wouldn't come back too soon again. Later, she learned that her police department was typical of Blane County, the most rural and poorest in all of Florida, where the average salary was $17,000. The high school drop-out rate was the highest in the state, and the number of advanced degrees was the lowest. For the PD, that meant lamebrain cops, lousy pay, antiquated technology, and plenty of dead spots where even if a cop were inclined to follow up on an infraction, he'd get no signal. Plus, there was little to no chance of moving up in the department.

While Maggie was reading the texts, she smelled Southern Blend, her favorite cologne since last Christmas when she worked at Tall and Wide Department Store. "Rugged and masculine with a hint of whiskey," she'd tell the customers. Had Jackson stopped by then—and he fit the tall-and-wide profile—she would've told him to grab it. That is, if she didn't know he was such a stupid-ass dick. Knowing that, she would've steroid-sprayed him with Diesel Fuel for Life—and let him deal with the aftermath.

"We use the nonthreatening, everyday texts as a means of comparison, looking for language similarities that *could* link one of the suspect's writings with the actual threatening texts," she said.

"Hmm." Jackson was staring out the window and his foot was still tapping with an audible thud each time his heel met the floor. "So? Find any?"

"Excuse me, Mag." It was Forrest, and he was standing in front of the booth. "Do y'all notice anything, Mag? Some folks here," he said with a grand arm gesture, "are needing some grub. Ain't fittin' for you to ignore us, even if you did find yourself a new, uh, customer. Howdy, sir. Name's Forrest."

Jackson nodded.

"Pleased to make your acquaintanceship," Forrest said as he strutted off.

"Backstory there," Jackson said to Maggie, clearing his throat unnecessarily.

"Isn't there always," she said.

Something about Jackson's eyes told her that in his case, there surely was.

After dealing with all the customers' orders, Maggie grabbed her backpack, sat back down across from Jackson, and got out her colored pencils. Looking over the pages, she began labeling each piece of paper: Suspect #1, #2, #3, #4, #5. Then she circled one sentence from each of these nonthreatening emails that seemed most typical of that suspect's writing. From her Forensic Stylistics class, she'd learned how to find indicative sentences by examining average syllable and sentence length, unique use of punctuation marks, grammar and syntax anomalies, and other telling marks. Highlighting these syntactical items made comparisons easier. Of course, if she couldn't come to a determination on her own, there were plenty of forensic software programs that spewed out that kind of thing. Authorship ID was huge in forensic linguistics, especially in determining the true author of ransom notes, suicide notes, signed confessions, wills—even threatening texts.

Maggie circled key sentences in each of the everyday emails from Known suspects:

From Suspect #1:

Politicians are champions of corruption and deception!

From Suspect #2:

Like I told Joey I ain't setting by and watchin my old man rune his sorry life and not do nothing this time you know what Im sayin.

From Suspect #3:

No way in hell I'm going along with that.

From Suspect #4:

So fkup 😬 mesd 1 time to mny dn trg to mk it 🖐 wk !!!!!

From Suspect #5:

What the shitshows going on anyway?

After a few minutes of hearing the background noise of Jackson's heavy sighs and seeing him fidget with the utensils, Maggie said, "Look, I need a little time. Either come back later or try the pie. Pecan's not that bad."

"Waiting."

"Suit yourself."

Maggie scanned the diner. Nobody needed anything, so she focused on the papers in front of her. Soon, the kaleidoscope of colors revealed clear patterns, like fingerprints. This kind of linguistic analysis was sometimes referred to as verbal DNA—although many if not most scholars in the field of forensic linguistics felt it was hogwash. Those who did believe in it said that a person's peculiar speech patterns, or idiolect, can help narrow down a pool of possible suspects. The debate raged on. Maggie was on the side of the verbal DNAers.

After a few minutes, Maggie signaled Jackson over. He'd been pacing by the front windows. Sitting down across from each other, she said, "Not one, two, or four."

"How'd you figure?"

"Full tutorial later. It could take a while."

"Short version?" Jackson said.

Maggie noticed that his leg was no longer bouncing, his fingers had stopped tapping, and he was leaning forward.

"Okay, in the everyday emails from the suspects, most of Suspect One's words are more than seven letters each. Keep that in mind. Suspect Two? His average sentence length is around seventeen words. Remember that, too. And Number Four uses emojis, SMS language, and punctuation marks on steroids."

"So?"

"Well . . ." Maggie strung out the pause before continuing. "You see, in the stalker's threatening texts, there are no big words, no long, rambling run-on sentences, and no emojis."

"And that supposedly tells you—" Jackson's cell rang. He looked down. "Sorry. Gotta take it. What's up, Duane?" Jackson stood up as he listened. "You shittin' me. Send it over."

"Get this," he said to Maggie, squeezing his bulk back into the booth. "Duane was standing watch outside our victim's hospital room. The victim tossed him her phone. Told him to read it."

Jackson's phone beeped. "Here it is." Jackson began reading the text silently.

"Here *what* is?" Maggie asked.

"A new text on the victim's phone that she gave to Duane." Jackson handed Maggie his cell.

Maggie read, You cunt. I ain't done with you. Gunna keep abusin' on you. You mine now. I fucked you good.

"What a goddamn—" Maggie stopped, closed her eyes, and forced herself to abandon her knee-jerk reaction. She reread the text.

"Anything there?" Jackson asked. "You see something?"

"Hmm. Could be," she said. "Give me a sec." Maggie kept repeating one phrase. "It's thin," she finally said, "but the guy wrote, 'Gunna keep abusin' on you.'"

"So?"

"He might be giving us a clue right there. Might."

"What clue?" Jackson asked.

"That's not standard grammar," Maggie said. "In fact, it's similar to Cajun syntax. Non-Cajun folk, like you and me, would say 'abusing' someone, not 'abusin' on.'"

"Okay, okay, okay. So what?"

"So he could be exhibiting something called unconscious utterances. Speaking like he did in childhood when he lived in, say, Southern Louisiana or thereabouts, not realizing that people here, where he is right now, don't speak that way. Kinda like someone living here saying catawampus.

Jackson's eyes were wide. "You sure?"

What was with this guy? He exhibited an unconscious utterance when he used *catawampus* speaking with the professor—and now, again, he totally ignores the reference.

"Of course," Maggie continued, not ready to let it go, "words like *catawampus* give away that the person comes from somewhere deep in the—"

"I said, are you sure?" Jackson repeated.

Maggie sighed—and gave in. "No," she said, "but it's a start."

"You're thinking Louisiana as a kid?" Jackson asked.

"Like I said, it's a start."

Jackson smacked his hand on the table. "I'm taking me a little ride." He slung his jacket over his shoulder and grabbed his Stetson. Maggie knew it was Cattleman from back when she and Lucy had made a detailed chart of each hat they saw in the Westerns they obsessively watched. Cattleman was their favorite.

"Sunshine and 105," Jackson said. "That's where I'm headed. Suspect Three dated the victim and she dumped him. That's why he's on our radar. Think I remember he lived in the Big Easy." As Jackson started toward the door, he turned and said, "This better not be a wild goose chase."

Maggie had expected he was going to shake her hand or maybe say thank you—but he was gone.

"Hey! You gonna take this shit away or what?" Forrest yelled.

Maggie sauntered over. "Six bucks an hour ain't half bad for a busboy. Want a job?"

"The blow kind?" he asked.

"Asshole."

Back in the kitchen, Maggie thought about what had just happened. Maybe, just maybe . . .

That was Lucy's favorite line from the song "Over the Rainbow." Maybe, just maybe, it could become hers, too.

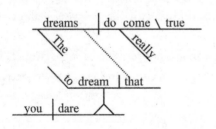

FOUR

After punching out at midnight, Maggie hopped on Annabelle and flew off along flat, empty, arrow-straight roads, aware, yet again, that Florida sucked for bikers. No hills—the highest elevations were the dumps—few hairpins to lean into, and way too many mega-highways. But she'd rather own a bike than deal with an overheating car. She'd bought Annabelle several months after her mother died—five-year anniversary this month—after Tidwell and Rodriguez had shown her the ropes on theirs. She'd fallen in love with the freedom and confidence a bike offered, so she sold the Camry, the *sensible* car Hazel had purchased ten years before she died. The last thing Maggie wanted was sensible.

On her way to Royal Palm Court, she made a pit stop at her home-away-from-home, the Black Dog bookstore, where she shopped weekly, sometimes daily. The repurposed barn was a rickety outpost run by sketchbag Jake, who for sure was dealing in something other than valued volumes, but that wasn't her concern. Right now, all she cared about was keeping busy so she wouldn't wig out at not having heard from Jackson.

Like Big Eats, Black Dog was open twenty-four seven. For sure, it wasn't because hordes of eager readers were knocking down the door of this long-ago abandoned barn. Truth was, you could count the number of literates in this part of Florida on one hand. At night, Black Dog was lit up like a football stadium, the only lights for miles, not that there was, in fact, anything around for miles. At midnight, it felt like not only did *nothing* else exist, but *no one* else did either.

Most times, she'd buy a bag of books sold by the pound, sight unseen. Why Black Dog sold some of their books by the pound was another thing Maggie never understood, but she didn't care. She'd end up spending less than a dollar on each book, plus she had the anticipation of a surprise as she unwrapped her treasure.

Right now, she wished she could talk to Lucy, not only because Lucy would bring her back from the brink, but also because Lucy would remind her that she was not a loser—that she was, in fact, a somebody.

Maggie couldn't remember a time before Lucy was in her life. On their first day of kindergarten, they'd been placed at the same table and given Play-Doh. Maggie created letters in various colors: yellow A; blue B; red C, and so on. Across the table, Lucy began forming words—*big, dog, hop*—using the colors Maggie had assigned for each letter.

At one point, Lucy sat down next to Maggie. Without speaking, the girls began composing short sentences with words formed from the Play-Doh letters. "Well, well, well," Miss Collum proclaimed when she saw what they were doing. "We have two budding geniuses here."

Ever since that afternoon, the two had been inseparable—until they weren't. Over the next eight years, when Maggie couldn't find the words to stick up for herself, Lucy did it for her. When Maggie's mother told her she'd never amount to anything, Lucy told Maggie she could be anything she wanted. "Don't be a fucking wimp," Lucy told Maggie over and over. When Maggie felt particularly useless and heavy-hearted, Lucy would magically show up, bolster her spirits, and in no time, Maggie would feel hopeful, even worthwhile—because she had seen herself as Lucy saw her. When Maggie was singled out in assembly for being "Spelling Bee Champion of Jefferson Middle School," Lucy stood up, whistling and hooting as Maggie walked to the stage, head down, shoulders hunched. Of course, Hazel hadn't come. All Hazel had cared about was that Maggie graduate high school and get a job right away. "Give me a little help around here, why don't you."

But in spite of Hazel's dismissive, disdainful, and degrading attitude toward Maggie, she loved her mother in a place so deep in her heart that it was accessible only rarely—but it was there. Maggie could still hear Hazel singing "You Are My Sunshine" as Maggie lay feverish in bed when she was six. That one song, sung so beautifully for Maggie and Maggie alone, ". . . You'll never know dear, how much I love you . . ." still echoed in Maggie's ears. Later, many years later, Maggie understood why:

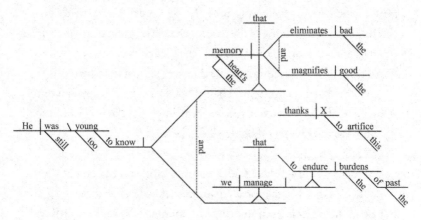

For sure, Gabriel Garcia Márquez had nailed that one.

"Whatcha after?" Jake asked Maggie as he sat splayed on his chaise lounge. He was busy, twitchy as usual, brushing imaginary dust from a book spine. "How about a little mystery? A dose of horror?" He took a toke. "Romance?" He tucked his chin and raised his eyebrows.

Right. Toothless Jake who hasn't showered in months sure seemed a likely candidate. Maggie figured that he and his buddies were making meth. Why else were aluminum cooking pots strewn around outside his ramshackle building? Why else would Jake complain that bugs were crawling up his legs and arms? And meth probably wasn't the worst thing he was into. One time, Maggie came upon a pair of girl's undies on the floor in a back corner of the barn. When she asked him what they were doing there, he joked, "Like sniffing 'em, ya know? No harm in that."

"No harm?" Maggie said. Then louder, "No harm? If I ever see you with jailbait, I swear I'll kick your damn balls so hard you won't be standing for weeks."

Another time, Jake was showing her some stupid pic on his phone when he inadvertently brought up a porn screen with guys getting it on with young girls. Seeing that, Maggie had thrown his cell at a tree. If it wasn't for the fact that Jake's was the only decent bookstore for a hundred miles, she'd never set foot in it again.

After choosing a five-pound bag of books, Maggie strapped it onto Annabelle, yanking two bungees to form a tight X. No way would she have those tomes flying off helter-skelter behind her.

"Later," she called.

"Hope to God so," Jake said, beaming. "Still waiting on y'all."

Once home, Maggie headed inside her pale stucco, next to all the other faded stuccos bordering the manmade lake, and dropped her bag of books at the edge of her previous pile. She had yet to put those in their proper places on the floor-to-ceiling shelves lining the living room, bedroom, even the kitchen walls. She'd already arranged some into neat stacks by category—novels, biographies, reference, true crime, etymology, forensics, linguistics, and Maggie's own sentence diagram notebooks—the antepenultimate step to giving them their forever homes. Alphabetizing came next. Buying books, stacking them, alphabetizing them—anchors all.

Maggie opened the fridge—plastered with Post-its of quotes she cherished—and cracked a Bud, draining half in one slug. She took off her jacket, lit up, downed the rest of the can, and stripped off her clothes. She was dripping wet—no A/C except for a window unit in her mother's bedroom, where Maggie never ventured. In her own bedroom, in front of the full-length mirror, she focused on her tattoos, looking for the perfect spot for the next one. She was due for another, actually overdue, according to a plan that had taken shape in the months, then years, after her mother died.

SHE RUNS. Maggie had gotten those words inked by her right ankle to mark three months of living on her own. *Run*, not as in what someone does in track shoes, but metaphorically. Gordimer's "She runs" was the last sentence in *July's People*. Maggie felt those words would set a clear course for what she'd planned for herself. She would run from the person she'd been and leave that sorry-ass loser behind. Over time, she figured, she'd build up metaphorical speed, veer left, swerve right, and sprint headlong into . . . whatever.

The following year, on her seventeenth birthday, Maggie chose a classic and elegant font for ARE THERE ANY QUESTIONS? She'd gotten that tattooed down the left side of her calf. It was indeed a handmaid's tale. She was still running hard and fast and hadn't been able to stop long enough to ask herself the only question that mattered: Why had she left her mother alone to die?

Maggie turned her right forearm to the mirror. ISN'T IT PRETTY TO THINK SO? She'd gotten the last line of *The Sun Also Rises* inked the following year, after she'd been awarded a full scholarship for her first two years of college, thanks to Ms. Barker, her beloved teacher of sentence-diagramming-and-Gertrude Stein fame. And, based on her perfect grade point average, she'd been given a free ride for the rest.

On her nineteenth birthday, Maggie had decided on I BEEN THERE BEFORE, Huck's summing-up. She still hadn't been able to stop running—blindly, madly, recklessly—into any bag-of-shit's arms who extended his toward her, however perfunctorily. She'd found the perfect distraction and at the same time, punishment. Mostly punishment. She kept right on doing all the other things she'd been doing—drinking and smoking too much, driving too fast, and popping too many pills of questionable origin.

But just last year, after having recklessly raced into more ravaging hook-ups than she cared to count, she'd finally made a change—and had stuck to it. A statement attributed to Philip Stanhope, Fourth Earl of Chesterfield, seemed spot on: "Sex: the pleasure is momentary, the position ridiculous, and the expense damnable." The expense for her—degradation, dehumanization, and debasement—had become so unbearable that even her need for punishment couldn't outweigh it, and she'd given up sex altogether. At least for the while.

Gordimer, Atwood, Hemingway, Twain. Famous last lines all. Endings were important. They presaged beginnings.

Piercings. She'd gotten plenty of those, too. The first was on a dare. Tidwell had said she'd never do it. Of course, he had nipple rings, a nose ring, ear piercings, and even a ring in his penis, which he was only too proud to show her every chance he got. He'd known the old Maggie forever and had bet her a hundred dollars she was too chicken-shit to get pierced.

The next day, Maggie became a hundred dollars richer—six small zigzagging rings gleamed proudly above her left eyebrow.

A few months later, she got a scaffold piercing in her right ear, which she connected with a thin barbell, along with seven lobe piercings running from the bottom rim halfway up her ear.

Last year, she added a delicate nose stud and a nipple ring.

Stepping even closer to the mirror—hello there, Maggie Moore—she saw a high, smooth forehead, wide-set almond-shaped brown eyes, olive skin, prominent cheekbones, thick pouty lips, always defined by bright red lipstick, and long, lean legs which, she figured, must've come from her father, along with her complexion. Sometimes Maggie felt she had a clear image of the man—dark brooding eyes, thick head of black hair, gentle smile. At other times, she knew she'd made him up. Her mother's refusal to say one word about him only fueled her imagination.

She thought again about what ink she'd get for her twenty-first birthday, which had come and gone several months ago. She'd been contemplating a few question marks or maybe an ellipsis. She could make a case for how each applied to her life. But now, considering how she'd fucked up with Jackson, she thought: COUYON. In Cajun, it described a foolish or stupid person. For sure, she could make a strong case how that applied to her life. She could get it as a tramp stamp or on the nape of her neck in a striking, bold font.

Maggie signed onto TruthFinder, a nightly ritual to see if any of the nicknames she'd input for Lucy had shown any sign of life. Nothing. She checked the Federal Bureau of Prisons—in case Lucy'd been arrested. No luck for Maggie. Lucky for Lucy. Next, she checked Pipi, then Zabasearch, followed by YoName. Nada.

By now, seven butts lay mutilated in the ashtray.

She checked NCMEC—National Center for Missing and Exploited Children—then the Department of Motor Vehicles records search feature.

She signed on to her account at NamUs—the National Missing and Unidentified Persons System. She'd added Lucy's name years ago, and every night she religiously checked to see if there was any action.

Then she went to Missing Children's Webring.

She followed that by popping into several of the chat rooms she usually visited: Has anyone seen a . . .

Maggie checked the time. It was nearly six a.m. and she'd exhausted her usual resources. It'd been almost eight hours since Jackson had dashed out of the diner. Surely, if anything had come of her idea, he would've contacted her by now. Maggie grabbed the bottle of vodka she kept in the side table cabinet and took a huge slug. Obviously, Jackson had spoken with Suspect Three, grilled him about where he was born and grew up, and had quickly crossed him off the list. She imagined that the next time he called, if he ever deigned to, he'd say, "Thanks for nothing, Ms. Linguistical Genius. Our Number Three was born and raised right here by the Everglades. Proved it. Never even been out of the state. Not once."

By seven, she'd showered, dressed, and was heading back to the diner. She'd agreed days ago to work the breakfast shift.

After her ritual of clocking in, donning her apron, grabbing her pad, and checking to see who needed anything, she went back to diagramming Proust. The hours slogged by with few customers—and no word from Jackson.

Since she'd already used up most of her tricks to halt negativity, she forced herself to relive a happy moment. Sometimes it worked. She closed her eyes and clearly saw the evening of her sixth-grade graduation dance. Of course, neither she nor Lucy had been invited by either a boy or some girls—Maggie because she was a certified weirdo nerd and Lucy because the boys were afraid of her trigger-ready fists and fierce mouth. But the two of them didn't care. They'd be a tight duo standing by the refreshments.

For weeks, they'd been watching Lucy's mom's video to learn how to line dance to "The Gambler." The students had been asked to vote on the songs that would be played, and Lucy had stuffed the ballot box with "The Gambler," her favorite and a reminder of when she'd been suspended. A pivotal moment.

They'd gotten down the basic steps: toe touches, crossovers, kicks, scuff heels, hitch knees, rocks, recovers, quarter lefts. Lucy had added her own touches—three grinds after a slow, sexy slide. They'd practiced till Maggie's pink rug was bare. Had Hazel peeked into Maggie's room then, she would've murdered them both.

That night, Lucy wore short-shorts and an American flag–type tank top—red-and-white stripes down the left, bright blue stars up the right. Her cowboy boots were purple and black with silver squiggles up the side. Maggie wore a white and black cowboy shirt, black jeans, and black cowboy boots. She'd been practicing dancing with her fingers in the belt loops like she'd seen on the video. Both girls were rail thin, but that was where their physical similarities ended. Lucy had straight blond hair, milky translucent skin, and a spray of freckles across her cheeks. Her eyes shone green and huge.

They spent the first hour of the dance chugging colas and eating cookies. Lucy had put a small flask of vodka in her boot. Drinking was a habit she'd gotten into to help pass the nights alone while her mother was out with yet another of her many boyfriends. That evening, with her back to the chaperones, Lucy added vodka to their colas. The girls downed the drinks. Maggie rarely drank back then. The only times she did were when Lucy offered it up and Maggie felt she couldn't say no.

But as Dylan says:

At one point during the dance, Lucy sauntered off to the ladies' room. While she was gone, a few of the popular girls clasped Maggie's hand and pulled her onto the floor. Maggie was stunned. Not one of them had ever even talked decently to her, much less hung out with her. Maybe, Maggie thought, the party was bringing out the best in them.

Once on the floor, Maggie started dancing—tentatively at first, but then little by little, more assuredly. As she became even more comfortable, she found herself sliding and grinding and doing cross-overs like she'd been rocking this her whole life. She heard a whistle and turned to see that Lucy had joined in from the bleachers—waving wildly, clapping, stamping her feet, and grinding right along with her. After a few more moves—scuff heel right forward diagonally right, hitch knee right, shake shake shake shake—one-by-one, the other girls started slinking away. Tired? Bored? Too hot? Maggie wasn't sure. Soon, however, Maggie realized that she was dancing alone, and the girls, now rimming the periphery, were raising one knee at a time, smacking it, and yelling, "Yee-haw."

That's when Lucy heavy-booted it up to Maggie, grabbed her hand, and whispered, "We got this."

Together they put on their best show, filled with slow sensual slides, seductive grinds, and plenty of booty shakes. When the music stopped, Lucy proudly held up her hand, raised her middle finger, and sprinted around the perimeter of the room, a victory lap of sorts. After she'd circled once, she took a grand curtsey and ran off with Maggie, yelling "Fuck y'all," before the teacher-chaperones could catch up with them.

Settled on the stool in Big Eats, Maggie started up again diagramming another of Proust's interminable sentences:

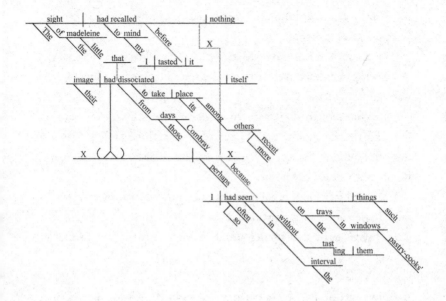

Maggie jumped when someone tapped her shoulder—and swiveled around. "Fuck off, Forrest."

"Name's Jackson."

The man's face was expressionless. Immediately Maggie knew that she'd done exactly what he'd admonished her *not* to do: She'd sent him on a wild goose chase.

"Hey, a little service around here?" Maggie heard Forrest yelling. When the hell had he come in?

Jackson still hadn't said anything, so Maggie figured it'd be easier to deal with Forrest than to suffer the oozing disdain that was sure to spill out of Jackson's mouth. "Back in a jiff," she said before grabbing the coffee pot and Forrest's favorite Key lime pie.

"Who the fuck's that dude?" Forrest asked as Maggie poured him a cup.

"None of your damn business."

"Seems he's *your* business," Forrest said, eyebrows raised, smirking. "Copper? You screwing—"

"Put a sock in it, asshole," Maggie said and walked back to Jackson.

Seeing the detective's frozen face, she said, "Sorry. Guess I was wrong."

Jackson remained stone-faced while Maggie shifted from foot to foot. Finally, he spoke. "So I went to Suspect Three's job. It was his day off. Found out where he lived. Went to his place. Didn't show for hours. Nice man. Nice home."

Seemed Jackson was going to drag this out for fucking ever.

"I said sorry," Maggie repeated.

"Turns out he grew up in Mamou. Know where that's at?" Jackson asked.

"No."

"Evangeline Parish, Louisiana." Jackson tipped his hat. "Chief wants to personally congratulate you. At the precinct tomorrow. Four p.m."

FIVE

"Noooo," Maggie moaned hearing the alarm's inner-ear-wrecking screech. Why'd she ever think that the sound of nails on a chalkboard would get her sprinting out of bed, pumped, and eager to carpe diem? There'd been tons of other choices: birds chirping, a flowing mountain stream, even the Beach Boys' "Good Vibrations," but she knew she'd never be persuaded to pluck the day with *pleasant*.

When she opened her eyes, she saw that she'd fallen asleep on the floor. Trying to remember how she'd gotten there, she went through details of the evening. After her shift, she stopped by Ink Station next to the diner and decided to celebrate what had become her very own success story. According to Jackson, she actually helped nab the bad guy! So, instead of having Henry ink COUVON on the back of her neck, she opted for **CHO! COL!** in a strong, bold font. In Cajun, it meant something like "Wow!" She'd gotten all her ink at Ink Station, thanks to Henry, who lived in the back of the shop and tattooed anybody anytime. Once home, she headed out back and polished off half a bottle of vodka with Rodriguez, Tidwell, Martinez, Smith, and Jankey. Her neck was burning, so she went back inside to get some aloe gel. Then . . . blank.

The alarm screeched again. She could easily change the ring tone, zip, zip, zip, but no way would she admit defeat, however inconsequential. Her shoulders were already weighed down by all her other poor choices.

Eventually, she persuaded herself that dormancy wasn't going to get her anywhere—and she had, in fact, *somewhere* to go. At eight a.m., she was to meet Professor Ditmire for her first RA meeting.

Lighting up, she turned on the shower and stepped into the tepid drizzle. Something about the pipes meant lukewarm was as hot as it got and something about the well pressure meant that a strong stream was a pipe dream. Ha. *Pipe* dream. Showering and smoking at the same time was a multitask she'd perfected long ago, as was reciting the alphabet backwards skipping a pre-prescribed number of letters in between, whistling while eating Moon Pies, and writing in mirror image with her right hand while drumming her fingers to any song that came into her head with her left.

Drying off, she considered the day ahead. First, her *first* meeting with Ditmire. Then the day shift at Big Eats. After that, off to the precinct at four, followed by a hang at the lake.

Dressing down and making sure that none of her ink or piercings showed—black jeans, black T-shirt—and only applying the lightest shade of lipstick she had, Love That Pink, she limited herself to two beers for breakfast before heading out. "And the beer I had for breakfast wasn't bad, so I had one more for dessert," she sang, a silent thank you to Kris Kristofferson for writing it and Johnny Cash for covering it.

Once in Ditmire's office, she sat at the round table in front of his desk and placed her pencils in a single line, sentries guarding her knowledge.

"Good morning," the professor said. "Chief Murray texted me last night. Seems you helped solve the case. You should feel very proud."

"Yeah, well . . . truth is, the cops had the suspects already lined up. All I did was analyze a few texts." Maggie looked down.

"Humility has its place," Ditmire said, "but not here."

She shuffled the pencils and opened her computer.

"Okay, let's get to it. How about we start with *Dialogue in Films of the Nineties.* Did you have a chance to take a look at it?"

"Yes."

"And?"

"I read it."

"The whole thing."

"Yes sir."

"It's well over three hundred pages."

"I learned a lot," she lied. She already knew almost everything in it from other books she'd read.

"Then, I suppose we can move on. Are you familiar with conditional formatting and advanced charting in Excel?"

"Yes." Maggie thought about the dozens of charts she'd created over the years, chronicling every detail and clue of Lucy's disappearance.

"This is good news indeed." He handed her a pile of papers. "Apologizing ahead of time," he said. "I know my notes are a mess, but do you think you could create order out of this chaos? Could you input the data on, let's see, some twelve different categories? I jot down things pretty much as they pop into my head, so these pages can be confusing. Take all the time you need. I have office hours all day."

"No problem."

The professor sat back in his desk chair and opened a book while Maggie looked over the notes, mentally placing each new thought into one of the categories she'd begun to create. He wasn't as scattered as he thought, and less than two hours later, she'd completed the task. She desperately wanted a smoke, so she said, "Excuse me. Bathroom break."

He nodded and quickly returned to reading. Maggie walked down the creepy, empty hall to the stairs, where she lit up. "I've got this," she said softly. "No-brainer." After taking a few drags, Maggie squirted her mouth with cool-mint mouthwash and followed that with a spray of rose water.

Back at the table, Maggie spent fifteen more minutes going over her work. "Done," she said after having made sure everything was perfect. "I think this is what you want."

Ditmire looked over her work. "Seems you've got this under control. Do you think we could set this up for twice a week? I'm submitting several proposals to my agent for books I want to write. I'm hoping she'll think one is worthwhile. Maybe you could look them over if you have time?"

"I could do—"

"Great."

Maggie sang as she biked to the diner, "Ain't nothing that a beer can't fix." It was stuck in her head, so she belted it out along the way. Right now, she didn't think things needed fixing, but a beer sounded good anyway, so she popped into Henry's to grub one off him. He was always good for refreshments of any kind.

After spending a slow shift of mostly reading and diagramming, she hopped on her Kawasaki and sped off to the precinct. Arriving at four on the dot, she parked Annabelle far enough from the building so she couldn't be seen and took a slug from the vodka she kept in a flask in her backpack. "Lucy, this one's for you."

"Chief Murray'll be right with you," the teenager manning the desk said, not taking his eyes off his cell. "Make yourself at home."

Sitting down in one of the green molded-plastic chairs that nobody could make themselves at home in, however hard they tried, she looked around. A wood sign announcing the Second Amendment hung on the wall: "A well regulated Militia, being necessary to the security of a free State, the right of the people to keep and bear Arms, shall not be infringed." Another proclaimed: "Duty. Honor. Courage." Below that was a Confederate flag, and next to it were the words "Blue Lives Matter."

Not sensing any movement from the hall behind the desk, Maggie took out her diagram book and began whacking away at Proust.

"Ms. Moore?"

Maggie looked up.

55–60
smoky gray hair
soft, tired eyes
gentle smile
rumpled clothes

"Chief Murray." He extended his hand. "Nice to meet you."

"Likewise," she said, cramming her book back into her backpack.

"Come, I'm right down here." Maggie followed him along a faded, green-walled corridor, past an empty water cooler, a file cabinet that had begun collapsing in on itself, and several closed office doors. The place smelled like burnt coffee and cigarettes.

rounded shoulders
lumbering walk
slight limp
portly

"Have a seat." He pointed to a chair at a small table and sat down across from her. A group of large photos on the wall behind the desk showed the chief proudly holding huge fish. Two trophies bracketed either side of his desk. One said, "1st Place Redfish Team Champions"; the other, "2nd Place Largest Kingfish." A small, gilded picture frame held two lines in calligraphy:

With a smile of Christian charity great Casey's visage shone;
He stilled the rising tumult; he bade the game go on.

Maggie knew those lines well. She could easily recite the entire poem—but she wondered why the chief would have part of "Casey at the Bat" beautifully framed. Maybe he'd been a professional ball player way back when?

"Nothing better'n the great outdoors," the chief said picking up one of the photos. "When I retire these old bones next year, that'll be all I do."

"Sounds like a plan."

"Been a long haul, but hey, we managed to make the world a little better," he said. "Not a bad legacy. Not bad at all. But we're not here to talk about me. I wanted to thank you in person."

The chief handed Maggie a plaque. "Maggie Moore. Honorary Member of the Olemeda Police Department. Our Sincere Thanks for a Job Well Done," he read.

"Sure didn't expect this," Maggie said holding the plaque. "Thanks. But really, it was all Jackson and you. You put the whole thing in motion, and then Jackson came up with—"

"First of all," the chief began, "may I call you Madame Genius?"

Maggie laughed.

"You did what we couldn't do. So as a result, I'd like to pick your brain some," he said.

"Might take some time," she said smiling, "considering my new identity."

"Ha! So, young lady, you blew us right out of the water. We'd been struggling with this one, making no headway whatsoever. What I'd really like to know is this. How'd you figure out Louisiana?"

"I got lucky."

"You make your own luck, my dear," he said. "That's a fact. So, clue me in."

"I'm sticking with a little bit of luck and a little bit of knowledge."

"The knowledge part is what I'm after," he said.

"It might be kind of boring. Technical. That okay?" Maggie asked.

"Go for it."

"Okay, here goes. First, I looked for similarities between the stalker's texts and those from the five suspects you had already fingered. Just like what was done with the Unabomber. In that case, as you well know, they compared his Manifesto with his other writings."

"Stalker *and* rapist in our case," the chief corrected.

"Right. I came to some tentative conclusions that ruled out three of the suspects because their writings were radically different from the texts the stalker-slash-rapist wrote."

"So *anything* anyone writes can give him away just like that?" the chief asked.

"Not anything. In his last text, sent while the victim was in the hospital, he used a regionalism without knowing it. 'Abusin' *on*.' Regionalisms are the most obvious kind of clue. So I asked Jackson if either of the other two suspects that I hadn't ruled out came from some area in the deep South. He said he was pretty sure one did. Truth is, I didn't do much. It was Jackson who—"

"Hit me again. What's this regionalism stuff?"

"Okay, here's the simplest example," Maggie began, "and the most obvious. Say you were born in Philly and moved to New Orleans. You go to the diner and ask for a hoagie. They look at you. Hoagie? That's because Big Easy folk call that kind of sandwich a po' boy. If you were in Boston, they'd call it a grinder. New Hampshire, a sub. LA, a torpedo. New York, a hero, and so on. Of course, it's not really that area-restricted, especially with everyone talking to everyone else all over the world. But certain words *can* be clues to where a person might have lived." Maggie caught her breath.

"Got it."

"Forensic linguists can never say for absolute certainty that it's this person or that who did or said something. What they can do is point a finger in a direction—in this case, a Louisiana direction. Then it's up to you guys to find the clues that'll nail him."

"I consider us damn lucky to have found you."

"You make your own luck, Chief Murray," Maggie said and smiled. Then, looking at a framed poem on the chief's wall, she said, "'Casey at the Bat'? May I ask how come?"

"My all-time favorite," he said.

"So that explains the framed lines on your desk," she said.

"Man, you're observant."

Not looking at the poem, Maggie recited, "'The outlook wasn't brilliant for the Mudville Nine that day.'"

"You know it?" the chief asked.

She continued quoting the poem and slapping her thigh to emphasize the beat. "'The SCORE stood FOUR to TWO, with BUT one IN-ning MORE to PLAY.'"

"'And THEN when COO-ney DIED at FIRST,'" the chief continued, also emphasizing every other word. "'And BA-rrows DID the SAME.'" He made a sweeping arm gesture for Maggie to continue.

"'A PALL-like SI-lence FELL upON the PAtrons OF the GAME.'"

"Good lord!" the chief said. "Never met anybody could do that 'cept me and the boys. It's part of the job description. I make 'em learn it. Da DUH da DUH da DUH."

"It's called iambic heptameter."

"What the hell's that?" the chief asked.

"Damn, I'll never get Ms. Barker out of my head. She was my seventh-grade teacher. Drilled Casey into our heads. Many poems are written in beats. In Casey, it's seven heavy beats in each line. That stuff's not really important. What I want to know is why's the poem so important to you?" Maggie asked.

"Guess it's 'cause I dreamed of being in the big leagues since I was five. Obviously, that didn't happen." He chuckled as he patted his belly. "I recite that damn thing all day long. Can't help myself. Most of the time, I don't even know I'm doing it, until someone like Jackson points it out," the chief said.

"Damn earworm," Maggie said. "You know the name Jean Harris?"

"Should I?"

"She murdered her lover, a cardiologist-slash-diet-doctor, Herman Tarnower."

"Right, right. I remember that."

"Turns out she had this song stuck in her head since childhood. 'Put the Blame on Mame.' Psychologists at her trial said the repetition served as a secret weapon to pump her up and justify her actions."

"You shittin' me? Just 'cause she was singing a song?"

"*That* song. Other lyrics have been linked to murder, too. Like 'Helter Skelter' and Charles Manson. 'Night Prowler' and Richard Ramirez. Prosecutors in that case had no doubt it had driven Ramirez to kill *and* provided him with an MO. I could go on." Maggie stared straight at him.

"Hey, don't be looking my way," the chief said laughing. "I'm an innocent man. All the Casey poem ever did was try to make me a better man."

Maggie chuckled. "Funny thing about earworm. Usually, it's triggered by a key incident in the past that has some deep significance— sometimes joyful, often painful. I bet your Casey jag started at some point when you were dreaming of the big leagues *and* you happened to read that poem."

"Hey, Madame Genius. You happen to be right. Me and Casey

have something in common," the Chief said. "It was the championship game. Stillwater High against Greely. Score tied three all. Two outs. Bottom of the ninth. I was up." The chief shook his head and looked down. "It was the most humiliating day of my life. I know it must've been for Casey, too."

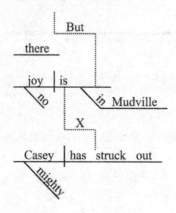

SIX

The following Thursday, after their fourth RA meeting—three hours of chart-creating—Professor Ditmire suggested they decompress at Muddy Waters, the local hangout where expensive coffee came with names befitting a wannabe intellectual mecca: David Coffeefield, For Whom the Bean Tolls, Lord of the Beans, The Count of Macchiato. As they passed the pastry display case, three trays high, Ditmire said, "I've got a serious sweet tooth."

"I might have to get one of each," Maggie said.

"I was thinking the same. I absolutely can't resist. My addiction."

Maggie realized that was the most personal thing he'd said in all the time she'd been his RA. Small talk played no part in their interactions.

"No way you're even a contender when it comes to chocolate," Ditmire said.

"Oh?"

"There's nothing *chocolate* that I don't know," Ditmire declared and then chose the Mississippi mud cake.

"Me neither," Maggie said ordering the deep-fried brownie.

"Do I hear a challenge?" Ditmire asked.

Maggie cocked her head.

"Challenge on!" Ditmire said. "A fight to the finish!"

They carried their desserts and coffee to a small table by the window.

"Okay, let me think a sec." Ditmire sat back in his chair. "Hmm. I've got one. Let's see who can name the most films with the word *chocolate* in the title. I'll start. *Like Water for Chocolate*."

"*Charlie and the Chocolate Factory*," Maggie said. "Easy peasy."

Ditmire took a huge bite of his cake. "Mmm. So good! *Chocolat*."

"*Lessons in Chocolate*," Maggie immediately responded and sipped her espresso.

"Hmm. Wow. Good one. Not sure I know . . ." Ditmire began drumming his fingers on the table. "Chocolate, chocolate . . . Oh of course. *The Chocolate Soldier*. Phew."

"*Blood and Chocolate*," Maggie said and chuckled. "Among the worst movies, ever."

"Hmm. Not so many titles with *chocolate* in it, come to think of it." Ditmire squeezed his napkin in his palm. "Give me a sec. I'm not sure there are any others."

Maggie smiled. "Is there a time limit?"

"Like you have one?" His eyes narrowed as he stared at her.

Maggie looked from his face to the floor, then back again.

"You have one?" he repeated. "If so, say it. Just say it."

Maggie hesitated. "Nope," she said and chuckled—not even considering saying any of the other films that'd come to mind: *The Chocolate War, Merci pour le Chocol—*

"That's a relief. Wouldn't want to be one-upped by a student."

Maggie had just lost all interest in finishing her brownie.

"So," Ditmire said after polishing off the cake, "aside from everything else I'm doing, I'm submitting a grant application on the idea that less is more when it comes to dialogue in film. That's the title. Less is more."

"From 'The Faultless Painter'?" Maggie said, clearly remembering the line from Browning:

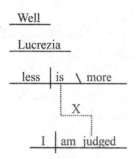

"Not sure what you're talking about," Ditmire said.

"The words. From the Browning poem, 'The Faultless Painter,' also known as 'Andrea del Sarto,' right?" Maggie asked.

"No," Ditmire said. "I took it from the horse's mouth. The guy who first said it. Van der Rohe. He was talking about minimalism in architecture."

"Oh . . . right." Maggie twirled a strand of hair.

"You know something I don't?" he asked.

Maggie stared intently at her espresso.

"Come on."

"Well . . . I'm not at all sure . . . I thought the painter del Sarto said 'less is more' in the poem. Obviously, I was wrong."

"I don't know the poem," he said. "But I highly doubt that was the source."

"Confused again," Maggie said lightly. "Chronic state of affairs."

Goddamn furor loquendi. Know when to hold 'em. Know when to shut the fuck up!

Maggie remembered memorizing the Browning poem in twelfth grade, along with what her teacher had said was the poem's theme of less is more. At the time, shortly after her mother's death, Maggie felt she should apply those words to her life. The feeling, however, didn't last long. More wasn't even enough back then. More. More. And even more.

"I footnoted van der Rohe. I know I'm right," Ditmire insisted.

Maggie nodded with certainty. "I'm sure you are," she said in a barely audible voice.

"Here's an idea. Take a look at my application. You might even research a bit more about 'less is more.'" He deliberately raised his eyebrows. "And then, let's talk."

Maggie rubbed her palms on her jeans.

"There's a section in the application about brevity in film dialogue," he continued. "So you'll be reading a bit about that."

Maggie shook her head. "I never studied film dialogue. I don't think I'd be your best reader. Maybe someone from your film class would be—"

"However, you seem to have great recall," he said. "There'd be no reason you couldn't simply give it a read. Okay, how about we try this. A little challenge to determine if, in fact, you're fit for the task. Can you give me one example of brevity of dialogue in a movie you've seen?"

Several immediately popped into Maggie's head. *2001: A Space Odyssey. Cast Away. The Revenant.* But she didn't say anything.

"Come on, I know you must have some in mind."

"No, I really don't."

"Think harder then," he said firmly.

Finally, after finishing her espresso, she said, "Maybe . . . maybe the line, 'Mmm. Juicy fruit.'" Her voice rose on the word *fruit*. "You know? From *Little Miss Sunshine*"?

"I'll take it," he said. "Maybe not the best, but, yup, it'll do."

Ditmire finished his second dessert, a slice of chocolate pecan pie, took several sips of coffee, leaned in, and said, "I'm real curious. How'd you land at Rosedale?"

Maggie couldn't tell from his facial features if he was really curious or simply filling the space with chatter.

"Trust me, it's so boring you don't want to know," she said gazing around the café.

"Please. Fill me in."

Maggie hesitated, then spoke so quickly that there was barely a separation between her words. "Okay, so I graduated high school a year early, went to college which I finished in three years, majored in linguistics 'cause I was told I might have some small amount of talent there, then decided to apply here for my master's 'cause it's local and not too expensive." Finally, she took a breath.

"Another?" he asked pointing to the empty cup.

"I'm good."

"That explains some things, but why forensics?"

"Long story. There's no short version. Another time."

"Well then, last question, how about in twenty words or less, what're your plans after graduation? If I'm not mistaken, you graduate at the end of the semester."

"Right. Yup." Maggie thought how to answer the question and then counted the words. "Not lots of choices for master's in forensic linguistics. Maybe FBI or a law firm. Might as well have majored in philosophy." She paused. "Twenty-two."

"Huh?"

"That was twenty-two words. Two too many."

"Geez. Idiot savant?"

"The former."

"Ha! So why not go for a PhD? At least then you could teach. I did that."

"For one, can't afford it. Besides, don't think I want to teach."

"It could open lot of doors. Trust me. The places you'll go!"

Maggie had to chuckle. That Dr. Seuss book was the first book she'd memorized word for word. From that time on, she was both proud—and ashamed—of her near perfect photographic memory. Ashamed because, once again, her classmates mocked her. But right now, at this very moment, she felt proud. "'You have brains in your head. You have feet in your shoes.'"

"'You can steer yourself any direction you choose,'" Ditmire continued.

Maggie clinked his mug with hers. "It was my favorite Dr. Seuss book."

Just then Maggie's phone pinged. "Sorry, sorry," she said. "It could be BJ. Her kid's been sick and I might need to . . ." She read the text. "Listen to this," she said. "Come to precinct at five tonight. Emergency. Oh shit. I wonder if . . . shit shit shit. Um, sorry." Maggie let out a huge sigh. "Maybe the Louisiana guy was *not* the one." Maggie saw that eight cops were on the chain. "Better go," she said. "Thanks for everything."

"I'm sure you got the right guy," Ditmire said.

Maggie raced out and quickly diagrammed a Marge Gunderson line from *Fargo* on the way:

As she started up Annabelle, Maggie forced herself to quit the pity party and start thinking positively, so that even if she'd led the cops to the wrong man . . .

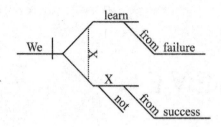

Bram Stoker's *Dracula* had just become her new source of positive thinking. Fancy that.

SEVEN

Maggie got to the precinct at 4:45 p.m. and stayed in the parking lot to smoke one last cigarette. Once inside, an officer from behind the reception desk extended his hand and said, "Captain Gutierrez."

"Hi. I'm Maggie."

"Figured. Great to meet you."

He hurried her in. "Meeting's about to start. Come on."

"Sounds serious," Maggie said.

"Never got a call like this. Chief's frantic."

"Um, could I ask if ... do you know if ... does it have anything to do with, you know, the stalker guy who raped—"

"Buddy Ray from Louisiana? Nope, you nailed that one." Maggie tried to stay up with the cop she now labeled Dapper Dan as he giant-stepped down the hall. His cologne wafted off his body and filled the hall, nearly masking the smell of burnt coffee. "Buddy Ray finally admitted it. This one's totally different. Something about the mayor over west aways. That's all I know. Chief'll tell us the rest."

"Take a seat." The chief gestured to one of the two empty chairs as they came into the conference room. Mr. Dapper held it out for her. The other cops were already at the table.

"Thanks for coming so quick. This here's Maggie," he said to the room of cops.

Maggie took note of each man as the chief said his name.

Huckabee
husky redhead, full beard, thick neck

Evans
overweight
porcelain skin, apple cheeks, jolly

Pickens
sloppy, straining at seams of uniform
uninterested

Carter
silent type; could be a bonehead . . . or a genius

Gutierrez
peacock
slick-back hair, clean shaven

Jackson
still a commanding presence
sad or angry or both

Maggie immediately recognized from the way they were sitting and the look on their faces that they were just like the cops she had tried to interest in Lucy's disappearance. Bored. Indifferent. And maybe heartless.

"So here's where we're at," the chief began. "The mayor over in

Birchbrook, Tom Hemphill, he's a friend of mine. Y'all know Birchbrook? Around forty miles up CR 345. The man does really good work. Helps out his community big time. He's been elected and re-elected for the past decade . . ."

The chief's words were fading. Did she really need to know background on a mayor in Birchbrook? Maggie's breathing began returning to normal, now knowing that her worst-case scenario had not come to pass—again. Her thoughts returned to the three different book proposals she was ready to email to Ditmire. He'd sent her rough drafts of each last week and asked if she could magically turn *these lemons into lemonade like you do with everything you touch*. Should he only know about her nonexistent culinary skills. But his flattery and encouragement were going a long way to overcome—

"Kidnapped!" the chief yelled. Maggie looked up. His face was red and twisted as he barked out words from the side of his mouth. "You heard me. Kidnapped! Now you gotta understand, this here's personal. I've known the mayor since before Heidi was even born for Chrissake. I knew him when his wife was alive." The chief took out a handkerchief and wiped his forehead. "Called me personally this afternoon, after Heidi'd been missing for several hours. Crying. For the love of Jesus, we've gotta bring her home."

Maggie diagrammed:

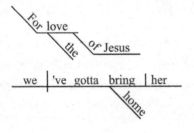

Beginning a sentence with an independent adverbial phrase—*for the love of Jesus*—indicated that the most important part was yet to come: *bring her home.* She began by placing *for* on the diagonal line leading to *love* and then she—

"Been gone since noon!" he yelled, banging his hand on the desk.

Maggie stopped diagramming.

"The mayor figured she'd show up any minute. Maybe she was hanging with friends or whatever. Kids, ya know? But then he called all her friends. No Heidi. He went to all the places he figured she could be. Even sent patrols out looking for her." The chief stopped and shook his head. "Then a cop found her bike on the side of the road."

The chief turned his back. Maggie assumed he was wiping away tears.

After a minute, he said, "Okay, here's what's being circulated online and what's appearing in tomorrow's paper. For sure, TV and radio are gonna cover it nonstop." He gave a copy to everyone.

FOURTEEN-YEAR-OLD MISSING

BLANE COUNTY, Fla. A frantic search is under way for 14-year-old Heidi Hemphill, daughter of Mayor Tom Hemphill.

Heidi was riding her bike to her martial arts class in Summit. But she never made it. The instructor called the mayor when Heidi hadn't shown up. The mayor called the police. They traced her route and found Heidi's bike on the side of the road on Lakeview near Dixie.

Heidi is 4 feet 11 inches, around 100 pounds, white, with brown eyes and short curly blond hair. She was wearing pink shorts, a white T-shirt with "I Heart Florida" on it, and red high-top sneakers.

"Things like that don't happen here," said Ellen Connelly, a neighbor of Mayor Hemphill. "Everyone's worried sick."

Martha Hemphill, Heidi's mother, passed away from cancer a year ago. Heidi is the mayor's only child.

Detective Henry Breakwater from the Wellingford Town Police Department is lead detective. All neighboring precincts have been notified and will be actively involved in the investigation.

"If anyone believes they may have seen Heidi or has any information at all about her whereabouts," Breakwater said, "contact the police immediately at 555-550-5755."

An Amber Alert has been issued.

Below the article was a photo of a young girl, Heidi, standing next to her father in front of Town Hall at a swearing-in ceremony for new judges. She was wearing a gingham pinafore and pink Mary Janes. The caption read: "Heidi Hemphill steps into her mother's shoes." Maggie sensed Heidi's shyness in the way her big brown eyes didn't look at the camera, but off into the distance somewhere. Her shoes were turned slightly inward. She had a deep cleft in her chin, like Kirk Douglas, and a single dimple on the left side of her face.

After Maggie finished reading, she said, "Chief, I'm really sorry about what happened, but I don't get why I'm here."

"Right. Well, here's what they're holding back from the public. The guy left a note in the bike spokes. I've got a copy. Breakwater's men have already combed the area where the bike was, cordoned it off, put sniffer dogs on it. They're fielding calls, interviewing folks, checking possible enemies the mayor may have. It was a hard-fought race last year. The yokels up there get all riled up about most anything, ready to grab their guns at the drop of a hat. One person's already come forward. The lady said she saw a truck in the area going kinda slow. Trucks don't go slow around here, she told the cops. She took down the plates. An APB's out."

Maggie's hands started trembling.

A sentence from Toni Morrison's *Sula* surfaced:

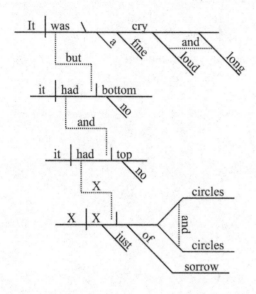

A harrowing howl of remembrance exploded in Maggie's head.

"For sure, it wasn't some spur of the moment thing," the chief continued. "The guy spent time composing the note ahead of time. He must've known Heidi'd be passing by that deserted stretch of road on Wednesdays at around noon. He must've been stalking her. I think he sat down, real calm-like in his living room or wherever, and wrote the damn thing out. Word by word. Each of you guys has a task. Go up there, Gutierrez, start by helping Breakwater's team interview neighbors, friends, teachers. Evans, assist them in checking out sex offenders. Last number on file here in this county is over three hundred. They've got their eyes on guys located within a twenty-mile radius of the mayor's house. Know how many that is? Wild guess. I'll tell you. Sixty-five. Jackson, you give another once-over to the area where the bike was. Pickens, I want you—"

Maggie grabbed her backpack and rushed to the door.

"Maggie?" the chief yelled.

"I'm sorry," she said. "But I can't help you."

"Why not? What the heck!"

"Not this," Maggie said as she raced out.

EIGHT

Maggie rode home in a fog. After she parked Annabelle, she ran into the house, grabbed a Bud, and went out back. For sure, the guys'd be there—and serve as the perfect distraction. The backyards around the lake flowed one into the next without so much as a fence or shrub barrier. It was as if everyone had silently agreed that this land is your land, this land is my land, and *mi casa es su casa*. Staking out ground was for rich folks, the small-minded and privileged. No one on Royal Palm would dare be accused of that.

All the kids who grew up on the block had each other's backs. In the twenty-one years Maggie had lived there, she never feared for anything. If anyone dared come at her in a threatening way, there'd be serious consequences. One time, when a gang member who'd been hanging with Rodriguez grabbed her and cupped her breast, the dude ended up limping to his Harley.

"Hey Sugar, wanna fuck?" Maggie heard as she neared the lake. Of course the guys were hanging out, smoking and doping in their outdoor club house.

"You wouldn't know where to put it," Maggie answered Tidwell automatically.

"Not what you used to say."

"That was then."

Tidwell had fought in Afghanistan, and when he came back, he was different. For one, he was minus two toes. For another, his once carefree, reckless attitude was replaced with a somber, brooding one, which he drowned in pills.

"You okay?" He gave her a hug. "Wassup?"

Rodriguez popped his head out his kitchen window. He grinned when he saw Maggie and started making a slurping sound. "Hey, Babe. Wanna?"

"What an asshole," Tidwell said.

"Things never change, do they?" Maggie said.

"Least you know what you got."

"Is that the good or bad news?" Maggie asked.

"Little of both, I suppose." Tidwell put his arm around her. "You wanna talk 'bout something? Don't like how you look."

"I'm okay."

"You sure?"

Maggie nodded.

"I'm always here. You know that, right?" He took a toke and passed her the joint.

"Of course, Tid. Thanks."

"Okay, so here's the thing," Tidwell said. "We're heading to Daytona for a rally. Think you could hold a little something for me? Don't want no one breaking in and stealing it."

"Sure."

"Be right back."

While Tidwell was gone, Maggie took long, deep drags and finished the joint.

Returning with a duffle bag, Tidwell said, "Feel free to indulge."

"Gotta go," Maggie said. "Hope the trip's the bomb."

Maggie gave a peace sign and headed inside. Once there, she grabbed her diagram book. She jotted down the next sentences she wanted to work on. They were from Joan Didion's *The Year of Magical Thinking. I know why we try to keep the dead alive: we try to keep them alive in order to keep them with us. I also know that if we are to live ourselves there comes a point at which we must relinquish the dead, let them go, keep them dead.*

True. So true. They remain. They occupy.

Maggie diagrammed those sentences, the next, and the next, and then she'd had it. Enough with the goddamn lines and pedestals. She lit up and checked her phone. Nothing. Good. Maybe that'd be the end of her and the Olemeda PD. Hearing revving engines, she saw dozens of bikes lining Royal Palm, poised to head off to the rally.

She'd been putting off writing a paper analyzing the syntax and sentence patterns in Son of Sam's letters to the cops, and she figured this could be the perfect time to tackle it. Delving into Berkowitz's words would keep her mind focused, tethered even. And that's exactly what she needed right now. Besides, the paper was due in two days. She reached over to grab her computer and knocked over Tid's satchel. Dozens of vials spilled out.

"Tid," she said to the living room walls. "What the fuck! You've enough shit here for every dude on Royal Palm—for a year."

Amazed by the sheer number and variety, Maggie decided to line them up alphabetically, creating order out of chaos. Surely, Son of Sam could wait. Starting with *Amphetamine* and ending with *Xanax*, she placed each drug in its correct place on the long, low table by the kitchen. Standing back, she marveled at the impressive array of uppers, downers, and just plain obliterators. Touching each one in turn, she paused at Dextroamphetamine and figured that a hit of speed would be just the ticket to get her focused on Mr. Murder's mocking letters. She plucked two and washed them down with a beer. Soon after, she found herself researching and typing furiously. Thank you, Tid. In one note, Berkowitz called himself, "the Chubby Behomouth." The insane jerk can't even spell!

Maggie heard a knock, and when she looked away from the screen, she saw that the sun had already risen. The rabbit hole of dexies had been a productive one. She'd already typed eighteen pages.

"Not home!" she yelled. In all the years she lived on Royal Palm, never once did any of her neighbors knock, and besides, they'd all left for the rally. She figured it must be a Jehovah's Witness. They often stopped by but always hightailed it away after hearing her refrain, which she yelled now: "Just outta prison. Ain't lookin' for religion." She typed the last sentence of her paper: "And thus the Son of Sam Law came into existence," when she heard the door open.

"What's with you?" Jackson asked as he stepped inside. "What the hell's the matter with you anyway?"

It took Maggie a second to comprehend that Jackson, Detective Jackson from the Olemeda PD, was inside *her* house.

"Excuse me," she said. "What the hell're you doing here?"

"Chief told me to get you on it." Jackson waved a sheet of paper at her. "Not my idea."

"I believe this is considered trespassing. Where's your warrant?"

"Right," he said. "Why don't you call the cops? So, you gonna explain yourself or what?"

"I don't need to explain anything to you."

Jackson took a few steps farther into the room. Post-its in a variety of colors covered the walls, tabletops, doors, even the ceiling. "What's going on?" he asked. "What the hell're all those things?"

Maggie stood with her arms across her chest. "That your business?"

"Weird."

Maggie let out a sigh. "So happens, Mr. Invasive Species, each one is a favorite quote. They enlighten, even inspire, me. Know anything about that?"

"Nope."

"Figured."

Maggie pointed to a neon pink stickie. "Try that one," she said.

From across the room, Jackson read, "People surprise you, Frank, with just how fuckin stupid they are."

"Richard Ford wrote that."

"So?"

"Right," Maggie said. "So."

Jackson moved farther into the room.

"Oh, please do come in." Maggie made a sweeping gesture. "By all means, make yourself comfortable. Sure, the couch is fine. May I get you something to eat? Drink? A beer, sandwich, snack?"

"I'm good, thanks."

Jackson strolled around the room. "This place could be a bookstore." He trailed his hand along the book spines. "Or a library. How many you got? Must be five hundred at least."

"One thousand, seven hundred and thirty-eight, for your information," Maggie said, hands on hips—and scowling.

"Yeah right."

"Yeah right is right," Maggie said.

"You keep count? Oh, you were kidding," Jackson said. "Ha ha."

"I was not kidding."

"Well then, that's nuts. Look, the chief's job is on the line. Mine too. So give us a hand here, will ya?"

"I'll find someone else to work the case. Give me an hour."

"What part of this am I missing?"

Maggie stood in front of him. "Look, I can't work this case. I won't work this case. Period. End of story."

"Why's that?" he asked. "'Cause you shot your wad on the last one?"

"Nice image, Jackson. Whatever."

"Give me one good reason and I'm outta here."

Maggie sipped the beer, sat down, lit up, and blew smoke rings. "Fine," she finally said. "I'll tell you but then you get the fuck out."

Jackson nodded.

"Okay, working this case would put me in a bad place. I can't go back there."

"Back where?" Jackson cocked his head. "Stop blowing that shit in my face. I'm gonna say it again. Chief's job is on the line. Long story. He needs you."

"I can't."

"Let's cut the bullshit, okay. You tell me why. I tell it to the chief. We all understand. It's over."

Maggie blurted, "My friend went missing years ago. She was fifteen. Still hasn't been found. The cops feigned interest. You know who you guys remind me of? All the cops back then, sitting around pretending to care. Same empty eyes. Same arrogant disinterest. I. Can't. Go. Back. There."

"Oh, okay, you got a backstory," Jackson said. "I get it. I'm real sorry about your friend. Now, returning to why I'm here. We're looking for Heidi Hemphill. The mayor's daughter. Today. Your friend, on the other hand, has been gone a long time. Truth is, she may never be found. But Heidi's fresh. A whole different enchilada. And why the hell wouldn't you want to help find a missing kid?"

"Tell the chief you did your best." Maggie opened the door. "Please go. I'll find you someone."

"Thick as I am," Jackson said circling the room, "I thought that brains brought some sides with it. You know, like courage or decency. Looks like those things passed you by."

"Don't guilt me, okay. It won't work."

"No one in their right mind wouldn't help." He stopped next to the table by the kitchen. "Hmm . . . I spy with my little eye. What do we have here?"

"Oh shit, shit, shit." Maggie quickly began stuffing pills back into Tidwell's duffle bag.

"You have a prescription for these?" Jackson asked.

"I'm holding them for a friend."

"Heard that one before."

"Helping him out," Maggie said.

Jackson picked up one vial. "Oxycodone." Looking at others, he said, "Codeine, Percocet, Dilaudid. Bet you're making some serious bucks."

"Right, I'm a dealer," Maggie said blowing smoke directly at him.

"Quit it, ya hear?" Jackson palmed half a dozen vials. "This much qualifies as intent to sell."

"Gimme a break, Jackson. I'm not that fucking stupid."

"Do you happen to know the penalty?"

"I said, they're not mine."

"Seven to twenty plus a fine," Jackson said.

"I swear, they're not—"

"Swearing doesn't make fact."

"I can't believe you're doing this."

"Believe it," Jackson said and picked up the duffle. "This is called evidence."

"I told you they're not mine."

"However," he said as he casually walked around the room, "I could be persuaded to look the other way."

Maggie stared at him. "You're kidding, right?"

"Not a chance."

Mr. Commanding Presence was *bribing* her. Goddamn.

"I'll forget I saw anything," he said. "And in return, you—"

"Don't say it. Just don't."

"And in return," he paused, "you take a look at this goddamn note. That's all you've got to do. That's the sum total. Tell me what you see." He waved the note. "Take your time to think about whether this is an assignment you're willing to accept. You've got," he checked his watch, "exactly one minute. Don't mind if I do take a seat," he said settling in on the opposite end of the couch from Maggie. "Fifty-nine. Fifty-eight. Fifty-seven. Fifty-six—"

"Come on, Jackson. This is insane. I'm in grad school for Chrissake. I'll get you someone way better. Trust me, I'd be of absolutely no use."

"Forty. Thirty-nine. . . ."

Maggie mentally diagrammed a sentence attributed to Norman Cousins:

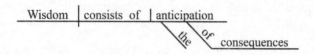

She began by placing the subject, *wisdom,* first, then the phrasal verb, *consists of,* next.

"Nineteen. Eighteen . . ."

Maggie crushed her cigarette.

"Eleven. Ten. Nine," he said. "Reminder, you're under arrest at zero."

"Right."

"Four. Three."

"You wouldn't," she said.

"I would. I will. Two."

Maggie grabbed the paper. "Fine," she said. "Satisfied?"

She began reading:

I'll poke her hard wit my bigg dick; she screem and purr and spin.

So love the sinner; hate the sin. It feel real good to win!

"Jesus." As she began to imagine the kind of pervert who could have written it, she once again reminded herself of Alcott's words: "Don't think about the meaning of what you're analyzing. Read the words without emotion. Do the job you're being trained to do."

"Whattaya see?" Jackson asked. "Anything there?"

"Shut up, okay? Just shut the fuck up."

She made a mental note of what she saw:

> *twenty-seven words*
> *one two-syllable word*
> *correct punctuation*
> *three misspellings—all suspect*
> *word-initial letter of each sentence in upper case*

"Anything?" he asked.

She mentally formed sentence diagrams but couldn't find any patterns— no consistent use of introductory adverbial clauses, no multiple compound-complex sentences, no regionalism, no misplaced modifiers.

handwritten

She considered what the words might reveal about the person's education. He correctly used the semicolon, an apostrophe, and end punctuation, so he probably graduated from high school. He spelled *sinner, poke, purr,* and *hate* correctly, but misspelled *with, big,* and *scream.* If he's trying to appear uneducated, he should've done better than that. The guy's had some schooling, but for sure he's not all that clever.

"So?" Jackson asked, pacing.

Maggie looked for age and ethnicity clues but didn't see any words that would indicate a specific decade, like *totally, Chicago overcoat, oh snap*, or any slang unique to a certain demographic, like *dang, fixin' to, britches, kin*.

"Not much here," Maggie said. "Except a Christian reference. 'Love the sinner hate the sin.' Maybe he's a preacher or minister or something. And he's a lefty."

"You know handwriting, too?" Jackson cocked his head.

"You asked me to help. We're on the same team, remember? I'm no expert, but I know a little. Took a course. Forensic document examination."

"Religion. Lefty," Jackson said. "Religion. Lefty. Lefty. Religion." He kept repeating the words. "Let's see," Jackson continued. "Dudes with religion? Why that's about every single person I know. Plus, it'd probably include the entire Southern US of A. And a lefty? I bet that narrows the pool by ten or so?"

"It eliminates approximately ninety percent of the population, Mr. Know-It-All. So maybe you'll consider opening your mouth when you know what you're talking about."

"Consider it considered."

Maggie went back to examining the note.

"Look, I've gotta get back to the shop," Jackson said and grabbed his hat. "Chief's waiting on a word. Hey, no pressure. Only thing is, chief's putting all his eggs in your basket. No pressure at all." He closed the door behind him.

"No pressure?" Maggie repeated. Her mother's words immediately, automatically surfaced: *You'll never amount to anything. You're a goddamn loser.*

But then she thought of the title of a Billie Jean King book: *Pressure Is a Privilege.*

Believe it, Maggie told herself. Get on with it.

"I can," she said out loud, closing her eyes and singing softly, "You'll never know dear, how much I love you." Relaxing back into the decrepit couch, she repeated over and over: "How much I love you. How much I love you."

"One more thing." Jackson had tornadoed back in. "I checked out where Heidi went missing."

"Please, just go!"

"Breakwater's men must've used toothbrushes to sweep the area. Nothing but dirt and more dirt."

"Thanks for the update, but that's not in my wheelhouse. It's yours."

"I did come up with something. An eyeglass screw, you know the kind that—"

". . . that's near the hinge and connects the end piece with the temple. Also known as the arm."

"Whatever, Miss Know-It-All."

"You saw a screw? A goddamn microscopic screw? That's kinda insane. But, seems to me," Maggie said, "not being a fancy detective or anything, that dozens of people've been combing the area, right? And I'll bet one or two of 'em wear glasses, right? And I'll further bet that any one of them could've lost their screws—literally—right? Or, how about this. Perhaps some hapless fella passed by there last week or last month and broke his glasses."

"If it's a winner, it could narrow the pool. Unlike your religion crap."

"By a whopping thirty-six percent," Maggie declared. "Not the best odds."

"You know that for a fact?"

"Yup."

Jackson shook his head. "I don't believe you. I'm checking it out."

"Trust me," Maggie said emphatically.

"The way to make people trustworthy," he said, "is to trust them."

"You didn't really say that."

"I did."

"And you know where it's from?"

"Hemingway. Wrote it in one of his letters," Jackson said.

"No friggin' way. You read them?"

Jackson had a wide smile on his face.

"Oh my god. You're not as thick as you look. Maybe."

"Chief said he'd like to see you back at nine sharp, that is, if I was successful. So, see you at nine." He tipped his hat and shut the door behind him.

NINE

At nine the next morning, Maggie showed up at the precinct. The place was swarming with press. Reporters from local TV stations and papers were camped outside. It had been reported that the Olemeda PD was assisting in the investigation. As Maggie walked inside, half a dozen reporters shouted questions: "What's the latest? Any suspects? Who are you? Are you involved . . ."

Maggie went directly to the chief's office. Jackson was already there.

"Thank you, Maggie," the chief said. "You've no idea how much this means to me."

"No problem," Maggie said, although it was a huge problem.

"First off, no talking to reporters. I'll deal with them. The word is, we're assisting Breakwater's team and they fully expect Heidi will be back home safe and sound in no time. Leave all that to me."

"Yes, sir," Jackson said.

Speaking to Maggie, the chief said, "Jackson here reported you narrowed down that the guy's a religious dude and a lefty. Any more you can say about that? Can you explain how you got there?"

"Well," Maggie began, "it's really not much and, truth be told, it might turn out to be a big fat nothing. But I'll tell you what I saw. He writes 'Love the sinner, hate the sin,' so the guy could be religious. But, on the other hand, anyone could use that cliché and have no religion at all. I'm just noting it, okay? And as far as being a lefty, I got that from several clues, like the slant to the left of his letters; like where the sharp point was at the end of a lowercase *t*, showing that the cross-stroke went from right to left, not like a righty's which goes from left to right; like the smudges on the words as his hand crossed over them when he kept writing. All pretty obvious clues. This kind of analysis is far from definitive. Graphology doesn't usually stand up in court, but I had these thoughts and figured I'd tell you all. Basically, they're just educated guesses."

"More educated than us here. So, you got anything else?"

"Not yet. I'm afraid there simply aren't enough words."

The chief pointed to the missing kids' posters on the wall. "Heidi being missing is the saddest thing I've had to deal with in all my thirty some years on the force. I can't hardly get these words out, but . . . we may have to add her picture here. Pray to Jesus not."

Of course, Lucy's picture wasn't on any poster of missing kids. Maggie knew that Lucy had long ago been relegated to the cold case files. Nobody was looking for her—if they ever had.

The chief sat down, elbows on knees, head in his hands.

"Missing kids do get found," Maggie said hoping to bring a sliver of optimism to the chief. "Like, for example, Jan Broberg, Jayme Closs, Elizabeth Smart, Jaycee Dugard, Katie Beers. All of them."

"I suppose."

"And how about Amanda Berry, Gina DeJesus, and Michelle Knight? And those are the ones I can think of right off the top of my head. For some, it took decades. But they did eventually come home. So there's hope."

"Chief here was voted President of the Find Our Missing Children organization," Jackson said. "One hundred ninety-seven cops and detectives from all over the country unanimously elected him."

"Impressive."

"We did help locate a few. Actually, seven. Kids from all over the country. Not a great percentage, but we're never giving up."

"Why don't you tell the chief about your friend?" Jackson said.

"Now's not the time," Maggie said.

"Yeah it is," Jackson said.

Maggie shook her head.

"The reason Maggie didn't want to work on Heidi," Jackson said, "was 'cause her best friend went missing years ago. This is personal for her, too."

"Jackson!"

"Now that's something," the chief said. "Where's she now?"

Maggie glared at Jackson.

"Maybe he can help," Jackson said. "No harm in letting him try. Truth is, Maggie's got no idea where she's at. Nobody knows."

"Damn, that's tough," the chief said. "I'm hoping and praying that's not the case with Heidi." He slumped in his chair. "I can't let myself go there. Tell me about your friend. What happened?"

Maggie looked at him, then down at her feet, then back at him. His focus had stayed steady, his eyes fixed on her, and he was nodding his head.

"Come on. Maybe I can help."

She bit her lip, held her breath for five, then asked, "You really want to know?"

"Wouldn't have asked if I didn't."

Maggie began telling the story, haltingly at first, but then furor loquendi took over. She ended by saying the cops who worked the case were useless.

"Real sorry to hear that. Our guys can be called a lot of things, but useless ain't one of them."

Yeah right.

"So we get together every month and invite a speaker, like a forensic sketch artist or forensic psychologist, to fill us in on what they do and the latest developments in their field. Then we break into groups and discuss any new info, insights, ideas, stuff like that on any of the kids. Of course, if anything comes up between meetings, we do a quick conference call. They're all over Heidi as of twelve hours ago. Soon as we catch a break, I'll tell 'em about your friend."

"That would be amazing," Maggie said, hoping her enthusiasm would encourage the chief to get on it.

"Tell her about the psychics," Jackson said to the chief.

"You tell her."

"Wasn't my thing," Jackson said.

"Jackson here goes by the book," the chief said. "Like when someone calls and *thinks* they *might* have seen something, he grills them so hard they give up. 'Are you one-hundred percent certain that the truck was a . . . ? Oh, only ninety-nine? Well then, when you can substantiate, blah blah.' Right, Jackson? For me, anyone who has anything to say is worth my time. Yup, I've consulted with psychics. Jackson thinks it's hoo-ha. So far, they haven't led me to anyone, but I'm not tossing 'em out just yet. I read about how they led detectives to a dead body in, I think it was Montana or Idaho. Somewhere, but damn, I'll follow up on anything and anybody."

"Even a forensic linguist," Maggie said.

"Damn straight," the chief said and he and Maggie high-fived.

Looking at Jackson, the chief said, "Did you ask her?"

"Ask her what?" Jackson said.

"Oh come on. I give you one goddamn thing to do, well maybe two and maybe you were successful in the most important one, but how about the other?"

"The chief wants you to join the Mud Hens," Jackson said.

"The what?" Maggie asked.

"Our softball team. The Mud Hens," the chief said. "Serves as decompression. This job can burn you out in no time. And now with Heidi," his voice cracked. "Two days missing. Stats are not good."

"Um . . . Mud Hens?" Maggie said. "Anything to do with Mudville Nine?"

"Damn straight." The chief wound up and threw a fake pitch. "I know it's kinda laughable."

"Better than Jacksonville Jumbo Shrimp," Maggie said. "Or for that matter, the Rocket City Trash Pandas. They're actual minor league teams. But, hey, sorry, I'm gonna pass. Thanks though."

"Come on. We have one helluva time, don't we, Jackson?"

Jackson rolled his eyes.

"Mind if I ask why me?" Maggie said.

"Lou Ellen had to quit," the chief said. "Sprained her ankle chasing her kid, and we need to replace her. A *female,* you know, good for the PC business. I figure we could use some brains on our team, too, you know what I mean? And I think you'd be a lot faster than any of our guys. All of 'em are a hundred pounds overweight, except Jackson here. He's only thirty. When they run, I'm scared to death they're gonna have a coronary."

"Sorry," Maggie said, "but I never played softball. Besides, I only smoke tobacco. Don't chew it and for sure I don't spit it."

The chief smiled.

"Plus, I've no balls to fiddle with."

The chief roared. Jackson managed a smile.

"We'll find us someone else," Jackson said.

Maggie stared at Jackson.

"Yup, no problem at all," Jackson said.

"Oh?" Maggie raised her eyebrows. "On second thought, I'm in."

"That's what I want to hear," the chief said. "Game's tomorrow. You free?"

"I guess I'll have to be. See you then, Jackson," Maggie said tipping an imaginary baseball cap.

TEN

Maggie kept checking her texts all night, but she hadn't gotten a word from the chief or Jackson. She turned on the local news. There was nonstop chatter about possibilities of what happened to Heidi, along with disparaging remarks about the PD.

Maggie tried to push all that negative talk to the back of her mind, because she needed to be ready for her seventh session with Professor Ditmire. She succeeded but immediately another bleak thought invaded. Was some kind of weird rivalry going on with the professor? At the café, she sensed he was desperate to one-up her, show that he was way more intelligent than she. Could that be? Of course it could, but . . . for sure, her mind must be playing tricks on her because at every session, Ditmire was 100 percent in her court. He'd been giving her more and more responsibilities: reading and revising his proposals, helping him prepare exams, grading papers, even rewriting huge chunks of his papers.

Where were the jackasses now who thought Brainiac Bitch was a nobody?

"To get you up to date," Ditmire said as soon as Maggie walked into his office, "I sent out the much-improved grant application you worked on—thank you very much—and I should hear back in a few weeks. April 25 to be exact. You did great work. An especially huge thank you for the Browning attribution. It wasn't van der Rohe after all who coined 'less is more.' However, in my own defense, I was also correct. He is the person credited with popularizing it. The disseminator of the concept in the aphorism."

"Yes . . . right."

"Now I don't mean to brag or anything, but I'm a shoo-in for this one. Totally qualified. Above and beyond. How can I ever thank you?"

"You just did."

"No, actually, I'm going to right now. Are you ready?"

"I guess."

"I got in touch with Dean Schmidt, my buddy at Grogan. He's head of forensics there. What do you think?"

"About what?"

"Applying to their PhD program."

"Nope right out of the gate," Maggie said. "Not a chance in hell. But thank you. That was awfully—"

"Why's that?" Ditmire asked.

"For one, I can't afford it, even if I did get accepted. And that's a huge *if.* And for two, I'm done with school. Wanna get out in the world. Look, I really appreciate it, but—"

"New worlds can open up," Ditmire said. "Listen to me. Grogan's PhD program is funded, so you'll have no worries about money. With a PhD, job prospects balloon. You could teach or do research. Maybe you could join the FBI, if that's what you want. Even work in trademark or copyright law. You'd be in huge demand. You've got to dream big, young lady!"

Maggie picked at a cuticle.

"You've got so much talent, I'm afraid it's going to be wasted. You'll graduate here and then . . . a big nothing. No prospects."

"I know there aren't many jobs out there," Maggie said. "But I'm willing to give it a try," she said. "Maybe I'll get lucky."

Maggie took out her computer to get to work. "Oh," she said. "I've got a bit of good news."

"Go on."

"Well, it all began about a month ago," Maggie said then wrapped her hand around her bleeding thumb.

"And?"

"Professor Alcott, you know her, right? She asked if she could recommend me for this government grant. It's to work on threat assessment. The grant is to examine language on possible terrorist websites and figure out if the threats are authentic or not."

"I didn't know you studied that."

"I don't study exactly that, but it's words words words—and I do study them. A whole lot." Maggie instantly saw Michael Ondaatje's words, which she had placed on a Post-it on her refrigerator:

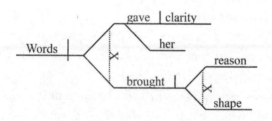

"I figured, why not apply? What harm?"

"Exactly," Ditmire said. "Why not?"

"Leaving aside it's the longest shot in the history of grant applications," Maggie said.

"Sounds like it, but hey, you never know."

"I only applied because I didn't want to seem rude or ungrateful. Professor Alcott's been so supportive."

"At least you're giving it a shot."

"There's more," Maggie said. "I got an email this morning. I made the short list. My head's spinning."

"You did?"

"Five of us. Down from over sixty," Maggie said. "Nuts, right? They'll make their decision on the same day that you hear about yours. Wild."

Ditmire turned his back. Maggie figured he was thinking of ways to congratulate her. "Never thought much of Alcott," he said.

"Oh? She's really nice," Maggie said. "And wicked smart."

"Insipid, if you ask me. A real loser."

"No she's not!" Maggie blurted, then trying to keep her voice calmer, she said, "She's been nothing but supportive and encouraging. I owe her a lot."

"You know, now that I think about it, that wasn't a strategic move on your part, becoming associated with her. Maybe you should've consulted me first. I mean, this ain't my first rodeo."

"She recommended me for a grant," Maggie said. "I'm very grateful. I don't understand—"

"When word gets around that she recommended you and you're passed over, you're going to look like a loser, like her. The buzz never stops around here. My opinion is that it would be better for you to enroll in a prestigious PhD program."

"I admire Professor Alcott. I think she knows what—"

"When I applied for my first grant, I'd already published a book. I was considered something of an expert in my field. The radio station had hired me for a weekly show. Look, you're talented. You just need to get some experience under your belt and learn how to be strategic."

Ditmire's *Psycho* ring went off. He looked at his cell and started reading to himself. A huge smile spread across his face. "It's from my agent," Ditmire said, "and I'm quoting here. 'Thank you for sending me your three extraordinary book proposals. Each one is innovative, well researched, and meticulously detailed.'"

"You sent them out already?"

"Backstory," he said. "I emailed them right after I got them from you. You totally transformed them. Within no time, Harriet got back to me. In all the years we've worked together, she's never moved so quickly. This is amazing. You did a great job. Of course, I made a few changes here and there."

"I hope you made a whole lot. They were totally not ready to go."

"So, here's the rest, and I quote. 'We will be having an editorial meeting next week in which I will present my thoughts. Of course, there's no way of knowing whether or not they will go along with my recommendation. Sometimes they do, other times they don't. But I'm going to give it my best shot.'"

"That's fantastic news," Maggie said.

"Indeed. Thanks to you. You know, we make a great team. Along those lines, I've been thinking—always a dangerous thing—but I've been thinking that maybe we could work on a book together. And now if they accept one and give me a contract, I'd like you to be a part of that, in some way, TBD. Okay?"

"Wow. Okay."

"Good good good. Now do you see what I meant about reaching for something when you're confident of success?"

"Yeah . . . well. It's done, so . . ." Maggie trailed off.

"Otherwise, you're just a loser. Trust me. I know what I'm talking about."

Professor Alcott had believed in her, singled her out. That affirmation would last far longer than any possible sting from a rejection. What was with Professor Ditmire?

Jodi Picoult's words came to mind. Maggie had diagrammed that sentence last night:

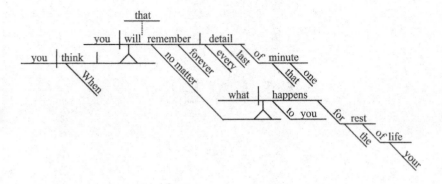

Maggie knew she would.

After preparing some charts for Ditmire, during which time neither she nor Ditmire had said a single word, Maggie declared, "Oh! I had no idea it's so late. I'd better get going or I'll . . ." Maggie trailed off as she collected her things. "I'm gone," she said at the door. "See you Tuesday."

As she headed across campus, she thought about what Ditmire had said—and was pissed off. Why should she have to defend something as positive as applying for a grant? Why should she have to defend Professor Alcott? She was the smartest professor Maggie ever had, Ditmire included.

Halfway to Annabelle, Maggie realized she'd left her notebook in Ditmire's office. Knowing she'd be diagramming late into the night, she rushed back. When she got to the fourth floor, she heard a man yelling. She slowed down, startled that someone was in one of the other offices. Walking toward Ditmire's, she realized it wasn't someone in one of the other offices on the floor. The loud voice was coming from 401—it was Ditmire's—and he was screaming at the top of his lungs.

". . . and if you ever, ever dare to doubt me again, I swear you'll be more sorry than you've ever been. Who do you think you are? Who? I decide . . ."

Maggie pivoted—and raced out of the building.

ELEVEN

As Maggie rode Annabelle to Poinsettia Park, she forced herself to find the positives in a softball game. She came up with only three. Maybe the chief will tell everyone that Heidi had been found. Maybe tonight they'd find time to talk about Lucy. And maybe the game would obliterate all thoughts of Ditmire.

As soon as she arrived at the wide dirt expanse of the park, the chief came shuffling over. He put his arm around her shoulder and handed her a cap. "It's official. You're a Mud Hen!"

"Quite an honor." Maggie put it on.

"Nice!" the chief said. He led her to the bleachers. Maggie felt the heavy drop of his right leg as he moved slowly. "Think it's arthritis," he said. "Can I tell you about the joys of old age?"

"You're not old." Maggie purposely slowed down.

"So we're playing the Croc Pots tonight. Number One in our league."

"Croc Pots?"

"You don't like the name?"

Maggie chuckled.

"Don't tell 'em. They think it's clever. I don't get it."

All the Mud Hens came to bump fists with her. "We took the liberty of putting you in left field," the chief said to Maggie. "That was

Lou Ellen's spot. Easier than moving these bimbos around. And if you see anyone watching the game from the bleachers, assume it's the press. Say nothing. Ignore them. I gave a statement before I came. Said I'd be giving my next statement this evening. No more words till I say them."

"Okay," Maggie said, seeing a few folks in the bleachers.

The chief handed her a mitt and tossed her a few grounders. She caught them and threw them back, overhand. "Impressive!" he said. "For a girl."

"Watch it," Maggie said.

The chief was up first. Before he picked up his bat, he sidled up to Maggie. "You call it. Should I bat lefty or righty?"

"Righty," she said. "You can do both?"

"Affirmative. But how'd you decide that?" the chief asked.

"No brainer," Maggie said. "Pitcher's lefty. Stats are clear on opposite-handed pitchers."

"Damn. Anything you don't know?"

As batter after batter struck out or flied out, the game dragged on. Maggie tried to appear interested, but it got harder by the inning. She came to bat four times—struck out twice, walked once, and got to first by running faster than the shortstop could throw. Now it was the bottom of the ninth, and the score was tied one-all. It was the Mud Hens' last chance.

Maggie watched the pitches being hurled at the chief. She hoped he'd be able to step out of the batter's box in time if one came too close.

"Streeeeeiiiike One!" the umpire called.

"Streeeeeiiiike Two!"

"Streeeeeiiiike Three."

"Sorry, guys." The chief limped off.

Maggie was up next.

"You can do it," the chief yelled. "Go get 'em."

When the pitcher saw her step to the plate, he walked off the mound and made an exaggerated gesture of adjusting his junk. The

Croc Pots howled. Maggie decided to step away, too, and stared at him before making the same gesture back. The Mud Hens roared. She waited a few seconds after he returned to the mound before getting set. No way he was having the last *non*word.

"Streeeiiike one," the umpire said as Maggie watched the ball speed by, dangerously close to wiping her out.

"You got this one," the chief yelled. "Eye on the ball."

Maggie watched the next pitch spinning toward her as if in slow motion. She pulled back, stepped heavily into her left foot, swung—and connected—sending the ball hard along the third-base line. She raced safely to first.

"Your junk back in place yet?" the chief taunted the Croc Pot pitcher.

Jackson was up next. He swung wildly at the first pitch.

"Keep calm," the chief said.

The pitcher became even more fierce. Although he was firing some serious heat, he threw two consecutive balls. On the next pitch, Jackson connected. It was a fly deep into center field. As soon as the fielder caught it, Maggie raced to second, then to third. She glanced over her shoulder and saw the ball careening toward home plate, but she sensed it'd be short. "Hold up," Jackson yelled. "Stop!"

Maggie rounded third and kept going. She slid into home plate—beating the catcher's tag by a second.

"Safe!" the umpire yelled, kneeling and crossing his arms. "Safe!" he cried again.

Maggie was on her stomach in the dirt and all she wanted to do was stay there. She'd run her fastest and had brought in the winning run. A few moments of indulgence seemed appropriate, but the chief grabbed her hands and brought her up to standing. "Knew you were magic!"

"Number One! Number One!" the overweight Mud Hens clucked as they raised her above their heads. She prayed none of them would drop dead of a heart attack.

After she was safely on terra firma, the Mud Hens collected the bats, balls, and gloves. "Come on," the chief said. "Let's head over to the Beer Shed. A celebration's in order. C'mon, guys. The shed in fifteen."

A beer sounded good to Maggie.

As they walked across the parking lot to the bar, the chief said, "And somewhere men are laughing, and somewhere children shout." The chief was beaming as he continued, "'Cause there's SO much JOY in MUDville—mighty MAggie DID not STRIKE out.'"

Maggie thought about mentioning that because he'd changed the last line, it was no longer in the strict iambic heptameter the poet had intended, but she knew to hold 'em. She said a silent thank-you to Kenny Rogers and "The Gambler," not only for giving her one of the best memories of her life with Lucy, but also because the lyrics have served as her mantra—and earworm—for almost a decade:

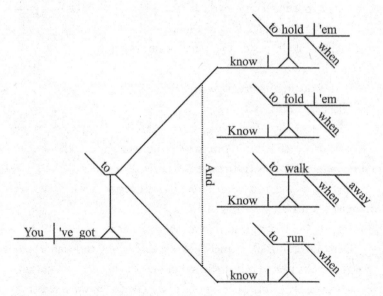

A few beers later, only Jackson, the chief, and Maggie were still kickin' 'em back.

"I didn't get to tell you this during the game," Maggie said, "but I was blown away. You can switch it up batting *and* throwing."

"My one talent. The Majors sure messed up not signing me. Even Casey couldn't switch it up like that."

"It's rare," Maggie said. "Fewer than one percent, I believe, are truly ambi. You might qualify."

"Everyone's got a talent of some kind or other. What's yours, Maggie? I mean besides knowing every single thing there is to know about every single thing. I bet you've got some linguistic specialty."

"No, I don't."

"You've got something."

Maggie shook her head and took the shells off some peanuts, munched away, and washed them down with a slug of Bud.

"Come on."

Maggie continued eating and drinking.

"Come on. It's there," the chief said.

Finally, Maggie spoke. "Okay, maybe one thing."

"Speak," said the chief.

"I can write in mirror image."

"Like backwards?"

"More precisely," Maggie began, "you start on the right side of the page and write each letter in reverse of its normal way. In school, they said I'd outgrow it. Hasn't happened. Well, that's about it."

"Like how you can read *ambulance* perfectly when you look through your rearview mirror?"

"Exactly, but that's print. A lot easier than cursive."

"Demonstration?" The chief opened a napkin and took out a pen.

"You know, this so-called talent of mine is no big deal. It's considered an extremely primitive form of cipher." Maggie wrote a sentence in mirror image while she was talking.

"Cipher?" the chief asked. "What the hell's that?"

"Code. Like if you're a spy, I suggest you don't use it."

"I'll keep that in mind," the chief said.

"I taught it to my best friend in fourth grade. From then on, we had our own secret way of communicating. Better than Pig Latin. This was our favorite sentence."

Maggie began writing in mirror-image on a napkin.

I missed the fucking bus (mirror-writing)

After looking at it for several seconds, the chief asked, "What's it say? Jackson, can you read it?"

Jackson shook his head.

"Take it to the mirror," Maggie said.

"Hold please. Hope the john's got one."

When the chief came back, he chuckled, "I missed the fucking bus."

"Lucy said that's how she felt every day of her life. I get it now," Maggie said.

"Damn, Madame Genius," the chief said looking at the napkin. "That's something else." The chief looked at Jackson. "While we're at it, what's yours? Your talent."

"Pass," Jackson said.

"This guy," the chief said to Maggie, "is a twenty-four seven certified workaholic. Too focused, if you ask me, but results? He's got 'em in spades. Go on, Jackson. Tell her."

Jackson said nothing.

"Okay it's his eyesight. You can't believe what this guy can see," the chief said.

"Born that way," Jackson said. "Not a talent."

"The man can read stuff from ten or more feet away. Wanna know how I found out? For sure, it wasn't because he told me. Two words strung together he calls a book." He smiled at Jackson. "We were at this conference," the chief said. "He was in the seventh row; I was in the first. After the meeting ended, he asked me why I was taking such detailed notes about a Mr. So-and-So. 'How'd you know what I was doing?' I asked him. He said he saw me writing the guy's name several times. He added that my penmanship could be improved."

"Knock it off, chief," Jackson said.

"Here. I'll get him to prove it."

The chief took the menu and walked around ten feet away and opened it, pointing to small type on the back. "Read it," he said to Jackson, "if you can."

"Really? Come on."

"Just do it."

Jackson read, "Gluten-free dishes can be prepared upon request. If possible, call in orders ahead of time."

The chief brought the menu back and he and Maggie looked closely.

"Goddamn!" Maggie said. "That must be seven-point type. You ever see this before?"

Jackson shook his head.

"What'd I tell you?" The chief clapped Jackson on the back. "The guy's got super vision. I made him get it tested. Turns out, he's got 20/10."

"Impressive. The only people I ever read about who supposedly have better than that are Australian Aboriginals," Maggie said. "Some have 20/5. But that's unheard of in the broader population."

"Jackson's unique. Out of this world."

"I repeat. Knock it off, chief," Jackson said.

"My shift," Maggie said looking at her cell. "I'm doing a huge one—ten to ten. I've gotta get going or I'm gonna be fired."

"Where do you work?" the chief asked.

"Corner of Cypress and 405. Stop by if you're in the mood for lousy food, shit decor, but damn good service."

"Roger that. And I'm real glad you're a Mud Hen." And to Jackson, he said, "Give the lady an escort so she can get to work on time. What're you driving, Maggie?"

"Kawasaki Volcan 900."

"You shittin' me?" the chief said.

"I'm afraid Jackson won't be much good," Maggie said, tipping her very own Mud Hen cap.

TWELVE

At four a.m., Maggie and Forrest were the only two in Big Eats. From midnight to five, the cook takes off and the kitchen shuts down for any specially made hot dishes. Most everyone who comes in then knows that the late-night service consists of sandwiches, pastries, and dishes that can be heated in a microwave—like mac 'n' cheese.

"Keep meaning to ask you," Forrest said when Maggie brought him coffee and slid in next to him, "when you gettin' outta this dump?"

"Keep meaning to ask you the same," Maggie said.

"Soon as you graduate, get a job somewhere nice, and take me with you." Forrest smiled.

"Better move on to Plan B."

"Now that's a damn shame." Forrest gave her neck a little massage. "Whoa! Think you might need a little R&R. How about it?"

Maggie kissed Forrest on the cheek. "I'm legal now, so I know that's not an actual offer. Still love you, though," she said. "In spite of who you are and your illegal preferences. Better watch your step."

"Speaking of which, I might be outta town for a bit. Requested a transfer to the West Coast. Figured I'd see me a new part of the country."

"You in trouble?" Maggie asked.

"Maggie, Maggie."

"You didn't do anything more stupid than usual, did you?" Maggie asked.

"All depends on your definition of stupid."

Other customers were arriving, so Maggie left Forrest nursing his coffee and took the orders. At six, she got a text from the chief. She read it while making a catfish sandwich for Forrest to take on the road.

> Another. Was texted to the mayor. Goddamn it! Find something, Maggie. Can you be here at 10?

Maggie quickly brought the sandwich to Forrest.

"You're the best," he said. "In a league of your own. I'm gonna miss you."

"Stay in touch. And stay the hell outta trouble. No way I'm bailing you out. Again." They hugged and Maggie watched him leave. Then she settled herself on a stool and read this latest text:

> I strike her, chain her, make her come, and tongue her cunt on fire. She pleeses, teeses, beggs then freezes; fuck her real real far.

Checking to make sure no one needed anything, she began to analyze the twenty-five words, keeping all emotion at bay. Then she started to compare them to the note left in the spokes. By the time her shift was up and she'd biked to the station, she felt confident she had something. Outside the precinct only a few reporters were awaiting news. Lucky for Maggie, no one perked up seeing her enter.

"Okay," the chief said after everyone settled in and Gutierrez handed out coffees and set a box of donuts on the table, "as you know, we got another text last night. You all read it. Least you better have. Before we do anything else, I want to ask Maggie to tell us what she found. Mind you, I know she's been working all night at Big Eats. You guys go patronize the place, hear? She's working triple time, seems to me. Okay, Maggie?"

"I might have a little something," she said. "But like I've said before, we're only eliminating folks here, not finding *the* one. You've got to bear with me, okay? So, I looked at the two notes. I'll talk about the bike note first, having looked at it with fresh eyes after comparing it to the new note. I noticed the writer's trying to rhyme the last word in each couplet."

"Couplet?" the chief said. "What the hell's that?"

"Listen to me read it. Pay attention to the words I speak loudest. They are the last words in a line. Sorry ahead of time for saying some, you know, grody words out loud."

Maggie read:

I poke her hard wit my bigg dick; she screem and purr and **SPIN**
　　So love the sinner; hate the sin. It feel real good to **WIN!**

"*Spin* and *win*," Maggie repeated. "Those words rhyme perfectly, right? Now listen to these lines from last night's note. Again, pay attention to the words I emphasize:

I strike her, chain her, make her come, and tongue her cunt on **FIRE**
　　She pleeses, teeses, beggs then freezes; fuck her real real **FAR.**

"Those end-of-line words in the couplet don't rhyme for most of us. Close, but no cigar."

"Yeah they do," Jackson said. "Fahr and fahr. Perfect. But what's that got to—"

"Listen to me," Maggie said. "Listen carefully. FI-er. Fahr."

"Sorry, Maggie, but what's this proving anyway?" the chief asked. "He's a lousy poet?"

Jackson tried to suppress a chuckle. "No difference in those words," Jackson said. "Perfect rhyme."

"Where're you from, Jackson?" Maggie asked.

"Alabama. Why?"

"*Fire* and *far* rhyme if you have a deep Southern accent or maybe a rural Western one. When I say those words, and this may also be true for some of you, they do not rhyme. So I'm suggesting this guy's probably from the deep South or somewhere in the rural West." Maggie offered up a silent thank-you to her dialectology professor.

"Last I checked," Jackson said, "that's where we're at. The South."

"The point is, we're narrowing the pool." Maggie glared at Jackson. "That's all I can do. The guy's not local. I've lived here my whole life. I know how locals speak. And he's not from Boston or Philly or the East Coast or hundreds of other places. You can exclude a lot of people by knowing how they talk."

"Makes sense to me," Gutierrez said. "Those words are definitely not rhyming in my book. Fi-er, Fah. Ya hear? I'm originally from Maine."

"Now adding on to that," Maggie continued, "he's purposely trying to mislead us with his spelling."

"Please explain," the chief said.

"You can see he spells *tongue* correctly. Which, I might say, is not the most phonetically spelled word. But somehow, he can't figure out how to spell *begs* or *pleases*. Obvious subterfuge. Now, his punctuation is perfect, so I'm thinking he graduated high school, at least. I'll bet he went even further. I'm thinking his job requires him to write. Maybe he takes meeting notes or writes reports. In spite of the disgusting content of his writing, his stuff's pretty sophisticated."

"Hey, is that another Christian reference?" Jackson pointed to the first line in the new note.

"What?" the chief asked.

"I'm not gonna say the sentence out loud—y'all can read it yourselves," Jackson said, "but it sounds a lot like, 'The tongue also is a fire.' James 3:6."

"I never figured you for a church-going man, Jackson," the chief said.

"Ain't, but maybe he can't get that Bible stuff out of his head, like me," Jackson said. "I haven't stepped foot in a church for decades, but I can recite every damn thing I studied in Bible school. 'The tongue also is a fire, a world of evil among the parts of the body. It corrupts the whole body, sets the whole course of one's life on fire, and is—'"

"Whoa," the chief exclaimed.

"But you know," Jackson continued, "like I said before, being religious doesn't leave out anybody around here."

"Does me," Gutierrez said.

"Me," said Evans.

"Gotta start somewhere," Maggie said. "I also did some research on the kinds of people who leave notes at crime scenes." She scanned the room. The cops seemed interested; none of them had dozed off. "That's not a common occurrence. The main conclusion researchers come to is that the guy believes he's smarter than everyone else, especially the cops—and he desperately wants to prove it. Think BTK. Think Son of Sam. Think the Zodiac Killer, for some examples."

"So he's taunting us?" the chief asked. "Is that what's going on here?"

"Yup. And here's some good news," Maggie said. "If he keeps on writing, and I suspect he will, we're going to get more ideas about who this guy is, and who he isn't, and maybe we can narrow this baby way down."

"Your mouth to God's ear," the chief said. "Okay, anybody got anything else?" The cops shook their heads. "Let's keep thinking while we're on duty today. Something's gotta come up," the chief said. "Get outta here now."

"You wanna know what was going through my mind when you were talking?" the chief asked Maggie after everyone had left. "I remember a case right here in Florida. A couple of years ago. A guy was taunting the cops by sending shit to them practically every day. It was a kidnapping, and the guy kept asking for ransom."

"Every misfit washes up on shore here eventually," Maggie said.

"You got that right. It was up north a ways," the chief said. "I heard about it on one of my fishing trips. But back then, I was a hundred percent focused on fishing. Big tournament was coming up. I was raring to go."

"How'd you do?"

"First place. For best total weight in three species. Redfish, speckled trout, and triple tail. Not bad."

"And the guy taunting the cops?"

"I'm gonna take a look back at the papers from then and see what came of it. All I remember is the guy kept asking for money. I'm hoping it turned out okay."

"So Son of Sam, up in New York City," Maggie began, "sent letters to the press, the police, and even his neighbor. He left the first one near the bodies of two of his victims. Handwritten. Addressed to Captain Joseph Borrelli at the NYPD. Berkowitz taunted the police for their inability to catch him. 'I'll be back!' he wrote. One of the most interesting statements about Berkowitz's letters came from Jimmy Breslin, a journalist with the *New York Daily News*. Berkowitz sent him handwritten letters, causing Breslin to say, 'He's the only killer I ever knew who knew how to use a semicolon.' Now that's really fascinating."

"Pervert," the chief said. "Hope the sicko never sees the light of day again."

"Let me know if you find anything in that other case," Maggie said.

"Will do. Meantime, gotta tell ya, Heidi's town's real shook up. Been five days. Everyone's been told to keep their doors locked. Not to let their kids go out alone. Vigilantes are roaming the streets. People are phoning in, reporting on their neighbor, their kid's coach, even their own husbands and brothers." The chief seemed to be fighting back tears. "Mayor called me last night. I could hardly figure out what he was saying, he was so shook up. Nobody should have to suffer the loss of a kid. Nobody. And his wife. Unthinkable. I'm gonna solve this one if it's the last thing I do. The mayor's counting on me. And the commissioner. He told me that my ass is on the line. Since I'm retiring soon—one hundred forty-seven days, not that I'm counting—he's looking for a reason to fire me first so I can't collect what I'm due. A vindictive bastard." The chief's eyes scanned the posters of missing kids. "Saddest damn thing in the world."

Maggie wanted to say something that could give the chief a bit of hope. All she could come up with was a quote from Scarlett . . .

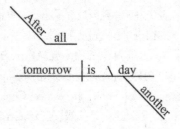

. . . but she decided that proclaiming false optimism would be too cruel.

THIRTEEN

"I did some digging on your friend," Jackson said when he showed up at the diner the next morning and took his usual seat in the last booth in the corner.

"Morning to you, too," Maggie said. "Coffee?"

"Sure. Thanks."

She brought him his usual, a maple-glazed donut, poured him a cup, then topped off Forrest's and George's. They had moved from their usual booth to the one next to Jackson's.

"Thought you went West, young man," Maggie said to Forrest.

"Worked it out so I could put it off for a bit. Wanted to say my goodbyes to Georgey here."

"Good move," Maggie said and went back to Jackson.

"What friend?" she asked him.

"The one you won't tell me about."

"Oh for Chrissake. Leave the guy alone. Tidwell fought in Afghanistan. He lost—"

"Tidwell? Name's Lucy."

"What?" Maggie asked.

"Your friend. The one who went missing. The one you wouldn't talk about. Lucy Wells."

Maggie closed her eyes and felt the sting. She diagrammed C. S. Lewis's line:

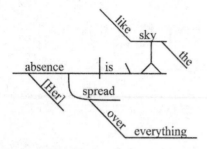

"Maggie?"

"How'd you find her name? I didn't tell you—"

"Excuse me. What the heck do you think I do for a living? I went to the Cypress Havens PD and had them pull the folders," Jackson said finishing the donut. "It looks like child services visited Lucy and her mom several times. Seems the neighbors complained about her being left alone a lot."

"I thought you were working on Heidi and doing your own day job. How'd you manage that, too?"

"Twenty-four hours in a day last I checked. Heidi and Olemeda take up about sixteen. Now, you do the math. I still got eight free hours. But here's what I came up with. Truant officers and government officials used to come around her trailer. Seems Lucy's mother, Luna, was never home."

"They pissed her off," Maggie said. "Nosing around where they had no business."

"Seems she was quite the looker. Found six guys to back it up. Your cops didn't bother talking to any of them."

"They're not *my* cops. They're your brothers in blue. Lucy hated her mom's boyfriends. That's why she spent so much time at my place."

"I followed up on all of them." Jackson drained his cup. "Grilled 'em."

"And?"

"Clean. So I checked out where Luna worked. The cops didn't follow up on that either," Jackson said.

"Surprise, surprise."

"The place is still there. Same owner. He remembered Loony Luna. That's what he called her. Said she was a great employee—polite, friendly, eager. But said she was also kinda flighty and loosey-goosey. He said that. Loosey-goosey-loony Luna."

Maggie said, "I loved Luna."

"Every lunch hour, the owner told me, she'd go to this church down by 505. Kind of a hippie hang-out. It's a Baptist church now. I called the minister, told him the story, and asked if he knew anyone from back then. He put me in touch with a few folks. I made some calls. The leader was a guy named Hank Earl Kennon. I did some investigating."

"Hey, what about a little service here?" Forrest was leaning over practically falling into Maggie's lap. "If you're still working that is."

Maggie got up. "Guess I still work here. What can I get you gentlemen?" she asked.

"Whatcha offering?" Forrest looked her up and down.

"The menu. Read the menu," Maggie scowled.

"Used to be some in-ter-es-ting specials."

"Used to be," Maggie said. "Those words are key."

"Thought for sure there'd be a special today," Forrest said. "Didn't you, George? Been a while."

"Are you going to order or what?" Maggie crossed her arms.

"You free later?" Forrest asked.

"When *later* comes, I'll be in touch."

"What? No send-off? I'm gone soon. What, copper's goods are better'n mine?" Forrest asked.

Maggie started to walk away.

"Pardon me, but I've been trying to get your attention forever."

"Learn a little patience, why don't you?" Maggie said.

"You never seemed to mind my abilities before." Forrest smirked. "Hey George, you know Maggie here's going after that kiddie snatcher. The one up over west. Mayor's kid."

"Shut up, Forrest," Maggie said.

All of a sudden, George bolted, spilling his coffee on the way.

"Hey man!" Forrest yelled. "What's with you?"

"Never saw George move so fast," Maggie said.

"Yeah, well, you oughta put two and two together. He served time, you know," Forrest said.

"For?" Maggie asked.

"Take a wild guess."

Maggie looked around the diner. "Gotta take some orders," she said. "Be back."

As soon as everyone was settled, she sat back down with Jackson.

"Turned out," Jackson continued, "it mighta been a cult. That's what the folks I spoke to called it. They said the group upped and left one day. Just like that. Here one day, gone the next. Kennon told his followers—these folks considered themselves followers—that friendlier skies awaited them in Montana. Whoever wanted to come was welcome."

"What was unfriendly about these skies?"

"Exactly. The folks who didn't go with the group had their reasons. One guy's diabetic and needs his doctor and drugs. Another has kids in junior and senior high. When they graduate, this woman said, they'd all reunite with their *family*. Another has a boyfriend who won't leave town."

"I'm still not sure why the others left," Maggie said.

"Neither was I, so I paid a visit to Kennon's assistant-slash-possible-lover-slash-possible dealer. Daisy's her name. Nice enough, but she wasn't giving up anything. I managed to get her talking."

"How?"

"I arranged for her to come to the PD and took her down to a special interview room. I set it up just right beforehand. Cigarettes, Coke, candy bars."

"That got her talking?"

"I asked why they left. She hesitated. I knew something was there. I asked again. Finally, she said they wanted more space to pursue their dreams. Open skies. Room to farm."

"And?"

"I didn't believe her. Told her she'd be spending the night if she didn't come clean. She swore up a storm. I said I knew some things about her that could get her in a heap of trouble."

"Did you?"

"No. But I figured there had to be something. Anyway, I said I'd get to that later, and I began by telling her that Kennon has a wife now; actually, three. Don't know that either. I said we'd been following him since he left. And one of his wives was his *new* personal assistant. Like *you* used to be, I said. You should've seen her face. But she recovered real quick. 'I'm happy for him,' she said with the saddest face."

"You know about a woman scorned, right?" Maggie said.

"We sat there for a while, her saying nothing, so I said I'd be taking a break and would be back. Plan to make yourself comfortable, I said. This could be a while. As I was leaving, she said she might know something.

"I sat back down.

"'He used to work for Parks and Rec,' she said.

"I know that, I told her.

"'He quit a few weeks before the group left town,' she added.

"I know that, too, I said. But I hadn't gotten that far in my interviews, so I actually knew none of that.

"'Do you know why he quit?' she asked me. I didn't. 'Maybe I know something that could help you out,' she said. 'Swore I'd never tell anybody.' Then she asked me real earnest if I'd be telling Kennon. Course not, I said."

"What'd she say?"

"Turns out, Parks and Rec let him go. Several mothers had complained he was acting wrong ways with their daughters. Their very young daughters. Including giving them drugs. They swore they wouldn't press charges if he resigned and got the hell out of there."

"Jesus."

"When I spoke to the head of Parks and Rec, after some pretty hard persuading, he said he was the one who hired Kennon in the first place. Said he didn't want to make the accusations public. Afraid of losing his job. He felt that if Kennon resigned, things could go back to normal and he could keep his position."

"So Kennon's a pedophile?" Maggie asked.

"Daisy said that she thought he had his eye on Lucy and Luna. Guess he likes variety."

"That's rare for pedos. Usually they stick to a certain age range, a specific look, like blond or black hair, and a body type, say skinny or kinda full-bodied."

"Anyway, Daisy admitted she'd always been jealous of Luna. Here's my theory. You ready for this?"

"You bet," Maggie said.

"Kennon persuaded Luna to go with. Probably didn't take much since it seemed she was in love with the guy. Least that's what the folks I spoke to said. He knew that getting Luna to go meant that Lucy would be going, too. So, they—"

"Wait! Stop right there. No way in hell Lucy would be caught dead in any group, hippie or otherwise," Maggie said. "She wouldn't even join a school club for Chrissake. And that was a requirement."

"Maybe," Jackson said, "and this here's my theory, Kennon had his henchmen quote, unquote *persuade* her. That could explain the blood in the trailer."

"No way Lucy'd ever be persuaded."

"Just for a sec, imagine a variety of persuasive tactics. Not unheard of. Think Jim Jones."

"Oh come on," Maggie said. "Lucy'd never drink any variety of Kool-Aid. Give her a bottle of vodka, then you'd be talking. No one could force Lucy to do anything she didn't want to do. She could take *you* on—and win."

"Somehow someone got them out of that trailer. That much we know. Why not consider that a manipulative, charismatic, maniacal guy, along with some of his crazed followers, figured out how to whisk them away."

"Luna was the most peaceful person I'd ever known. She adored Lucy. She'd never make her do anything like that."

"Love can make you do some messed-up shit." Jackson grabbed his hat. "Just consider it." He tipped his hat and left.

FOURTEEN

The following night was the university's annual party in honor of the professors and students. It was to celebrate the hard work they'd all put into their classes. The get-together was extremely popular and everyone looked forward to attending, except Maggie. But Ditmire insisted she come.

"I might be on the inside track for Professor of the Year," he had said at their last RA meeting. "You wouldn't want to miss that. I wouldn't want you to miss it. Plus, with only some thirty students in the grad program, it wouldn't look good if you didn't show."

"Fine, I'll be there," she'd told him.

Maggie arrived at the auditorium as everyone was settling in. She grabbed a glass of wine from the elaborately laid out buffet and took a seat in the back row. The president welcomed everyone and spoke at length about the linguistics programs, as well as the other departments. He praised the amazing group of students attending the university.

"I know you're all curious who will receive top honor this year. The tally's complete. Votes from the students and faculty are in. It's a great distinction to be chosen Professor of the Year. So without further ado . . . drum roll, please."

He opened an envelope.

"Just like the Academy Awards," he chuckled. "Okay, here we go. For this year, the award goes to . . . Professor Edward Ditmire!"

Ditmire shot up, scanned the room, and bowed slightly in several directions. "Thank you. Thank you!"

"Come up here," the president said. "Congratulations!"

Maggie applauded along with all the others.

"I must say, I'm not the least bit surprised." The president handed him his trophy. "In celebration of your excellent work. The committee read all the comments your students wrote when nominating you. Their remarks were quite laudatory. Anything you'd like to say?"

Looking around the room, beaming, he said, "You like me. You really like me." He held up the small trophy. "I'm humbled and honored. Thank you, one and all." He clasped his hand over his heart and walked off the stage.

Maggie wondered why Ditmire would misquote Sally Field at such an important—and public—moment. Did he not know that what she had in fact said was:

For sure, she'd never bring it to his attention.

"Before we disperse for some libation," the president continued, "I'd like to take a moment to recognize another person. Professor Ditmire's assistant and a star in our forensics program."

Maggie had already stood up and was about to head out, but she quickly sat back down.

"A double honor for the professor tonight," the president said. "Ms. Margaret Moore helped the Olemeda police department solve one of their most heinous crimes using her forensic linguistics expertise. And they've asked her to work on another case. We could not be more proud of her. Stand up please, Ms. Moore. Ms. Moore? Are you here? Ah, yes, there she is."

Maggie stood up halfway, then immediately sat down. Everyone clapped.

"Okay, let's get this party going!" the president said.

Maggie gave a slight wave to Ditmire before heading out.

"Wait," Ditmire said as he jogged up next to her outside. "Hold a sec."

Maggie had been checking her phone to see if the chief had sent any update.

"Go back in," she said to Ditmire. "It's your party! The man of the hour!"

"What a shockeroo," Ditmire said.

"You so deserved it," Maggie said. "No shock at all."

"No, no, I mean the shout-out to you."

"Oh, that? Blah blah blah."

"Certainly not blah blah blah to me. More like stealing my thunder, you know?"

FIFTEEN

Maggie drove Annabelle directly to Big Eats even though she'd be hours early for her morning shift. She didn't want to go home. She didn't want to be alone with her thoughts. Stealing his damn thunder? That's fucking unbelievable.

As soon as she saw BJ, Maggie said, "I'm giving you a break. Go home. Get a life."

"Your man's here," BJ said.

"Fuck Forrest."

"No . . . him," BJ said, pointing to the back booth.

Jackson waved her over.

"I'll hang a bit," BJ said, "you know, in case you want some alone time."

"Stop winking. He's just a cop."

"And you're just a girl. Who can't say no?"

"Go home," Maggie said.

"I'm waiting." BJ gave Maggie a hug.

Maggie grabbed a cup of coffee and sat opposite Jackson in what had now become his booth. "What're you doing here?" she asked. "Hey, how'd you even know I'd be working now? It's not my usual—"

"I'm a cop, remember?"

"You've been . . . wait. You've been following me?"

"Didn't want to disappear without giving you a heads-up. Came to tell you I'm taking me a little trip."

"You need to tell me that now?" Maggie drank the entire cup of coffee.

"Just made the final plans. I'll be gone a few days. Stay in touch directly with the chief." He took a long look at her. "You okay?" he asked.

Ignoring his remark, Maggie said, "You're here to tell me that you're taking a trip knowing the chief might lose his job if Heidi isn't found?"

"Yup. Union regs."

"What are?" Maggie asked.

"Gotta take a certain number of days every year. R&R. I'm long past due. Chief says I gotta go now. He insists. Doesn't want any trouble with the reps. Besides, he thinks I need a fresh POV about Heidi. At this point, I'm thinking we're not finding anything but a body."

"Don't say that."

"You know the stats better'n any of us. Long and short of it? I'll be out of town a few days. Maybe it will do some good."

"Where're you going?" Maggie asked.

"Somewhere in the Panhandle. Aunt Bertha's Motel to be exact. Chief stays there every year. Fantastic fishing, he says." Jackson was ripping his napkin into pieces. "I was debating with myself whether or not to tell you," he said.

"I would've figured it out. Or the chief would've said something."

"No, not that. Tell you where I'm going."

"You just did."

"There are a few cults near where I'm staying."

"And? Oh, I get it. You're thinking of joining one? Haha." Maggie inspected his face. He looked like the cat that swallowed the canary. Satisfied. Proud, even. "Oh, wait a sec. Wait one goddamn second."

"Yup," Jackson said seeing the wild look in her eyes.

"A cult that *Lucy* might be in?" Maggie asked.

"I was thinking that maybe the yahoos went there after they were forced out of Montana."

Maggie looked confused.

"I spoke with the sheriff out there. Seems the knuckleheads'd been shooting up their neighbors' livestock, and he ordered them out. Said they headed for the Panhandle. Long as they were out of his jurisdiction, he could care less."

"Let me make sure I've got this straight," Maggie said. "You're going to the Panhandle to look for a cult that Lucy might be part of?"

"I called around a few places up there, said I was interested in investigating cults. Several folks confirmed there're a bunch of folks living off the beaten path in their neck of the woods. I also circled back to the old church members who said they'd join back with the group one day. Some of them thought they'd be coming back to Florida."

"You wanna know something, Jackson? You're fucking pissing me off." Maggie leaned across the table. "I get that you're trying to help. Very nice. Thank you. But anything you do concerning *my* friend involves me. I've got to be part of it."

"Better this way," Jackson said. "I've been doing this a long time. Besides, it's a hundred-to-one odds, but if anything comes of it, I'll be in touch. I promise you that. To quote a famous person—that'd be you—we're on the same team here. I'm trying my best to help out."

Maggie spoke through clenched teeth. "I don't give a fuck. Besides, Mr. Been-Doing-This-A-Long-Time, Lucy would never speak to you. I know her. You don't."

"I'm flying to Pensacola. Plane's around noon. Then two hours to Aunt Bertha's. Look, all that's gonna happen is that I'll unwind some, do a little fishing, check out a cult or two, then come back refreshed and ready to dive back into Heidi. If a miracle happens, you'll be the first to know. Promise. You gonna wish me luck or what?"

"Break a goddamn fucking leg," Maggie said. "Then call me for backup."

"Adios."

As soon as Jackson left, Maggie broke out her computer and checked the airlines. The only plane leaving around noon from Miami to Pensacola was on American Airlines. She figured that was the one Jackson was on. Next, she checked Ft. Lauderdale to Pensacola flights. A plane was departing at two-thirty p.m. She called to see if any seats were available.

While on hold, she calculated that it could take her three hours—more or less, depending on traffic—to get to the airport. If she hustled after her shift she'd have enough time to grab a few things from home and then bike to the airport.

When the representative came back on, he told her the flight was half empty. "Be at the airport an hour and a half before take-off."

"Sure thing."

Maggie worked till eight a.m., when BJ came back. After arranging with her to cover her shifts for the next few days, Maggie rode home, packed some clothes, grabbed a beer, and headed to the airport. Once there, she parked Annabelle in short-term parking and raced to the terminal. She asked the first official person she saw where Silver Air was—and ran to the counter. The plane was due to take off in half an hour. After handing the attendant her passport, she was given a boarding pass. "This is my first flight," Maggie said. "Ever."

"You're in safe hands with us. Or should I get you a chaperone?"

"If he's handsome, it could work," Maggie said.

"I'm with you there," he said. "You'll be fine. And you sure you want the last row? It's right next to the restrooms. Plenty of empty seats up front."

"That's okay, but thanks."

"If you change your mind, speak to the attendant. Any baggage you'd like to check?"

"Nope. Quick trip."

"All right then. Gate Two, down the promenade and to the right. Pass through security and you're good to go. Better hustle."

After security, Maggie found Gate Two and was quickly ushered on. A flight attendant checked her ticket and motioned her to the back. "But take any seat you like. Not a whole lot of folks flying today."

"I'm good. Thanks."

As soon as the FASTEN SEAT BELT sign was turned off, Maggie pulled up her hoodie, stretched out across three seats, closed her eyes, and started imagining different scenarios as to how she'd greet Jackson. She envisioned knocking on his motel door and saying . . . what would she say? "Fancy meeting you here." Nah. "Howdy, partner." Ridiculous, although maybe he'd smile. She remembered the assignment in Ditmire's class to come up with as many greetings as they could. Back then, she'd come up with thirty-nine in under two minutes, which had caused him to declare that she was brilliant. Maybe she'd try one of—

"Uh, excuse me." Someone was touching Maggie's shoulder. She opened her eyes and shook her head. "We're preparing for landing," an attendant said. "You need to fasten your seatbelt."

"Landing?" Maggie pulled off her hoodie and sat up.

"You slept the whole two hours. We should be on the ground in ten minutes."

"Wait!" Maggie said as the attendant turned to go. "Could you help me out? I need to rent a car. Where would that be?"

"As soon as you deplane, follow the signs for car rentals. It'll be down the corridor to the left."

Once off the plane, Maggie ordered an espresso at the first kiosk she saw. Downed it. Then another. She hadn't eaten since last night, so she grabbed several Snickers.

At Quality Car Rental, the rep offered her several choices. "The cheapest," Maggie said. "I'm on a tight budget."

"I suggest the Chevy Spark. It'll get you where you need to go. No frills."

"Four wheels and an engine?"

"That's about it! It's the white one, third down, first row."

Maggie had already checked out where Aunt Bertha's Motel was in the Panhandle. Only one choice came up, in a place called Masonville. It was an hour and forty-five minutes from Pensacola. Maggie prayed that it was the right Aunt Bertha's.

After missing the exit out of the airport two times, she finally managed to get on the highway. She turned on the radio, lit up, and found herself edging toward a good mood. She made it! Her first plane ride ever and it was painless. As she drove on the first of what she'd mapped out to be three different highways, she noticed the landscape. Only ugly scrub pines. Florida never fails to disappoint, she thought.

About an hour later, she saw a tattoo parlor next to a bar in a small strip mall and pulled in. Bubbles Bar was blaring honky-tonk as she ordered a beer, then a second. No reason to rush.

"Do you know the place next door?" Maggie asked the lady bartender.

"Do I?" She thrust her arm toward Maggie to reveal an elaborately drawn, multicolored serpentine sleeve. Coming out from behind the bar, she showed Maggie her calf. Dozens of butterflies flitted all around it. "Luke's the best artist around," she said.

"Does he do piercings, too?"

"Sweetie, he does anything." She smiled. "I mean, anything."

After Maggie downed a vodka shot, she went next door. "How long will it take for a navel piercing?" she asked the man she assumed was Luke.

"Depends how complex. Ten, fifteen minutes tops, unless you're going for something way complex."

"And some ink around it?"

"Like what?"

"I'll write it down. Could you copy it?"

"Ain't much I can't do," he said licking his lips. "All you gotta do is ask."

"Navel piercing. Ink. That's it."

An hour later, after Maggie bought two bottles of tequila next door, she was back on the road, having fulfilled her quota of ink and piercings for the next year—and booze for the rest of the trip. A barbell adorned her belly button and circling it in mirror image was one of Lucy's favorites:

Dreams can come true.

It read *Dreams can come true.*

She swallowed several Advils, and when the pain eased, she belted out "Tennessee Whiskey" along with *the* Chris Stapleton. After an hour with plenty of wrong turns, she finally pulled up to Aunt Bertha's. It was a sorry-looking one-story motel with a blinking neon sign that promised vibrating beds. Welcome to the Redneck Riviera. She wondered why the chief didn't treat himself better when he came up here on his fishing vacations.

Sitting in the motel's parking lot, the neon blinking in her eyes, she began rehearsing her greeting. "Yo! Wassup!" No, that wouldn't do. "I couldn't not." Short and to the point.

As she was trying to muster up the courage to find out which room Jackson was in, she saw him leaving the office, suitcase in hand. He strolled past a line of doors, stopped at the last one, Number Seven, and went in. After giving him what she felt was enough time to settle in and unpack, she knocked.

The door opened.

"I couldn't not," she said.

Jackson slammed the door.

SIXTEEN

Maggie went back to her car and tried to regroup. After smoking two cigarettes, she had a plan.

"I couldn't sit home and wait," she said to the wood door. "It's not like I'm going to turn around and go back or anything. So you might as well open up."

She gave it five minutes, then she banged again. "You know, this was my first plane ride. Maybe you want to congratulate me."

Still, nothing.

"I couldn't not come!" she yelled. "Don't you get it?"

It was looking like she might be camping for the night on the concrete walkway outside Room Seven at Aunt Bertha's stupid friggin' motel in the stinking Panhandle knocking every ten minutes just to piss him off—when she came up with Plan B. She'd go to the office and tell Aunt Bertha she was worried that the person in Room Seven might be dead. Why, Bertha might ask? She'd explain that she was acquainted with the gentleman in that room, in fact, she was there to meet him—let Auntie think what she would—but because no one was answering her knocks, she became concerned.

She banged harder. "Can we talk! Please!"

No response.

She slid down, her back against the door. A few minutes later, the door opened and she fell in. Jackson didn't attempt to help her up but looked at her in disgust.

"I'm exhausted." Maggie got herself up and tried to smile. "Flying is stressful."

"Seeing you is stressful. You're going back," Jackson said.

"I'm not."

Jackson started tapping away on his computer. After a few minutes, Maggie said, "I'm not good at this silence thing. Can we talk?"

Silence.

"This makes me want to scream."

"I'm warning you," Jackson said without taking his eyes off the screen.

"I could help," Maggie said. "Really."

She sat on the couch, knees to her chest. Jackson mumbled something she couldn't make out, but no way would she ask him to repeat it.

"Mind if I smoke?" she asked.

"Yes!"

"You don't have to yell. I have very good hearing."

Jackson continued tapping away.

"A smoker needs a smoke in times of extreme stress," she said. "This is a time of extreme stress."

Silence.

"Look, this isn't working," Maggie said.

"No shit."

"My mother used to give me the silent treatment after chewing me out and it drove me crazy—not the chewing out part, the silence part—and I hated it so much and I still do and it makes me want to jabber on and on and not ever stop talking just to fill up all the empty—"

"Shut up!"

Maggie put her head between her knees. She felt herself beginning to cry but forced herself not to. "I was trying to tell you that my—"

"I. Heard. You." Jackson spit out the words. He came close to her. "I don't care about your sad story. You're no longer a kid. Your mother's not here. Grow the hell up. And shut the hell up!"

"I can't. That's just it. That's what I'm trying to tell you."

Jackson slammed his computer shut. "Goddamn it!"

"I could tag along. You could think of me as a sidekick. Every cowboy has one."

"Please just be quiet," he began pacing. "I need to figure this out."

"The Lone Ranger and Tonto."

Jackson shook his head.

"Roy Rogers and Gabby Hayes."

Silence.

"Rex Allen and Slim Pickens."

Silence.

"Calamity Jane and Wild Bill Hickok."

No response.

"Gene Autry and Smiley Burnette."

Jackson stopped pacing. "You know Smiley?"

"Tattered black Stetson. Turned up brim." Maggie thought she saw the beginning of a softening around his eyes. "I'm sure you have one. You have every other kind. Brick. Gambler. Gus. Tom Mix."

"How do you know all those?"

"Because of Lucy. Everything I know is because of her. That's why I'm here."

"Please, don't talk. Let me think."

Maggie made a sign of zipping her lips.

After a few minutes, Jackson said, "I've got a plan. No flights leaving tonight, but there's one outta here tomorrow afternoon. You'll be on it. Meanwhile, I'll get you a room."

"I'll stay in the car. No problem."

"No you won't."

"I'd prefer to," Maggie insisted.

"I was raised to be a gentleman."

"I sure as hell wasn't raised to be a lady. I actually like sleeping in cars," Maggie said.

"For Chrissake. C'mon. We're going to speak to Aunt Bertha." Jackson held the door open.

"This is ridiculous. Okay, I'll stay on the couch."

"We're getting you a room."

Jackson left for the office. Maggie followed.

"Please," she said to his back. "Totally unnecessary."

"Well hello again, Mr. Jackson," Aunt Bertha said. Bertha seemed more like someone's bodyguard than their aunt. Big and solid, with huge hands. She seemed able to slam an axe into a thick tree trunk or a person she didn't like so much.

"Everything okay?" she asked.

"Perfect. My um—"

"Daughter," Maggie said quickly. Seeing the wide-eyed look on Bertha's face, she added, "I'm adopted."

"Oh, honey, isn't that wonderful!" Aunt Bertha said.

"But I'd like my own room. Being with parents, well, my daddy, you know, kinda sucks."

"Oh, honey, we're all booked," Bertha said. "I'm sorry." And to Jackson, she said, "You've got yourself a beautiful daughter here."

Jackson's mouth was stuck open.

"Oh heck. We'll figure it out, somehow, won't we, Pops?" Her smile stretched across her entire face. "Oh, also, do you have a map or something? We, uh, we're looking for a place for dinner."

"Always love seeing fathers and daughters here together," Aunt Bertha said. "Like me and my daddy used to. But he's passed. May he rest in peace."

"Sorry to hear that," Maggie said. "Bless his soul."

"He was getting on," Bertha said. "But we had plenty of good fishing years." She took out a map and highlighted roads to several restaurants. "You fish by any chance?"

"Yes, we do," Maggie said. "That's why we're here."

"Figured. Well then, if you're looking for redfish or speckled trout, Lake Malory's the place. Best spot for miles. And for a quick dinner, if I was you, I'd go up the road apiece to Wicked Willie's. Close by. No fuss. Good grub."

"Perfect. We really appreciate it." Maggie grabbed Jackson's hand. "C'mon, Pops."

"Now y'all enjoy. And if there's anything I can do, be sure to come see Aunt Bertha."

As they walked to Room Seven, Jackson said, "Don't say another word. Just don't."

Maggie suppressed a laugh until they got inside, then she howled.

"Quit it," Jackson said.

"Can't." Maggie kept laughing.

"Damn it," he said softly. "You have officially ruined my trip."

"Sorry."

"Too late for that. And by the way, do you have a lot of practice doing police work?" he snarled. "How many years on the force? Oh, none you say? Then tell me something. How the hell do you think you could possibly help?"

"I thought . . . I figured if you were onto something, I needed to be there. So kill me for believing in you."

"Don't make the offer a second time." Jackson stared hard at her.

Maggie grabbed her backpack and slammed the door behind her. When she got to her car, she started crying. In no time, she was sobbing. After a few minutes, she started up the car.

"Wait," Jackson said reaching in and turning the key. "Come on back. C'mon." He grabbed her hand and led her back inside. "Sit," he said practically pushing her onto the sofa. "And don't cry!" Jackson said. "I can't stand to see anyone cry. Maud cried whenever—"

"Who?"

"Nothing! Just be quiet. You can drive a person crazy."

He looked over the map. "Wicked Willie's is only a few miles down CR 13. Things always look better after some grub. You up for it?"

Maggie nodded. She wondered if she'd just gotten her very first glimpse into his private life. Maud. She took her backpack into the bathroom. In the mirror, huge sad brown eyes stared at her. She took out her makeup and glommed it on. She changed out of her black T-shirt into one that said, 'I hate mayonnaise.' At least it was clean. She tried to replace her negative thoughts with positive ones but all she could come up with were words from *To Kill a Mockingbird* about real courage:

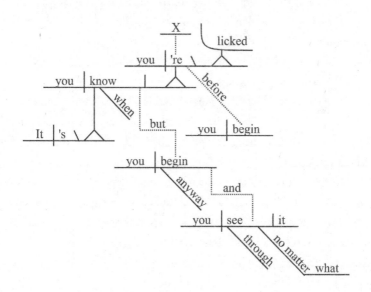

Thanks, Atticus Finch. I'm with you.

"Howdy!" the bartender said standing by their booth. "Fix y'all up with some libation?"

Maggie smiled. Ms. Barker would have called that a ten-dollar word. "Use one whenever you want to impress someone," she'd say. Right now, Maggie wished more than anything that she was back in Ms. Barker's class attempting to figure out the intricacies of diagramming—and thinking that would be the most difficult task she'd ever have to tackle.

"What do you recommend?" Jackson asked. "Something local?"

"Craft beer your thing?"

"Sure," Jackson said. "Your pick. Got anything to go with it?"

"Depends on what you're after. Plenty of fresh fat oysters. Fried green tomatoes. Key lime pie donuts, apple fritters."

"Anything chocolate?" Maggie asked.

"Best Kentucky Bourbon pie south of the Mason-Dixon line."

Looking at the menu hanging on a chalkboard behind the bar, Jackson said, "I'll have dill pickle chips and fried wings."

"Best choice," said the bartender, who doubled as the waiter.

"I'll have the pie," Maggie said.

She took out a pen and started making a list. "I'm keeping tally," she said. "I'll pay you back when we're home. I didn't bring much cash."

"Long as you're here, you're my guest. Or adopted daughter. Or whatever."

"Sidekick works," she said without looking up.

"Come on," Jackson said. "Cheer up. I hate seeing unhappy people."

"You guys choose one of these brews for your next round." The bartender set down two glasses. "And if this ain't the best damn pie you ever ate, it's on the house."

"It's not," Maggie said before taking a bite.

"Ha! Two on the house." The bartender saluted her.

For the next half hour, Maggie and Jackson barely acknowledged each other. Jackson devoured his wings and ordered a second round, and Maggie concentrated on the pie.

"Hey, you see that?" Jackson pointed to the mini juke box at the end of their table. "Haven't seen one of these since Alabama." He put in a dime. "Your choice. Pick a song."

"Why are you being nice all of a sudden?" she asked. "Totally out of character."

Jackson looked out the window. "I get why you're here."

Maggie slid over and flipped the pages on the juke box. She pushed the buttons for "The Gambler." In honor of Lucy, of course. Maybe the fact that the song was there was a good omen.

A couple passed by their table. "Come on! We can't be dancing alone."

Jackson stood up. "May I?"

Maggie took his hand and they walked to a small center area left open for dancing. As the song played, Maggie's body remembered her sixth-grade dance, and she found herself side-stepping and pivoting, like she'd been doing it every day of her life.

"Not bad," Jackson said.

"Your mama did a good job in the manners department," she said as she sang along.

> *You've got to know when to hold 'em*
> *Know when to fold 'em*
> *Know when to walk away*
> *And know when to run*

Jackson put his arm around her waist when Randy Travis's "Forever and Ever, Amen," came on—and he held her tight.

His hand felt good on her back. For a few seconds, Maggie suspended disbelief and allowed herself to enjoy being in a man's arms, in

Mr. Commanding Presence's arms, and smell his Southern Blend. She tried to blot out what she felt Jackson must be thinking: Long as the chick's staying, I got me a live one.

When the song ended, Maggie found herself wanting to linger, but Jackson had abruptly pulled away, turned around, dropped money on the table, and strode straight to the door.

Maggie stood frozen in the middle of the dance floor—a sickening throwback.

"C'mon," he said.

By the time she got outside, he'd already started the car and was drumming his fingers on the wheel. The entire ride back, neither spoke as Jackson blared the radio.

When they got to the motel, Jackson grabbed some blankets and a pillow from the closet and set them down on the couch. "I'm sleeping here. You take the bedroom."

"You won't fit," Maggie said gesturing to the couch.

She threw herself down on the sofa and pulled the covers over her head. "Good night."

Jackson banged the bedroom door shut.

After half an hour, Maggie assumed Jackson must be asleep. She grabbed a bottle of tequila from her backpack and headed outside. She drank and smoked till the sun rose, then she went back in and made coffee in the automatic coffee maker, the one "luxury" item in the place. As she was waiting for the coffee to perk, she glanced into Jackson's bag, which lay wide open on the kitchen table—and saw photos of a teenage girl. No, two girls. Many pics. In one, a blond, blue-eyed girl was posing in a string bikini, a sultry come-on smile on her face. In another, she was wearing shorts with the barest midriff top. Then the other girl, a light-skinned Black teenager, was doing some kind of ballet move, holding one leg high over her head. Then she was doing a split. What the hell were these girls' pics doing with him, here?

Maggie forced herself to come up with benign explanations—a cousin, the daughter of a colleague, a next-door neighbor. Yes, of course, it was one of those.

But in the next minute, she began ruminating: I know nothing about him. Maybe he's like all the other sick cops I've known or read about. Maybe he was let go from his previous cop gig because . . .

She made herself stop and forced herself to repeat what was on the mug she drank from every day:

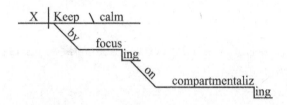

Yup, compartmentalization has its advantages. Ask any serial killer.

SEVENTEEN

"Morning," Maggie chirped as Jackson shuffled from the bedroom to the bathroom, fully dressed. "Coffee's ready."

Coming out a few minutes later, Jackson said, "Let's get going. I checked the map. Plenty of bars and shops along the strip. I'm thinking someone'll point us in the right direction."

"Here," she said handing him a cup. "You sleep okay?"

Jackson downed the coffee. "No time to waste," he said grabbing his keys and going to the car. "You've a flight to catch in a few hours."

Maggie had no intention of getting on any plane today. She'd made it all the way up here and wasn't about to leave until some resolution was reached. Was Lucy here in some cult—or not?

Jackson's rental was a few grades above hers. The seats were leather; the radio didn't blare half-static, half-music; the windows were automatic, not roll-downs. She settled in, turned on the radio, and found a country station she liked.

"You wanna hear this or do you prefer rock 'n' roll or maybe it's jazz or—"

"Would you mind not talking?" Jackson said.

"Yeah, actually, I would. But, okay, fine."

This morning, Maggie was filled with hope, so there was very little that Jackson could say or do that could take that away. Something inside her—and she was hoping it wasn't the tequila—told her that today was the day, the day she'd find out something about Lucy. Something definitive. She could feel it in her bones, like arthritic people feel when it's going to rain, like—

"Whattaya want?" Jackson said as he parked outside Krispy Kreme.

"Hard liquor'll do."

Maggie thought that her comment would make Jackson crack a smile or even say something disparaging—anything—but the man was as close-lipped as a shut-tight Venus flytrap. Perhaps he saw her as an insect and wasn't going to open up until she was gone.

Jackson brought back half a dozen donuts and two coffees. They drove another twenty minutes, while Jackson annihilated heavily glazed donuts: banana pudding, Key lime pie, chocolate with sprinkles. Maggie drank coffee.

Once they got to what the map called "the strip," Maggie said, "Party just beginning and it's only 7:30 a.m."

"I think they're still on last night's."

"So you're not mute after all," Maggie said.

As they drove past bar after bar, Maggie said, "I'm thinking no one here's going to be talking to you. No disrespect intended."

"Why's that?"

"Let's start with you're a cop. Plain as the nose on your face. You know, Jackson, you give off serious police pheromones, like it or not."

Jackson took his eyes off the road long enough to sneer at Maggie.

"Plus, you're Black. Plus, you're with me. Three strikes. They don't call this the Redneck Riviera for nothing."

Jackson pulled in front of The Barracuda Bar. "Stay. I'll say I'm looking for my sister. No prob."

"Jeez, this place is white like the purest coke," Maggie said.

"Guess I have more faith in people than you."

"Oh? When did that happen?" Maggie asked.

Carrie Underwood's "Before He Cheats" blasted as women in bikinis and men with full-body tattoos stood three deep at the outdoor bar. "Stay put," Jackson said.

Maggie watched as Jackson approached several different groups. Person after person turned away after talking with him for a few moments. Once he was back in the car, Maggie said, "I'm not going to say I told you so. That would be cruel."

They drove a little farther down the road. "Pull over," Maggie said, seeing a crowd. "My turn."

She tied her T-shirt below her bra and pushed her already low-rise jeans lower so her new piercing and ink showed, and she approached a white Ziggy Marley look-alike.

"Hey, you new here?" he asked.

"I'm looking for a friend. Wondering if you could help."

"Wanna smoke?"

Maggie took a toke.

A heavily pregnant woman with blonde dreads pressed her body into "Ziggy's" and wrapped her arms around him. "Decision made," she said. "Baby Moon will be born in a warm tub. Palm, Lucky, Trent, Jade and you will have front row seats. The more the merrier."

"Whatever you say, baby. This here's—"

"Maggie."

"She's looking for a friend."

"Ain't we all." She walked away. "Peace."

Ziggy passed Maggie the blunt again. She inhaled deeply.

"My kid's on the way. That'll make number five. Probably today. Moon's mom is over the moon. Ha! That's a good one, no?"

Maggie chuckled.

"I think Lotus could help you," Ziggy clone said. "She's behind the bar. Knows everyone and everything. Might even be acquainted with your friend."

At the bar, Maggie ordered a vodka shot and in no time was chatting with Lotus and River and Zeus and Venus. Half an hour later, after she'd been propositioned four times, she got back in the car, a Dixie cup of vodka tonic in hand.

"Slug?" she asked.

"It's eight-thirty," Jackson said.

"And?" Maggie raised her eyebrows, tilted her head, then finished the drink.

"So here's what I got. There's this place off 114." Maggie pointed to the left. "Lotus says a cult's there, three miles back in the woods. The people come down once in a while to stock up. Then there's this other place where homeless kids hang. It's under the trestle by Bimini and Clark. After I described Lucy—you know, the Lucy I knew seven years ago—Lotus said she saw someone who looked like it could be her. Said she'd seen a blonde kid with freckles and two dimples. Used to sit on the bench across the road. Just sat and stared, she said. Oh, and Lotus also mentioned there's this huge field about six miles down CR 11 where a bunch of loonies in long robes live. Her words."

Jackson's face remained expressionless. "You just finished a twelve-ounce cup of vodka."

"Plus two shots at the bar."

"You've got a problem," he said.

"Is that all you have to say?"

"A huge problem."

"How about a congrats, then?"

"How 'bout you try getting your shit together. Or is it you wanna die?"

"How about acknowledging what just took place. And then saying sorry that you doubted my skills."

Jackson grunted.

"I figure that counts."

Maggie stretched her legs onto the dashboard, lit up, and turned the radio so it was blasting. As if cued, the radio played David Allen Coe singing "Jack Daniel's, If You Please" and Maggie sang along:

> *Jack Daniel's, if you please*
> *Knock me to my knees*
> *You're the only friend there has ever been*
> *That didn't do me wrong.*

EIGHTEEN

For the next few hours, they drove from homeless hangout to cult hideaway to parks to bars. They stopped at each place suggested by someone that Maggie had spoken to, smoked with, drank with, promised to fuck—later. None of the folks had ever actually seen Lucy, but all were eager to make suggestions about where she might be.

At the third stop, an open-air bar with music blaring, Maggie thought she saw Lucy. She held her breath and put her hand over her heart. "Let it be her," she whispered. The girl's back was facing Maggie, but something about the bony shoulders, long straight blond hair, narrow hips, plus the short cut-off jeans and bright pink tee suggested it could be Lucy. Maggie walked slowly toward the girl and put her hand on her shoulder.

"Yes?" the girl said.

"Oh! Sorry, sorry. I thought you were . . ." Her voice trailed off as she walked away.

Stupid, stupid, stupid!

"Your plane's at three," Jackson said when Maggie got back in the car. "This is our last stop." They pulled into a wooded area far off any main road. "This should be it," Jackson said taking out binoculars. "The one Zeus told you about."

"His girlfriend's named Hera. Do you think she changed her name after she heard his, or vice versa?"

"Don't care."

"Curiosity, it seems to me, could be the most important attribute for a detective."

"I'm curious about what matters."

"Anyway," Maggie said, "Emerald Rain told me that she and Adolf come up here to get away from it all. Can I take a look?" Maggie motioned for the binoculars and peered through. "Tents, yurts, teepees. Can we get a little closer?"

Jackson started up the car. After bumping along, they pulled up a few hundred yards from what seemed to be a tent city. "Here goes," he said. "Wish me luck."

"You? How about me?"

"I got this one," he said getting out and banging the door shut.

"Fine. Only, I hope I don't have to say it again. Or *not* say it. Again."

Maggie watched him take long, purposeful strides until he was out of sight. For a few minutes, she allowed herself a version of the dream she'd had a thousand times before. This time, Lucy is hanging out in a tent and Jackson is sitting beside her. He tells her that Maggie is in a car right now, only a few hundred yards away. Lucy immediately grabs Jackson's hand, and they race to Maggie.

Finding herself getting antsy—Lucy! Are you there!?—Maggie took her diagramming book from her backpack and picked up where she left off. She was on her fifty-seventh opening line, this one from Hunter S. Thompson's *Fear and Loathing in Las Vegas*:

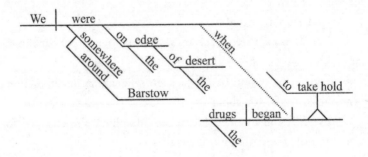

Not a hard one to diagram, as these things go. Subject, intransitive verb, three prepositional phrases, one adverbial clause. Piece of cake.

Thinking about drugs taking hold, Maggie recalled reading Thompson's details of his breakfast which included, among other things, four Bloody Mary's, sausage, omelet, milk, Key lime pie, two margaritas, and six lines of the best cocaine. Maggie wished she'd breakfasted with this man.

"Freaky!"

Maggie jolted. Apparently, she'd fallen asleep.

"What! What's going on?"

"You ready for this?" Jackson asked. "Who do you think's the leader of the group?"

After a second, Maggie said, "No way!"

"Way. Kennon. The very Kennon who left Florida, who went to Montana and then came back here. With his followers. The sheriff out West was right. The group had gone to the Panhandle after he tossed them out of his state."

"The same group that Luna supposedly was part of? For real?"

"Yup," Jackson said.

"And? And? And? Hurry up. Tell me everything."

Jackson and Maggie sat in the car, windows and doors open. A light breeze blew through, helping keep the temperature bearable. "He was real nice," Jackson said. "Cordial. Friendly. Looked me straight in the eye. He was calm."

"What'd he say? Does he know Lucy? Luna? Jackson, hurry up!"

"I told him I was looking for my friend's best friend. Said her name was Lucy. And also Lucy's mom, Luna. The guy put his arm around the woman sitting next to him. Her head was bowed, but she nodded and Kennon went on."

"You shittin' me? Was that—"

"He said that Lucy was with them a long time ago, but she had left.

'Everyone is free to come and go as they please,' he said. Then he shook his head and stared at the ground. 'She lived with us for a while,' he said. 'Unfortunately, she decided to leave.'"

He touched the hand of the woman next to him.

"This is Rainbow. She used to be Luna."

"No!" Maggie screamed. "No way!" Maggie flung her arms around Jackson's neck.

"Calm down," Jackson said.

"Are you fucking kidding me? Calm down? Now? Me? Oxy-fucking-moron."

"Okay, okay," he said taking her arms off him. "I think Luna, or Rainbow, is his wife or something."

"Do you think it's really Luna?"

"Said she was. She was wearing a long dress. Flowers on it. And sandals. She was thin, had hair to her waist. Kinda dirty blonde, you know? Bracelets up and down both arms. Necklaces. Plenty of them."

"Did she have a mole or birthmark above her lip? And freckles, just a few?"

"Yup. Both."

"Oh. My. God."

"Rainbow Luna said she hasn't seen or heard from Lucy in years. 'People find their own light,' she said. 'Lucy's on her own journey.'"

"What did you say?"

"I told her Lucy's childhood friend Maggie was with me. I asked if you could talk to her."

"What did she say?"

"Kennon answered. He said of course."

"Holy shit!"

"They're ready for you."

Maggie buried her head in her hands.

"Buck up, Maggie. You've gotta stay strong and focused. Here's my advice. Don't be aggressive or pushy. Stay calm. Allow for silences. They force the other person to speak."

"Sometimes they do." She winked.

They walked down a long dirt road until they came to a clearing. In front of them was a huge open tent with fifty or so people sitting on colorful pillows around the perimeter. A heavily bearded man greeted them. "I'm Hank Earl Kennon. I understand you're looking for Lucy," he said, approaching Maggie.

"Maggie Moore," she said. "Pleased to meet you. And yes, I'm looking for Lucy. She was my best friend when we were growing up."

"Rainbow?" Kennon said. The woman who'd been sitting next to Kennon looked up, a small smile on her face.

"Luna!" Maggie rushed over and flung her arms around her. "Luna! Luna!"

Luna pulled away. "It's Rainbow now." She took a long look at Maggie. "You're all grown up."

"It's been . . ." Maggie tried to catch her breath and be measured. "It's been a long time. Where've you been? Where'd you go? Why'd Lucy leave without saying bye? Why was there blood? Oh Luna! I've so many—"

Jackson interrupted. "Maggie's wondering if you can help her find Lucy."

"I wish I could. She stayed with us for several years, maybe four?" Luna asked Kennon, who nodded yes. "Then she decided this life wasn't for her."

"What life? What do you mean?" Maggie asked. "Where did she go? Where is—"

Jackson interrupted. "Maggie wants to know if you have any info where Lucy might be today." He gave Maggie's hand a hard squeeze.

"I don't," Rainbow said calmly. "She was one hundred percent on board with the plan. In the beginning that is. She thought it'd be a fun

---

---

adventure. When we were getting ready to head out to Montana, we needed to make it look like something terrible had happened so the cops would spend their time searching for home invaders or robbers or whatever. We didn't care, as long as they didn't come for us." She smiled at Kennon.

"Lucy *wanted* to leave?" Maggie asked.

"Wild child. That's what we called her, remember? Of course she wanted to leave."

"Yeah, but we told each other everything," Maggie said. "Why wouldn't she have told me?"

"Kennon made it clear that nobody could know where we were headed. They'd come looking for us and mess up his plan. Lucy was totally on board with it. In fact, she couldn't wait to get going. As it turned out, however, not long after we got to Montana, Lucy began to feel bored. She wanted more action. Seemed gardening, chanting, dancing, praying weren't quite what she expected. Guess the fun was wearing off, but we were about to embark on a new adventure and decided to head here. Lucy again was all-in. Excited. Thought it'd be an exciting trip. Unfortunately, it turned out that the beauty we created among ourselves, the love, our special family," she put her hand on Kennon's, "didn't mean that much to her. I tried convincing her, Kennon did, too, of course, so did everyone else, but it just didn't work. One day, she didn't show up for communal breakfast. Neither did her best friend. We looked all over for them, but after a few days, we realized that both Lucy and Ella were gone. Of course, that was their prerogative. It's everyone's prerogative. No one stays if they don't want."

"And you have no idea where Lucy is?" Maggie asked.

"I never heard from her. Not from Ella either. It's been a few years. Truth is, Maggie, Lucy never shared a whole lot with me."

"She did with me," Maggie said.

"Maybe you didn't know her as well as you thought. She's quite capable of being on her own, keeping secrets, leaving the past behind. She's moved on. We have to respect that. Sometimes, we have to let go."

"I can't, Luna, she was—"

"Oh Maggie, you two were jump-rope friends. Little girls who liked to pal around. We've all grown up. Charted new paths."

"We lived for each other."

"Go home, Maggie. Move on with your life," Rainbow said. "I did. Lucy did. I'm kind of surprised that you're still living so far back in the past."

"I can't believe she wouldn't have—"

"It seems that Lucy meant more to you than you did to her. I'm sorry, but that's the truth and it's all I have to say. I pray you find your own light."

"Come on, Maggie." Jackson tried to take her hand. She pushed his hand away.

"She's here!" Maggie yelled. "Or someone here knows where she is."

"Excuse me," Kennon said. "This is a loving family. We have no need to raise our voices. If she were here, she would have no need to hide from you or from us or from anyone. Please go now. It's time for chanting. Thank you for visiting. We wish you peace."

Kennon took Rainbow's arm and together they strolled out of the tent. Maggie started to follow, but Jackson grabbed her, turned her around, and gently ushered her toward the car.

Back at the motel, Maggie downed several gulps of tequila. "Liars! Lucy's there. I know it."

"Didn't Luna make sense to you? It sounded like an adventure, but then it turned out not to be," Jackson said. "Could be."

"She would've gotten in touch. I know it. Luna knows where she is," Maggie said. "I could see it in her eyes. They kept darting, And she didn't look at me when she said she didn't know where Lucy was. She's lying."

"You said Lucy would never go anywhere, stay anywhere, do anything if she didn't want to. Luna is believable. Maybe you need to let it go. It's been a long, sad road and a tough pill to swallow, but—"

"I want to go back," Maggie said. "I need to make sure. We've come all this—"

"Okay, okay. I get it. But we can't now. You've a plane to catch and clearly Kennon is done with this round. Let's give it a little time. We can come back in a few weeks with a clear plan. We'll get a warrant. I don't think they're gonna let us waltz in there again without one."

"Jackson, I need to go back now."

"I'm telling you, that's not the way to find Lucy. If she's here, or if someone knows where she is, I promise you we'll find out. But not right now."

Jackson went into the bedroom. Maggie stood alone in the musty, stinking living room of Bertha's goddamn gross motel. She went to light a cigarette but stopped.

This was Jackson's motel room. He'd come up here to help her. And he did! He was on her side. This was the closest she'd come to finding Lucy in seven years. She had to acknowledge that, and that that was really something.

After a few minutes, Maggie opened the bedroom door. Jackson was lying on his back, staring at the ceiling.

She lay down next to him.

Jackson touched her cheek.

Maggie buried her face in his chest.

Sometime later—a minute? An hour? Jackson's phone woke them.

"Get back here," Jackson read. "A break in Heidi."

A few minutes later, Maggie's phone pinged. "Eight tomorrow morning. Be here. Urgent."

NINETEEN

Jackson booked the only flight going to Miami, where he'd left his car. It would take off half an hour after Maggie's. Before they went their separate ways, Jackson said, "Of course, the chief has no idea we're, you know, together here," Jackson said.

"Right. No worries. It's staying that way."

"Safe flight," he said as they headed to their rental cars outside of Bertha's. "But before you go, I've gotta tell you something. While you were chatting with Kennon and Luna or Rainbow or whatever her name is, I took a look around and saw something way back."

"Me too. A yurt."

"That, but also a concrete slab. Barely visible."

"Hm. Didn't see it. But of course you did," she said. "Maybe it's the top of an underground bunker or something. A place to go when doomsday arrives."

"Or they're making drugs there," Jackson said.

"Or, they're using it as . . ." Maggie couldn't finish. They couldn't be that cruel, could they?

The next morning, the chief led Maggie to a room in the basement. "We've got a two-way set up here," he told her once she settled in. "You can watch him the whole time. We got us a good suspect. Cedric. Maybe you can figure out something from how he talks. And these here, they're some of his writings. You ever been in on an interview before?"

"No."

"Me and Jackson, we'll be grilling him. Take notes. Watch and listen. This could be our man."

Maggie saw the chief enter the interview room. Jackson followed. They sat on the opposite side of the table from the suspect. A pack of cigarettes and a few sodas were set out.

Jackson began. "Hello, Cedric. Chief Murray here and I would like to ask you a few quick questions. We're going down our list and eliminating folks right and left. No worries. You'll be on your way in no time."

"Good thing," Cedric said. "I've got a class to teach at three and I never like to miss school 'cause it's my life, my whole life and—"

"So whattaya teach," Jackson asked relaxing back in his chair.

"I teach a survey of European literature, but because I'm partial to poetry, that's where my focus is even though it's not the students' favorite so I try to make it as exciting as I can by bringing in poems that I think they can relate to like the kind that tell about relationships and friendships and love and things that they—"

Jackson cut him off. "How long have you been teaching? And where is that?"

"I'm going on five years at the junior college off Swamp Road in Island Park, you know the place, the kids come from all over the county, even the state because—"

"A fine profession," Jackson said. "I admire teachers. Raising our next generation."

"I take my work seriously even though it seems I'm the only person at the college who does and for sure I'm the only one with a PhD and that's saying something because it—"

"Moving right along." Jackson interrupted again. "Where were you on March 10?"

"If it was a Monday, Wednesday, or Friday, I was in class all day because it's my biggest teaching load and I—"

Again, Jackson cut him off. "It was a Thursday, three weeks ago," Jackson said.

"I can't say for certain, but I sub for the librarian on Thursdays from ten to three after I—"

"We took the liberty of contacting the dean," Chief Murray said.

Cedric squirmed and grabbed a Mountain Dew.

"He said you didn't show up that day. He said you called in saying you were visiting your mother in the nursing home. Seemed she'd taken a turn for the worse."

"I'm not so good on exact dates especially when they happened weeks ago 'cause I can barely remember what I did yesterday." He chuckled—a nervous laugh.

"We spoke with the staff at the home where your mother is." The chief put his elbows on the table and leaned forward. "They said you haven't been by in a month."

"They're wrong. I know I was there even though I can't pinpoint that exact day but I know that whenever I don't show up for work for sure that's where I go 'cause I take my teaching seriously and my mom's health, those are the two constants in my life and there's nothing else I do any day of the week except one or the other and—"

"I'm thinking maybe you went off on your own for a little extra-curricular activity," the chief said.

"I don't have any extracurricular activities." Cedric guzzled the drink.

"Why not explain to Detective Jackson here what we found on your phone. It was awful nice of you to let me take a look-see."

"That stuff doesn't prove anything," Cedric quickly responded.

"No worries," Jackson said. "If anyone went through my stuff, I'd be accused of being a killer, a deviant, a burglar, or worse. Just tell me what it was and we can take that off the table."

Cedric didn't speak.

"I'll tell you, detective," the chief said. "Photos, and plenty of them. Of who, you might wonder. Young girls doing things with guys who looked like dirty old men, am I right, Cedric?"

"Do I need to lawyer up?" Cedric asked.

"That's certainly your right. But we're gonna give you a few minutes to think about anything you might want to tell us."

Chief Murray and Jackson left the room.

"Whattaya think?" the chief asked Maggie when he and Jackson joined her in the viewing room. Before waiting for her answer, the chief said, "Guy's lying through his teeth. Told us he was visiting his mother the day Heidi disappeared. Wrong. When I spoke to him yesterday, he got all flustered after I asked him if he had any interest in porn. I told him I'd done some checking. He sputtered, turned bright red. I've done enough of these to know who's lying and who's not. So what've you got, Maggie?"

Maggie took out her notes. "With all due respect, in fact, with all the respect in the world, I didn't see anything linguistically speaking that would link him with the note-writer. But, you know, that's based only on speech and writing patterns, not on real detective work."

"Lay it on me," the chief said. "What did you see or hear?"

"The way he talks, his idiolect, is totally different from the kidnapper's style. This guy speaks in long run-ons, going on and friggin' on. I don't think he finished one complete sentence before one of you had to interrupt him. The Heidi guy writes tight, neat, short sentences."

"Nerves can do that," Jackson said. "I ramble when I'm nervous."

"Guess I've never seen you nervous, Jackson," the chief said and smiled.

"This man is articulate and smart. Doesn't let out a curse or a foul word like in the notes. Then as far as the handwriting goes, I couldn't find any similarities there either. None of the letters were formed in the same way. Different loops, different spacing, different slants."

"All the lies he told, Maggie. The phone porn," the chief said.

"You've got me there. Not my wheelhouse. I can only talk about words."

"Jackson, whatta you think?" the chief asked.

"On the fence."

"Why's that?" the chief asked.

"He lied about where he was the day Heidi went missing. He lives a few blocks from Heidi. The guy teaches and loves poetry. All that points in his direction."

"It adds up," the chief said.

"Except for what Maggie's found. Can't discount that," Jackson said.

"Hate to say it," the chief said standing and ending the meeting, "but this time, Maggie, I think you missed the mark."

"Sorry," Maggie said. "Wish I could've been of more help."

"I'm booking him," the chief said. "No doubt about it."

TWENTY

Maggie started up Annabelle. "I think he's wrong," she said. "But he's the chief. He's convinced. Guess that ends my gig with the PD."

On her way home, Maggie's phone pinged. She pulled over and read a text from Ditmire: You missed our session.

Quickly, she texted back: Sorry, something came up. Later today? Say 3?

Ditmire wrote: 3 sharp

In all the excitement about Lucy, Maggie had forgotten about Ditmire. Good thing that her ability to isolate unneeded or unwanted thoughts had kicked in.

She got to the university a few minutes before three. After taking a slug of tequila, now her favorite drink of choice, she ascended the endless flights to Ditmire's. Of course, Jackson was right. She was drinking way too much. But in her defense, alcohol had been her most loyal friend since Lucy had gone, and she wasn't about to give it up now.

When Maggie got to 401, Ditmire waved her in. "Sit," he said. She noticed he had a strange look on his face, one that Maggie hadn't seen before. Upset? Angry? Perplexed?

"Bad news," he said before she'd even put her backpack down.

That must be it: upset.

"But I've got good news. For you anyway. Which first?"

Maggie quickly realized why she couldn't read his emotions. Compound facial expressions are harder to analyze than single ones, such as pure joy or sadness or anger. She'd studied compounds, such as happily surprised, sadly angry, disgustedly surprised, and so on, and was now witnessing one firsthand.

"Are you ready for the good news first?"

"Okay."

"You've been formally invited to meet with Dean Schmidt, who only sees candidates he's certain to accept to the PhD program at Grogan. It's the most prestigious one in the country. Scholarship and teaching responsibilities would be included. Ta-da!"

Maggie didn't know how to respond. She'd already told him that she didn't think a PhD was for her.

"Well?" he said. "No 'thank you very much'? No 'this'll change my life'? No nothing?"

"Um . . . it's great news," she began. "It's amazing. Really. Thank you. But, you know, like I told you, I want to—"

"What? What do you want to do?"

"I'm not a hundred percent sure a PhD is right for me at this time. You know, I've been in school a million years and I think I need a break."

"Now that's a slap in the face," he said. "It's a rare opportunity. And, in my opinion, one too good to pass up."

"I don't think it's where I belong." Maggie looked down at her clasped hands in her lap and pressed her nails into her palms until they hurt.

"And I'm one hundred percent sure it's exactly where you belong." Ditmire shook his head. "Truthfully? I'm offended."

He sat down across from Maggie at the small round table. "After all I've done," he said softly. "I'm taken totally aback."

"It was very generous—"

"A kick in the teeth." He glared at her.

"I'll reconsider. Promise. Maybe I'll just meet with him and—"

"You have no idea how far I've stuck my neck out."

Maggie bit her inner cheek hard and diagrammed a sentence from Jane Austen's *Pride and Prejudice*:

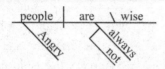

"I'm really grateful," she said, "but I've got to do, you know, what I think is best for me at this time. I had no idea this would affect you this way. I'm really sorry. But I'm going to think it over. Maybe I was too—"

"And I thought that was the good news. I must be delusional. Well, okay, I suppose I'd better get to the *actual* bad news I wanted to speak to you about. I've never mentioned my private life to you. I didn't think it was appropriate. And I still don't. But something's come up and I simply need to vent."

"Okay."

"Damn it, I could spit I'm so angry!"

"What happened?"

"My wife, my ex-wife, was just named provost at Nadler University."

Maggie felt blood in her mouth. She had no idea he'd ever been married, no less separated or divorced.

"Youngest person ever. Thirty-one. She's a medievalist. Done real well for herself. La-di-da for her!"

Maggie unzipped her backpack and fished for a tissue. Her cell, a notebook, and a pack of cigarettes fell out. She wiped the blood from her lip.

"And the grand finale? Wait for it. I got turned down."

"For?"

"The grant. The goddamn grant," Ditmire said. "The grant that I was a shoo-in for. The grant that I was more than qualified for. Nothing like this has ever happened to me."

"Can't you apply for—"

"That's not the point! The guy who got it? Thirty years old!" Ditmire banged his hand on the table. Then he got up and began pacing. His fists were clenched. "You wrote the damn thing," he barked.

"Wait. What?"

Pointing a shaking finger at her, he said, "You know damn well what I mean. The grant proposal. The goddamn proposal that was rejected. You wrote every single word of it."

"So are you saying I'm respon—"

"Goddamn it! What does some no-name kid have over me?"

Maggie began shoving her things back in her backpack.

"What about yours?" Ditmire asked.

"My what?" Maggie said as she walked toward the door.

"Grant. We were supposed to hear on the same day. Remember?"

"I forgot all about it. I'll check it when I get—"

"Check now!"

Ditmire grabbed her backpack and took the phone out of the front pouch.

"What're you doing!" Maggie reached for her cell, but Ditmire was holding it too high.

"I'm looking to see what happened with your application. Let's just take a moment here and find out," he said as he gripped her wrist and turned his back to her.

"Give that to me!" Maggie yelled. "What the hell do you think you're doing?"

"It's here. From the Federal Bureau of BLAH BLAH."

"Let me have it."

"Congratulations!" Ditmire read. "You have been selected..."

Maggie snatched the cell and raced to the door. "What the hell happened to you?" she screamed.

Ditmire caught up to her and blocked the door. "Don't go!" he said. "Don't you dare go!" Then squeezing her wrist tightly, he spit out each word. "Don't. Be. Ungrateful."

"You're fucking crazy."

As she tried to pull away, he wrestled her to the floor.

"I got you started," he said, his acrid breath close to her face. "Schmidt is willing to meet with you. Because of me. Only because of me. You were honored at *my* cocktail party. That would not have happened if I hadn't put you in touch with Jackson. I'm letting you help me write one of my books. Don't you think you... don't you have any sense of..."

Ditmire's words began fading as he pinned her down harder.

Ten minutes later? Half an hour? More? Maggie pulled up her jeans and ran to the door.

"You. Raped. Me," she screamed as she ran down the deserted hall.

TWENTY-ONE

For the next week, Maggie lay low. She didn't go to classes, and she called in sick to Big Eats. She couldn't eat. Anytime she wasn't sleeping, she hung by the lake—and that was her only happy place. Taking in the beauty of a flock of ducks all in a line, she barely thought about Ditmire—and about the fact that she'd kicked him so hard in the balls that he had collapsed screaming on the floor. She answered the few texts she'd gotten from Jackson with a quick Slammed with exams. Get back to you soon as I surface. End of that chapter.

Her only goal was to finish the twenty-six remaining days before graduation—and steer clear of Ditshit. As for Grogan, she'd tell Dean Schmidt that she'd have to decline the extremely generous offer to meet him in person. Maybe one day in the future, she'd tell him, she'd see her way clear to re-opening the possibility of a PhD.

When Maggie finally returned to school, she headed straight to her discourse analysis class, taught by Professor Edgerton. It was in a different building from where Ditmire's classes and office were. However, when she got there, Ditmire was standing by the door. Maggie froze.

"I need to speak with you."

Had he come to every one of her classes for the past week, waiting to see if she'd show?

Right there in the hall, he spoke to her softly. "I took some time to look over your papers and tests this semester," he began. Maggie figured he was going to praise her work first, then apologize. "I discovered much to my shock and dismay," he said, "that you lifted several sentences, even an entire paragraph, from some of *my* writings."

"I did what?" Maggie asked. "Is this some kind of joke?"

"Far from it."

"What are you talking about?"

"Do you deny it?" he asked.

"Oh, for Chrissake this is ridiculous."

"I have the proof right here." He waved several papers in front of her.

"I don't know what you have, but you know damn well I don't need to cheat. This is about last week, right?"

"I compared your papers with my own writings," he said, "and, word for word, you lifted entire passages. I don't know why I didn't see it earlier."

"You're sick," Maggie said. "You're a goddamn sick motherfucker."

"I suggest you admit it. You'll save yourself not only from failing my class but from possible expulsion. This *can* remain between you and me, if you agree to certain conditions."

"Wait. Are you bribing me to keep quiet?" Maggie came close to his face. "Stop it. Just stop it," she said. "If you think I'm going to report you for . . . for . . . you're wrong. I have no intention of doing that. Just let me finish the semester and graduate."

"I'm assuming you know the university's zero tolerance policy on plagiarism," he said. "It's suspension or expulsion."

"What the hell's the matter with you?"

"You're not admitting it?"

"No fucking way!" Maggie turned to get away from him. "You can go fuck yourself."

He walked quickly and caught up with her. "You leave me no choice. There'll be a disciplinary hearing. You'll have the opportunity to defend yourself. But let me warn you: I'm the one with the proof," he said waving papers again. "I'm telling you: You have no leg to stand on. You lifted passages. You plagiarized. You're going to lose. It's an open-shut case."

Maggie hopped on Annabelle and sped home. On the way, she cursed the wind, the smelly swamps, the fetid Florida countryside. She damned the potholes, the old people, the tourists, the locals, the germ-carrying steroidal water bugs, the alligators, pythons, snakes, and hurricanes. For Chrissake, the hurricanes! They were always just coming or going.

Once home in her living room, she screamed at the walls and threw an ugly vase across the room. Who bought that piece of crap anyway?

An email pinged. It was from the president of Rosedale.

Dear Ms. Moore,

This is to inform you that you have been . . . plagiarism . . . zero tolerance . . . a hearing . . . present your side . . . the committee . . . ten sharp on Tuesday . . . all supporting materials with you . . .

TWENTY-TWO

The next five days were a blur of writing and rewriting her defense. Maggie barely slept. She barely ate. And she didn't drink at all.

In half an hour, she would be defending herself, fighting for her academic life. She put on a peach-colored skirt and a floral-print blouse in soft pinks and greens. She'd bought the outfit the day before, thinking pastels would send the right *innocent* message. She tied her hair back so tightly that her head throbbed. She wore no lipstick. She reminded herself to look and act demurely and not to lose her cool—no matter what.

When she got to the meeting room, eight people including the president were there. "Good morning, Ms. Moore," President O'Malley said as he stiffly gestured Maggie to a seat. Chairs were arranged in a circle. Everyone's eyes could clearly see everyone else's.

"Good morning." Maggie nodded.

"May I introduce the Ethics Committee," the president said as he pointed to each person in turn. "Professor Radley, Professor Alcott, Professor Robinson, students Jason Mirtz and Shannon Brown, and administrators Mr. Gansfort and Mr. Hawthorne."

"Nice to meet you all," Maggie said. "And to see you again, Professor Alcott."

"Likewise," she said.

Maggie was glad that Alcott was there. One person in her court, possibly.

"Ah, welcome Professor Ditmire," the president said as the professor strode to the empty chair. "Nice to see you."

hair closely cut
worn brown leather briefcase
impeccably dressed
erect posture, confident walk

President O'Malley handed a sheet of paper to each person. "Why don't we begin by taking a moment to read the rules and regulations of this meeting?"

After several minutes, he asked, "Are we ready to proceed?"

Everyone nodded.

"Professor Ditmire, we're going to start with you. Would you please fill us all in as to why we are here today?"

Ditmire hung his head and took several halting breaths. Maggie thought that perhaps he was having second thoughts. Maybe he realized he didn't have proof after all. Perhaps he was getting ready to apologize and say that everyone could go home. Case closed.

"It's with a very heavy heart . . ." He looked down. "Sorry. This is harder than I imagined." He paused, pressed his palms together, and looked up with heavy eyelids. "You see, Ms. Moore was a star student. Remarkable. Even brilliant."

He locked eyes with each committee member, then continued. "I was so impressed that I asked her to be my research assistant."

He stared directly at Maggie. "And even more importantly, as I assume you all know, she helped the police put away a very bad guy using her superior language skills." He looked at Maggie. "I had such faith in you. That's why this is so heart-wrenching."

"Why are you—" Maggie began.

"Ms. Moore," President O'Malley cut in. "You read the rules. You'll have an opportunity to speak when the professor has finished. Continue, please."

Ditmire took a deep breath. "Ms. Moore became my RA in February, at the start of the semester. She helped me organize data concerning my latest funded project. She glanced over several book projects I was about to submit. From time to time, I would have her generate spreadsheets, grade exams, fact-check my papers, that sort of routine work. You know, help out with the myriad responsibilities we all have."

Everyone nodded.

Ditmire lowered his head again. "As a way of saying thank you, I would sometimes treat Ms. Moore to a cup of coffee at Muddy Waters after our meetings—if you can call that coffee."

A few members chuckled.

"It was during our times there that I sensed Ms. Moore was taking our friendship, our *professional* relationship, to a different and totally unintended level."

"That's a lie!" Maggie said.

"I assure you, Ms. Moore, you will have your chance," the president warned.

"Thank you," Ditmire continued. "Immediately, I pulled back. We stopped going for coffee. It was then that I noticed Ms. Moore becoming pouty, even angry and, one might say, aggressive. At first, I assumed she must be experiencing difficulties in her personal life." He looked at Maggie and shook his head before continuing. "Ms. Moore kept doing what I'm calling *acting out* until I finally had to ask her to stop working on the projects she'd begun. Her lack of concentration and her antagonistic attitude were impeding progress. I told her that since the semester was coming to an end and because I had so many other things on my plate, we'd have to stop our work sessions.

Of course, I thanked her profusely for all she'd done." He took a long pause. "But she wouldn't accept it. She cried. She pounded the desk. She said she'd do anything to continue working with me. She begged me to keep her on."

Maggie began diagramming a line from *The Wizard of Oz*:

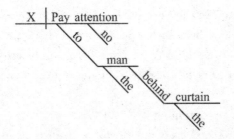

Damn him! Ditmire, like the Wizard, was all smoke and mirrors, pulling strings to get the effect he wanted. Maggie hoped they'd see through him. She hoped she'd be able to unmask the sick fabulist.

Ditmire cleared his throat, took out a handkerchief, and blew his nose. "A few weeks ago, I gave a midterm exam. Ms. Moore's was the best in the class, miles above the others. However, after I let her go, after she'd been acting so strangely, I began to think back on her work, and something hit me. Her papers were almost *too* good.

"So I reviewed some of my own work, work that I had written and that she had proofread as my RA. And then I reread her papers and the tests. To my astonishment, word-for-word, she had lifted entire sentences from *my* work. I'm pained to say this, but I have irrefutable proof."

The professor reached down, unzipped his briefcase, and took out several pages, each with yellow highlighted sentences. "And here it is. I'd like to offer up several examples."

He passed out a small package to each person, including Maggie, and waited while everyone looked it over.

"As you can see," he continued, "the similarities speak for themselves. Barely a word changed. Eight to ten separate examples. I can't tell you how sick this realization made me feel. Not only because I'm calling out a person I considered a superior student—and I want to point out that this is the first time in my nearly two-decade career that I've ever done such a thing—but also because I'm deeply disappointed in myself. How could I have been such a poor judge of character? I always prided myself on . . . but this isn't about me. It's about integrity. Honor. Truthfulness. The principles on which our great university was founded."

He paused again before continuing.

"I'd like to thank each and every one of you for your time and attention. Again, I want to say how sorry I am that we all have to be here today."

"Thank *you*, Dr. Ditmire," President O'Malley said. "We certainly understand how difficult this must be. Please know that we will come to a quick and carefully thought-out decision in a matter of days. A lot is at stake here." He nodded to Maggie. "Alright, Ms. Moore. Please, go right ahead."

Maggie patted her skirt and folded her hands in her lap. She reminded herself to keep her voice low and steady, not to flail her arms, and to make eye contact with each person in turn.

"Thank you, President O'Malley," she began. "I apologize for having interrupted before, but Professor Ditmire has not spoken the truth. What he is alleging is, quite frankly, laughable were it not so serious.

"I'd first like to say that I was valedictorian in high school *and* in college. Further, I've maintained a perfect 4.0 during my three semesters here and that has continued during this, my final, semester. In other words, I have no need to lift anybody's work. I have never been accused of plagiarizing before.

"In my own defense—because I now see the similarity in some of the examples in front of us—I am going to make it crystal clear what happened. Professor Ditmire asked me to write many of his applications, proposals, exams, and even huge chunks or sometimes entire papers he was submitting. I did that and was thanked profusely. So if some sentences in my papers were close to some in the professor's papers, it was one-hundred percent unintentional—and, ironically, I seem to have lifted from myself."

The committee members glanced uncomfortably at one another, all except for Professor Alcott, who steepled her fingers and leaned forward. Very interested.

"I don't know how to prove to you that those were my sentences in the first place—that I in fact wrote them. This is a he-said, she-said situation. I am well aware that the professor has been here for almost a decade and that he is highly respected. I cannot compete with that. I can only hope you will recognize that he asked me to be his RA because he felt I was the most highly qualified student. Furthermore, he also asked me to assist the police department to help nab a serial stalker-turned-rapist and, as he mentioned, I did point them in the direction of the perpetrator. He also asked me to be what amounts to a ghostwriter, not actually get credit, on a book he'd be writing. It was accepted based on a proposal I had written. I *alone* had written.

"If you still question my abilities, I humbly ask you to speak with Dr. Alcott." Maggie nodded toward her. "I hope I am not speaking out of turn, Professor, but I'd like the committee to know that you asked me if I'd be willing to apply for a prestigious grant, one set up to investigate terrorist threats. And, against the odds of sixty-seven highly qualified candidates, I was the one chosen. A truly humbling honor.

"From all of this, I'm hoping you can see that Professor Ditmire's claims that I copied sentences from his work is not the whole story. If I inadvertently lifted parts of eight sentences, they were mine to begin with. I did the research. I did the writing."

"She can't prove it," Ditmire blurted.

"With all due respect," Maggie said calmly, "neither can you."

"Okay, okay," President O'Malley said. "Ms. Moore, you have three minutes left."

"The total number of papers I submitted at this university is thirty-four, that's more than a million words, and includes twenty midterms and fourteen finals. I counted." Maggie paused, scanned the faces of the attendees. "At issue here are some sixty-seven words. Not having a calculator, I'm estimating that's under point-one percent.

"And now, if I may, I'd like to end by saying I've dreamed of becoming a forensic linguist since I was thirteen, although back then I'd never heard the term *forensic linguist* nor was I aware that it was an actual field of study. I beg you," Maggie pleaded, "do not let my dream die. I've worked so hard to try to achieve it."

"Like I didn't work hard to get to where I am—without cheating!" Ditmire yelled.

"Please, professor, I've asked you—"

"You are a liar," he blurted.

"Professor, you must refrain. You've had an opportunity to speak. It's Ms. Moore's turn now."

Maggie had finished saying all she'd intended to say, but now, she was seeing red.

"I hadn't intended to say this, but because of how the professor has portrayed me, I feel I must relate why this plagiarism issue arose in the first place. I know that my saying this out loud, in front of all of you, will be the hardest thing I have ever done, but I've got to do it."

"Ms. Moore, according to the rules, you have a minute and a half left," the president said.

"Thank you. I will stay within the timeframe. This cheating accusation is Professor Ditmire's veiled attempt at beating me to the punch, so to speak, of taking a preemptive strike. I was reminded of a line from *On the Waterfront*, which was part of an assignment the professor gave us, analyzing how dialogue in the film offered up info about life on the docks in the fifties. It's this: 'Do it to him, before he does it to you.'" She paused. "You see, we are here today," Maggie raised her voice a notch, "because Professor Ditmire was afraid that I would bring *him* up on charges."

The committee members looked confused.

"The very awful truth is this. Professor Ditmire raped me," Maggie said quietly.

"What? Are you crazy!" Ditmire stood up, yelling. "Stop this! Stop talking nonsense. How dare you!"

"Please," the president said. "Take your seat. Ms. Moore, uh, this is very serious. A deeply disturbing accusation. But continue. You have . . . thirty seconds left."

"He asked me to come to his office a few weeks ago and told me he'd gotten terrible news. First, he said that his wife had been made provost of the college where she teaches. Youngest person ever. I had no idea he even had a wife, or ex-wife as it turns out. Next, he reiterated that I had stolen his thunder at the annual cocktail party when I was mentioned for having helped the police nab a rapist. Then he said he'd been turned down for the grant that he was certain he'd get. He said it was given to some no-name kid. He then demanded to see if I had gotten the grant that Dr. Alcott had suggested I apply for. We were to hear on the same day. He grabbed my phone, looked for the email, found it, and then sputtered out that I had gotten the grant. He was enraged. His face contorted. It was purple. He couldn't control himself he was so so mad."

Maggie looked around at the attendees again.

"I'd like to end this excruciatingly painful meeting by saying I trust you all and believe that you will do what is right. Not one word I said was a lie. Everything is one hundred percent true. Sadly."

"Ms. Moore," the president said. "This is very, very serious. Since you are accusing the professor of rape, of course we will immediately look into it. We have systems in place to deal with this kind of thing. If you wish, you can also hire a lawyer and file a formal complaint. Please meet me at HR after the meeting so we can go over some next steps.

"Professor Ditmire, we also have systems in place for you—for the accused. Feel free to come to my office if you would like direction in dealing with this. Certainly, this is not what we expected to be hearing today but deal with it we will. For now, I ask the committee to take up the issue of plagiarism and plagiarism alone and meet me back here tomorrow, same time. We will make our determination then on that one issue. The accusation Ms. Moore leveled is one we need to delve into more thoroughly, of course. Thank you one and all. This meeting is over."

Ditmire caught up to Maggie as she raced to her bike. Coming up close, he said, "Cunt, goddamn fucking cunt. You'll get what's coming to you. I'll make sure of that."

Maggie hopped on Annabelle and sang from Dylan's "Buckets of Rain":

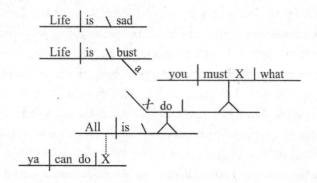

TWENTY-THREE

Two days later, Maggie received an email from the university. "Please, please, please," she said as she opened it.

Dear Ms. Moore,

After many hours of careful consideration, the Committee has weighed in on the issue of plagiarism.

The members noted that seven of the sentences from your midterm exam and other papers were, in fact, close to or exact copies from various writings of the professor's. However, the members did not feel qualified to weigh in on who originated those sentences—he or you.

"Yes!" Maggie yelled. "Yes! Yes! Yes!"

Therefore, we are not prepared to come to a conclusion on the issue of plagiarism. However, Professor Ditmire has requested that you not return to his class. He will give you an incomplete and suggests that you check with your academic advisor as to how you can fulfill your course requirements.

"Fine," Maggie said quietly. "Who the hell wants to be near that fuck anyway."

A permanent record of the Ethics Committee meetings will remain in your file and could be read by any potential graduate school admissions department as well as by potential employers who . . .

Maggie's eyes glazed over the rest.

Thank you for . . .

Maggie stopped.

How come Ditmire had a chance to speak with the president? Why hadn't she?

Ditmire's accusation of plagiarism was now on record, as was her accusation of rape. No one would want to risk hiring a person who has accused someone of rape, especially not the FBI, and for sure no PhD program would accept her now, not that she cared all that much about that. And the terrorist grant? Probably that would be rescinded.

From those thoughts, other negative ones flooded:

No mentor. No supporter. No FBI work ever.
Betrayed. Used. Lied to. Fucked over.

Maggie made it to the bathroom before throwing up.

An hour later, after nothing was left in her stomach, she called the diner. "I'm swamped," she lied to BJ. "You know, finals, papers. Suppose you could sub for a week? I'll owe you my life."

"No prob, babe," BJ replied. "Rhonda's been looking for more hours anyway. Call when you're up for air. Good luck, sweet pea."

Maggie recounted for the hundredth time the arguments she'd presented. She thought she'd made a strong argument for reasonable doubt—and she had. A victory of sorts. Yet now, a permanent record of all of this would exist. And it was fucking bullshit.

Maybe there was an appeals board she could speak to and see if this could be expunged. She'd investigate. And now, it was up to her to figure out how, or if, to hire a lawyer and bring a formal charge of rape. If she did, the school would no doubt hire their own lawyer, and for sure Ditmire would hire his—and it seemed he'd be taking this on as a fight to the death.

Hoping that a ride on Annabelle could help switch up her mood, she headed out, determined to focus on only what was right in front of her: potholes, swamps, roadkill. When she finally pulled in back home, she forced herself to open her notebook and diagram more Proust. One line would lead to another, the next, the next, and for sure in no time, there'd be no more thoughts of the whole sickening issue.

When she looked up, the sun was just going down—and the diagramming had worked. Thank you, Ms. Barker, again and again. But now, she found herself slipping back into negative territory. "Do something useful when you're at sixes and sevens," Maggie recounted her mother's words. Although Hazel had never come up with any useful suggestions, Lucy had. They would bake. Sometimes, their creations were edible. More often, the girls would end up flinging chocolate bits or handfuls of flour at each other across the kitchen. The cakes would never even make it to the oven.

Maggie hopped back on Annabelle and zipped over to the Piggly Wiggly. After buying ingredients for Key lime and brownie pies, she biked back home and began furiously mixing. One pie, two pies, three pies. In the oven. Out of the oven. Hot. When they cooled, she packed them up and put one on Tidwell's front porch, another on Rodriguez's, a third on the steps of Jankey's house. None of them were home, she knew by the absence of bikes. Probably just cruising the hood.

Now what?

She headed to Black Dog. Since Jake never locked the doors, she could go in any time. When she got there, she heard sounds coming from a small room in the back. It was where Jake kept his special trove of books: signed ones, first editions, beautifully illustrated ones. She went closer. "Jake? You there?"

A young girl, maybe twelve, thirteen, came racing out holding her clothes. "Sorry," she said as she left the barn. Right after, Jake came out, stoned, with only a towel around his waist. "Thanks, Mag. Would've been nice to give a fella some notice."

"Notice? What the hell're you doing with jailbait? That's a goddamn criminal offense. You're too old for this kind of shit. And too ugly."

She flung book after book at him.

"Now Mags. Jealousy ain't got no home—"

She picked up an aluminum pan and heaved it at him.

"If I ever get wind of this again, I'm reporting your ass to the PD before you even have time to get your dick back in your pants, hear?"

"Okay, okay, no harm intended. Just try to calm—"

"Shut the fuck up!"

Maggie headed home in a fury. Jake. Florida. Tim Dorsey got it right in *Pineapple Grenade*:

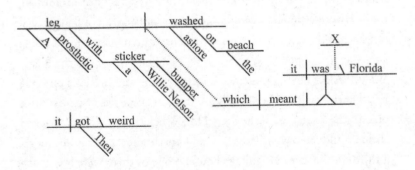

Now what?

In her living room, she alphabetized the tilting piles of books and put each book in its proper place on the appropriate shelf.

Now what?

She diagrammed the next three paragraphs of Proust.

She moved the novels that were in the kitchen into the bedroom.

Now what?

She spied Tidwell's backpack and spilled the contents on her bed. She saw the Quaaludes. She could use a little help. She swallowed one.

"I could kill you, Ditshit!" she screamed. "Fucking a-hole."

She downed another with a slug of tequila. And waited. She finished the bottle. And waited.

She swallowed two more pills.

Next thing she knew it was noon. The next day? The same day? How long had she slept? Wasn't she supposed to be at work?

She made it to the shower, washed, dried, and managed to put on some clothes. Her head ached and she felt nauseated. "Eat something," she said out loud and startled herself with her own voice. She stood at the refrigerator, opened it, peered in, closed it. What was she doing there? She headed to Annabelle and managed to get her leg over. After a few tries, she started her up. On automatic pilot, she drove slowly to the diner. She thought about calling Jackson but decided against it. How fucked up did she want to look?

"You look like hell," BJ said as Maggie walked in. "What're you doing here anyway? I thought you were taking the week off."

Maggie teetered to the kitchen to clock in. BJ put her arm around her. "Honey, let me give you some advice. Go home. I got this. You look like shit. You aced those exams, right? Better have."

"I'm fine." Maggie sat on a counter stool—and nearly fell off.

"You can't be here." BJ got Maggie to her feet and together they walked to the door. "I'll drive you, honey. We've got you covered." BJ motioned to the cook to do double-duty for an hour.

Maggie didn't have the energy to object.

Twenty minutes later, BJ helped Maggie out of the car and into her house. Settling her on the couch, BJ fluffed up a few pillows, put Maggie's cell and cigarettes on the table, and covered her with a light blanket. "Get some rest, honey. I'll call you later. Everything's gonna be okay."

As soon as BJ left, Maggie rifled through Tidwell's stash and found a Dilaudid. Down the hatch. Everything would certainly *not* be okay was the last thought she had.

The next thing she knew, a phone was ringing from somewhere far away. Swimming up from the bottom of the ocean—she'd been backstroking with a pod of whales—she surfaced, forced her eyes to open, reached for her cell but knocked it off the table. She slid off the couch and fumbled around for it. "Helloooo?" she said.

"Maggie?"

Why did that voice sound familiar?

"We got a new note. Chief wants you back. Real different from the others. I'm sending it over. Take a . . ." Jackson's voice started to fade.

"My dad," tumbled out of her mouth. "Operation . . . hips . . . taking care of him."

"Huh?"

She hung up.

She saw a lone pill on the floor.

She swallowed it.

TWENTY-FOUR

Beep, beep, beep. Rhythmic bleeps ping-ponged inside Maggie's head.

"Close call," she heard. Then, "Hello. Hello? Ms. Moore? Hello?"

Maggie opened her eyes.

"Well, hello!" a voice chirped.

Maggie's eyes scanned the room. Dull green walls. White sheet over her torso. Silver rails around the bed. An IV attached to her inner elbow. Blinking, flashing readouts.

"I'm Jennie May. Nurse on duty," the voice said. "We're glad you're back."

"Where am I?" Maggie mumbled. Her head ached, but the rest of her body was numb. She wasn't sure she even had a body. She told herself to wiggle her fingers. They moved. And her toes. She still had a body.

"You're in Holy Name Hospital in Summerville," Jennie May said. "Emergency Room."

"Why?"

"You'll have to ask the doctor. He'll be by any minute. But a very nice gentleman's been waiting to see you. Dr. Simpson said you could see him when you wake up."

"Gentleman? What's happened?"

"The doctor will explain everything. Shall I ask Detective Jackson to come in?"

"Jackson?" Maggie shook her head, trying to let a clear thought come in. "What's he doing here?"

"I'll let him explain."

Maggie figured that she must have fallen off Annabelle and got herself a concussion. The police must've found her lying in the middle of the road somewhere. She closed her eyes and tried to recount what had happened before this moment. She saw herself on the couch, then standing to get something, then lying back down. What was she looking for? She remembered Jackson calling—right!—and asking her . . . what did he ask her?

"You look like hell." Jackson was standing by her bed.

"Oh, Jackson. What's going on? What's happened?"

"That's what I want to know."

Just then, the doctor appeared. "Looks like you're among the living," he said to Maggie. "Good, good, good." Then to Jackson, he said, "Mind leaving us for a few while I take some vitals?"

The doctor closed a curtain around Maggie.

"Nice fella," the doctor said. "Got you here in record time."

"I don't understand. Why . . . why am I here?"

"You're fine now. You're going to be fine—if you stay off the pills. You came in not fully unconscious. In and out. We induced vomiting and let you rest. You've been sleeping on and off for over twelve hours now. Do you remember talking to me?"

Maggie shook her head.

"You did. Then you'd slip off to another deep sleep. Just what you needed. I don't think anything's left inside. You should be good to go in a few hours, after we talk about a drug program, even though the detective said you're no druggie. He swore that you must have misread a vial of something very strong for an aspirin or whatever. He said you'd been complaining of a headache when you were on the phone with him earlier in the evening."

"Oh."

"He assured me he'd stay with you twenty-four seven and keep an eye on you. You're a lucky woman."

"I . . . I know."

After taking her blood pressure and checking her heart, the doctor gave her some juice and told her to drink it slowly. He said, "Stay here till around two. I'll come back and make sure everything's okay. Just rest a while. And listen, I don't want to see you here again, Ms. Moore. From what the detective said, you're way too valuable to be taking time off from school due to some stupid mistake. Read those labels carefully next time, you hear?"

"Thank you."

"Mind standing up and let's see how steady you are?" the doctor asked.

Maggie concentrated hard on remaining upright.

"Good. Let's see how your brain's functioning. Tell me some things about yourself. I'll stop you at one minute."

"Can do." Maggie told the doctor where she lived, went to school, worked, and that she rides Annabelle.

"Very good. No slurring. No lack of recall. Last little test. In ten seconds, say as many words as you can that begin with . . . f."

"Falsified. Fabricator. Freaky. Fuck. Flabbergasted. Foreshadowing. Fasciculation."

"Okay, okay, enough." The doctor laughed. "Brain works better than most. Rest for a while, and when I release you, don't you dare come back," he said.

"Definitely on it," Maggie replied. "Thank you for all you've done. I'm very grateful."

"I'll have the detective come back in."

Seconds after he left, Jackson asked Maggie, "Doc says you're free to go this afternoon. Will you need a lift?"

"Oh, Jackson. I'm so confused. What happened?"

"We'll get to that later. Just close your eyes now."

When she woke up, it was the afternoon. The doctor checked her out again and she was set to go. Jackson put his arm around her to keep her steady, and they walked to the parking lot.

"You saved my life," Maggie said.

"All in the line of duty."

Once settled, Jackson asked, "Do you remember when I called last eve? Around six."

"That was last night?"

"You were slurring your words. Couldn't get out a logical thought. You said you were taking care of your father. But something seemed off."

"So you came by?"

"I did."

"And?"

"We'll get to all the details later. Let's just say you needed some help."

"I'm really sorry. I think . . . I remember . . . pills. Sorryyyyy."

"No need to apologize to me."

"I let the ball drop on . . ." Maggie looked out the window. Tears started falling.

"Bounce back and it's only a pothole. Dwell there and it's a sinkhole," Jackson said. "Besides, you know I can't stand to see anyone cry. Maudie would . . ." Jackson stopped, then quickly added. "Especially you." He handed her a handkerchief.

As they pulled into Maggie's driveway, Jackson said, "I rode your bike here from Big Eats."

"Oh, right. BJ drove me home. Said I didn't look so good."

"You need a new back tire, and brake pads could use a replacement."

"No shit. On my list. And thanks. I hope you wore a helmet."

"Don't even try to tell me how to take care of myself."

Jackson helped her out of the truck and settled her on the couch. On the table he'd laid out juices and Moon Pies. "Got these while you were heaving at the hospital. Doc told me to make sure you have plenty of liquids and to slowly start putting things back in your stomach."

"Beer counts, right?"

Jackson handed her a glass of orange juice. She took a bite of a Moon Pie. "Damn, this is good."

Maggie leaned back and let out a huge sigh. "Wanna know what happened?" she asked. "What landed me in the hospital?"

"If you feel like talking."

"That's the least I owe you," she said. "I'm no pillhead addict. That's the truth. Some pretty awful things happened."

"I'm all ears."

"I'll start with my professor." She drank the glass of juice. "You know, I'm more clear now than I've been in a really long time. All that shit out of my system. Maybe this whole thing is a blessing. You think?"

"If it gives you a fresh start, I'd say so."

"Okay, look, I'm not gonna beat around the bush? Here goes. He raped me."

"Whoa. You're not hallucinating or anything?"

"Absolutely not. Like I said, I've never felt more lucid. All the bad shit inside must've come right out of me. So, I'll leave out the sordid details and just get to the point. About a week ago, he brought up trumped-up charges against me that I plagiarized. I was hauled in front of the Ethics Committee. They came to the conclusion that they couldn't come to a conclusion on the plagiarism. Brilliant, no? But I'm royally fucked anyway. The charges stay on my record, so landing a job is out of the question. I'm no longer an RA. I can't finish the semester in his class and, well, because I told them about the rape, I'm now expected to hire a lawyer and file formal charges against him or, presumably, I would have been lying. Oh, and the rape accusation goes on my record as well."

"Jesus Christ."

"On top of that," Maggie said, "I couldn't get over the fact that, according to Luna, Lucy had no interest in seeing me. Or, if I don't believe Luna, Lucy could be dead. On top of that, well, depending how far you want to go back, the list goes on and on."

"Oh?"

"Well, yes. I'll go all the way back to me killing my mother. That's always there but stays successfully buried most of the time."

"Wait. What are you talking about?"

"Oh, I didn't shoot her or anything," Maggie said quickly. "I killed her by neglect. I've never told anyone about what happened. I've been too ashamed. Hey, what truth drug am I on now?" Maggie stopped and looked at Jackson. "Am I really telling you all this? Do you know if the doc gave me amphetamines? Fuck, I'm going to regret it. You're not leaving, are you?"

"Go on."

The words tumbled out. "I'd been taking care of her for over a year, after she'd been diagnosed with breast cancer and after the doctor said she'd be better off at home. I was a junior in high school. I'd go to school, race home, and sit with her, feed her, make sure she was totally comfortable—arrange the pillows, pull her sheets up to her chin, fix the blankets so she wasn't too hot or too cold."

"Florence Nightingale or Mother Teresa?"

"Neither."

"One night, after she'd been particularly ungrateful—whacking the hairbrush away, jerking her head when I tried to kiss her, stuff like that—she asked for a sip of juice. I screamed, 'Get your own damn juice. I'm done.' I'd never yelled at her before."

"Taking care of a person is stressful," Jackson said.

"I decided to go for a walk, a long, leisurely one. I deserved it. As they say, if you're not there for yourself, you can't be there for anyone else. An hour or so later, after I'd looped around Royal Palm Court several times, I strolled back in, calm and refreshed and ready to start taking care of her all over again. I cut mom a slice of the raspberry Key lime pie I'd baked that afternoon. It was her favorite. Every single day I did as many things I could think of that might make her happy. I was hoping that she'd be so grateful that she'd sing a song that she sang once to me when I was a kid. When I was really sick. *You'll never know dear, how much I love you.*"

"You Are My Sunshine."

"I'd read about such switcheroos that take place before a person dies," Maggie said. "I figured she would do it now, show me finally that she loved me, before it was too late."

"Fast forward, will you?"

"I brought the slice into the living room, the spoon poised to give her a tiny bite and then . . . well, then . . ." Maggie stopped.

"Go on. Just say it."

Maggie took a deep breath and let the words fall out of her mouth. "The first thing I saw was the juice glass on its side. Next was liquid pooled on the floor. And then my mother's vacant, staring eyes."

"Dead?"

"Dead." Maggie was sobbing. "If I hadn't screamed at her, if I hadn't gone for a meandering stroll," she mumbled, "if I had only given her the damn juice in the first place, if, if, if, I know she wouldn't have died."

Jackson was quiet as he took a bite of the ham sandwich he'd brought. Then he said, "She was dying, right? That's why the doctors felt it was best for her to be home?"

"All she wanted was some juice. She might've lived another . . . who knows how long."

"It must not've been easy taking care of her all that time. And I'm sure she wasn't enjoying a slow death or even having to depend on you. If it hadn't happened that day, it would've been the next day or the next. I consider you a saint."

"Not one day has gone by that . . . Oh shit, did I just unload all that on you?"

"You did. And I'm not the least bit sorry."

Maggie leaned over and gave him a hug.

"Maybe you want to rest now?" Jackson asked.

"Actually, I want to know why you called?"

"Now?"

Maggie nodded.

"It's a big one. You think you can—"

"Lay it on me."

"Okay. A new note had come in."

"No shit."

"What'd it say?"

"I've got it. You up for taking a look?"

"Nothing I'd rather do," Maggie said. "Except have a smoke. You mind?"

"Yup I do. But it's your life. And it's your house. Seems you've found quite a few ways to get to the pearly gates in record time. You sure you're ready for this?"

Jackson handed her the printed-out note. "Chief sent it to our squad. I saw your name wasn't on the list."

"Guess he's done with me. Can't say I blame him. After the Cedric thing."

"I'm not giving up on you."

Maggie felt tears welling up. This guy . . . Her voice quivering, she read: *"Lust. Whack. Writhing. Sneer. Cruel. Violence. Kill. Laughing. Dum as dirt; y'all ain't got know clue."*

"Wanna know what I think?" Jackson asked. "See the words *kill* and *laughing?* It's been eleven days. I think he's telling us something. I think we're looking for a body."

"Nothing about this suggests it was written by the same person as the others," Maggie said. "Maybe a copycat, looking for some attention?"

"Damn. I was hoping we were getting closer."

"Jackson, all of a sudden, all the air's gone out of this tire. I'm sorry, but I think I've reached my limit. I've gotta rest. Things are starting to get foggy."

"No prob. Nap time," Jackson said.

"I'll be back on it. Just gotta . . ."

Before she finished the sentence, she was asleep.

TWENTY-FIVE

When Maggie woke up, it was afternoon and Jackson was gone. "On duty," the scrawl read. "Be back at six. Rest. Eat. Drink. Rest. Eat. Drink. Repeat."

Maggie realized she'd slept through the night and most of the next day. She sat up, lit up, and looked around—and felt hopeful. The sun was shining, she was back on her feet, and Jackson was still around. She decided to shower, get dressed, and go to Big Eats to thank BJ. Jackson told her that she had stayed at the hospital with him most of the night.

As soon as Maggie walked in the diner, BJ raced over. "You poor baby! But look at you! You look like a new person, thank Jesus."

"Oh, BJ. Thank you. Thank you doesn't begin to cover it. Guess I fucked up royally."

"Plenty of time to talk 'bout that later. Meanwhile, Rhonda and I've got you covered for the next week. Go get cozy with your man. He seems like a keeper."

"Nothing happening there," Maggie said. "Except that I owe him, and you, my life."

"Well then," BJ said, a suggestive smile on her face. "Get started with payback."

"I love you," Maggie said. "See you in a week."

"One sec. You take care of yourself, ya hear. Before you head out, see those two sitting in the center booth? They asked for you. I told them you weren't working this week, but I guess they figured since they were here, they might as well chow down. College buddies?"

Maggie glanced over. "Oh, Ashley and Brittany. Not exactly buddies but real good study friends. We worked on several papers together, grilled each other before exams. They were the only people in the whole damn school I ever hung out with. You know, in the parking lot after class shooting the shit, smoking weed. Really cool. But I've no idea why they're here."

"Go find out."

"Hi Ashley, Brittany," Maggie said sliding into the booth. "How the hell are you? It's been a while."

"We miss you. Class just isn't the same without you."

"Miss you guys, too. But, you know, some shit came up. Life. Sometimes gets in the way of living."

"Ain't it the truth."

"But might I ask what brings you to this fine eating establishment? Don't tell me you looked up five-star restaurants in the area."

Maggie hadn't spoken to either of them for several weeks since they'd given a group report on forensic odontology. "If you're after a decent meal," she said, "I suggest you make a beeline for the door."

"We think we have an idea why you haven't been around," Ashley said.

"Okay," Maggie said.

"We read the Ethics Committee minutes. You know, they're public."

It took Maggie only a second. "Fuck. I didn't think any students actually read them."

"Ditmire's been on our radar for a while," Brittany said.

"What? Why?"

"Backstory in a sec. But for the past few months, we noticed all the attention he'd been paying you. It was familiar to us. Of course, it could've been because you're, like, brilliant," Brittany laughed. "But we'd seen him do that kind of thing before."

"To both of us," Ashley admitted. "Only I'm not brilliant."

"Me neither," said Brittany.

"What am I missing here?" Maggie asked. "So he paid you a lot of attention. I think you both *are* brilliant."

"Lately, he's been totally wigged out. Lost. Confused. Angry. Just plain weird. And we noticed you'd stopped coming to class. We happened to hear about the Ethics Committee meeting and decided to see what it was all about," Brittany said.

"Turns out, my story's pretty much the same as yours," Ashley said. "Part of it anyway."

"Wait a minute. He accused you of plagiarism?"

"The other part," Ashley said.

"No."

"You ready for this?"

"Not sure but go on."

"It was about a year ago," Ashley began, "after a group study session at Muddy Waters. We'd been going over dialogue from *No Country for Old Men*. Ditmire was cool. A real approachable professor. I stayed after everyone else had left. For some reason, Ditmire and I had a lot to talk about. He told me about his wife, how she'd upped and left him one day for a job opportunity and how angry he was, how he felt he'd been taken advantage of. 'After all I did for her,' he said. I told him my boyfriend had just dumped me. He implied that he was real lonely. Guess I did the same. Anyway, he started telling me how much he liked talking to me. That he loved chatting with smart people. So that was that. A cool connection. I was, you know, stupid as this sounds, flattered."

"I get it," Maggie said.

"So a few days later, after class, he asked if I wanted to take a drive. He'd seen this fantastic view from some place not far. He said I'd be blown away."

"Uh-oh," Maggie said.

"While we were sitting there looking at this gorgeous sunset," Ashley said, "I disagreed with the words he was quoting from *No Country for Old Men*. I know the film really well. I wrote my college thesis on it. At first, I thought we were just playfully disagreeing. But then he kept insisting he was right, and I knew I was right. I wouldn't back down. I didn't realize until too late that he was livid at having been wrong, or shown up, or questioned, or something. Clenched fists. Red-faced." Ashley pushed her food around before going on. "I couldn't get away."

"Damn," Maggie said. "I'm so so sorry."

"It was like he flipped out. Became a totally different person, one I'd never seen before. His eyes glazed. He was almost grunting. It was . . . the worst day of my life."

"Here's where it gets even weirder," Brittany said. "I didn't know anything about Ashley and Ditmire until one day she and I started talking, maybe a month, a month and a half ago. One thing led to another, and she warned me. She said she'd seen how much attention Ditmire was paying me. I figured she was jealous and blew her off."

"A few days after that," Ashley said, "while she and I were hanging out, I noticed that she looked terrible. I asked her what was going on. After a bit, she broke down and told me. That was my aha moment. Our aha moment."

"I'd been at his office," Brittany said. "He said he'd help me with an essay I was writing. A little while into it, I was joking around. I don't even remember what I said but it pissed him off. I tried to get out."

"Shit," Maggie said. "Shit shit shit."

"Look, I'm not naive. Neither is Ashley, but we didn't see it coming. In retrospect, now having given it lots of thought, we had seen that in class he was a kind of know-it-all who didn't like to be challenged. But truth was, we admired him for it. Seemed he was always right. Nothing like having a wicked smart prof."

"And he kind of lured us with promises. He said I could be his RA next semester," Ashley said.

"He promised he'd write glowing recommendations for a job I was applying for," Brittany said.

"We did some research on the kind of person who quickly can go into a rage, and then takes his anger out sexually. We came up with a diagnosis. May not be right, but we think he has intermittent explosive disorder with eroticized rage. But whatever. He's a threat and will continue to be."

"We never reported him. We never said anything to anyone. We figured we wouldn't be believed," Brittany said.

"Besides, and here's the shameful truth, we both decided that all we really wanted was to graduate and get the hell out of there. If we started proceedings, for sure it would muddy the situation, possibly even get us kicked out. Besides, a huge part of me felt it was all my fault. Maybe I'd led him on. I blamed myself. What the hell was I doing going for a drive with a professor in the first place?"

"If we'd been stronger . . ." Brittany said.

"But then we read the Ethics Meeting minutes," Ashley said. "We started thinking that we needed to report him now. It's a clear pattern. This can't keep happening."

"Jesus Christ. Both of you." Maggie shook her head. "That fucking goddamn prick."

"We decided we needed to go to the president. Tell him our stories. We thought about the consequences but now we don't even care," Brittany said. "We plan to hire a lawyer."

"No pressure on you in any way," Ashley said. "But if you want to be in touch, maybe come to the president with us or hire a lawyer together, text us."

"Let me give it some thought. It's really unbelievable. Group hug," Maggie said.

The three held each other tight. "We're strong," Brittany said. "And we won't let him get away with this."

"I've gotta get back to class. It was really great to see you again. Let's get together, whether about this or . . . forensic odontology. Our paper was rad, wasn't it?"

"We aced it, didn't we?" Maggie said.

"We're quite a team!"

"Here's a twenty for the grub," Ashley said as they got ready to go. "It wasn't that bad."

"That'd be the highest compliment Big Eats ever got. Put your money away. It's on me," Maggie said.

After kissing BJ goodbye and thanking her again, Maggie decided to take the long way home, knowing she could gun Annabelle on the back roads. She needed a long, head-clearing ride before giving all this info the attention it deserved. When she got to Moray Road, she made herself slow down. Cops always patrolled that stretch, so she kept checking her mirror. No cop was behind her, but a pickup was closing in. Maggie figured he must not be from around here, because every local knew not to speed. She inched over to let him pass, but he didn't. He came up beside her and stayed close, nudging her over until she was nearly off the road, inches from the swamp. She tried to look into his window—maybe it was someone she knew messing with her—but it was tinted and she couldn't see in. The truck had a crushed passenger side door she hadn't seen before. It was probably just some jerk high on something, trying to impress himself or whomever he was riding with. The driver kept nudging her closer to the shoulder, and several times, she missed spilling by inches.

"Fuck off!" she yelled as her foot dragged through the wet grass. This was the closest she'd ever come to wiping out. Her hands were starting to shake and sweat dripped down her body beneath her leathers. She slowed down to give him another chance to pass, but he stayed alongside her—so she floored it. He did the same. Where were the goddamn cops when you needed them?

A car was now coming toward them on the narrow two-lane road, so if Mr. Pickup didn't want to die, he'd have to gun it or pull in behind her. He slowed down—and Maggie took off. She cut a quick right onto a local road, then a left, a right, another right, a left, up and down side streets, all the while checking her mirror. No one was following. When she was sure she'd lost him, she pulled into a secluded spot and dragged Annabelle with her. She was trembling.

Was someone deliberately trying to wipe her out? With so many assholes in Florida, it was possible. Most likely, though, it was a bunch of bored kids pumping themselves up by having a good time at her expense. She remembered the last line of *Catch-22*:

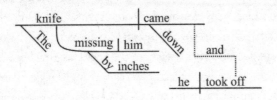

But, she thought, knives—or pickups—don't come out of nowhere.

TWENTY-SIX

Jackson's truck was in front of Maggie's when she got home.

"I thought we made a plan," Jackson said sitting on the front step. "You were supposed to stay here, rest, eat, drink."

"And I thought you were coming back at six."

"Looks like neither of us can be trusted," he said.

"Bombshell." Maggie took off her helmet.

As she came closer to Jackson, she saw the look on his face change.

"Hey, what happened to you?" he asked. "Accident? Don't tell me . . ."

"No, no, no. But I was an inch from wiping out. In the goddamn swamp! Thanks to some douchebag who was trying to run me off. He kept coming up behind me, beside me, then speeding off and—"

"Slow down. Who tried to run you off?"

"And that's not even the bombshell!" Maggie collapsed on the couch.

"What the hell's going on?"

"In chronological order or reverse?"

"Whichever," Jackson said.

"Reverse." Maggie recounted the saga of the shadowing truck.

When she finished, he said, "You're saying someone's targeting you?"

"Yup."

"You specifically?"

"Sure seemed that way."

"I think you need a few meals and a few good nights' sleep. You? Maggie Moore, student, waitress, sometimes genius, is in someone's crosshairs?"

"Just a feeling."

"You thinking maybe the professor?" Jackson asked.

"Joke, right? The dick drives an old beater, and from what I've seen, he probably never passed his driver's test. Plus, he wouldn't have a clue how to handle a pickup. Definitely not him."

"What else you got?"

"Ever hear the one about two college students walking into a diner?" Maggie asked.

"A bar, yeah. Diner, no."

Maggie recounted what Ashley and Brittany had told her. "So I'm thinking," she said, "do you know what I'm thinking?"

Jackson didn't say anything right away, but then, "A serial, uh, rapist?"

"Yup. They're reporting him to the president."

Jackson grabbed his phone and dialed. "Ms. Ginny Myers, please," he said.

"Who's that?" Maggie asked.

"Yeah, I'll hold. . . . Hello? Ginny? . . . Jackson here . . . fine, fine. You? . . . Great. . . . Everything's calm on that front, for now anyway. . . . For sure I will, but that's not why I'm calling. It's about something that took place at Rosedale. Real serious. I'm wondering if we could meet you soon. Great. Your office, an hour. Thanks, Ginny."

"Who's Ginny?"

"My lawyer," Jackson said. "Ginny Myers. Come on. If anyone can help you out, she's the one."

A few minutes later, they were ready to go. On their way, Jackson said, "I found out more about Cedric. Cedric Smith. His cousin does pool maintenance. Guess who's one of his clients?"

"For real? The mayor?"

"Smith picked up his cousin there more than a couple of times."

"So now you're also thinking the chief got it right?" Maggie asked.

"Gathering the facts. It's my job, you know. Still on the fence."

"Still, nothing about him rings true," Maggie insisted.

When they got to Ginny Myers's office, they parked and went right in. It was in a single-story detached building. A receptionist greeted them. "Ms. Myers will be right with you."

Ms. Myers gave a quick hug to Jackson and shook hands with Maggie. "Nice to meet you."

tall, thin
black skirt and blazer; white collared blouse
pearls
sharp features, thin lips

"Come on back," she said moving confidently down the lush carpet. The furnishings in her office were a cut above any lawyer's office that Maggie had seen around town, not that she'd been to many, but she had visited at least two—one after her mother died and she needed to know how to deal with the two-line will, and another when Maggie went with Lucy and Luna in an attempt to sue the neighborhood's management company for not fixing the broken water pipes. Ms. Myers's office had a beautifully carved mahogany desk, along with a couch and two big, deep chairs. Rows of books lined the walls.

"Is your ex behaving?" Ginny asked, motioning them to sit on the couch. She sat across from them in one of the flowered swivel chairs.

"No," Jackson said, "but at least she agreed to the entire month of July." He looked quickly at Maggie, then back at Ginny.

"I'd call that progress," Ginny said. "Keep me posted. If she messes up again, it's off to court. Again. How about the other, uh, you know, any progress on—"

"Fine, fine."

"I thought for sure something would've—"

"Moving along," Jackson said. Jackson's leg had begun bouncing.

"Alright, let's see what we've got here." Ginny took out her phone. "Do you mind if I record this? A whole lot easier."

Maggie looked at Jackson, whose eyes stayed locked on Ginny. Maggie wanted to stop the meeting right then and say, "An ex and something about a summer visit? That could explain some things," but Maggie thought about the photos Jackson carried with him and how he'd just cut off Ms. Myers from—

"Maggie? Can you begin now?" Ginny asked.

"Uh . . . okay. Sure."

Maggie tried to include everything that had taken place. When she finished, Ginny started firing questions. Maggie answered each one:

On the day of the rape, where were you?

What had taken place before the incident?

Did you have a relationship with the professor? How long?

Did you have expectations that it was leading toward something?

Tell me about the things you did together.

Was anything radically different leading up to this incident? Had his behavior changed? Do you have any explanation as to why?

What are the names of the girls who came to the diner? How can I reach them?

What did they tell you?

What were the results of the Ethics Committee's findings? Was any disciplinary action taken?

When they completed the Q and A, Ginny said, "I'll be in touch as soon as I've got something. In the meantime, I'll be contacting Ashley and Brittany. Of course, I can't promise anything, but I'm thinking we might have ourselves one helluva case here."

"I really appreciate this." Maggie got up and shook her hand. "Thanks so much."

"My pleasure. And Jackson, call if Madame Ex's behavior goes south."

"You know I will."

"And on—"

"Yup. Bye," Jackson said as he cut her off and walked quickly out.

Back in the pickup, Maggie waited for Jackson to explain. He didn't, so Maggie began.

"A daughter?"

"Yup."

"Maud?"

Jackson nodded.

"'Miss Maudie Atkinson baked a Lane cake so loaded with shinny it made me tight,'" Maggie quoted.

"You know that, too? Jesus, Maggie. Harper Lee grew up in our hometown," Jackson said. "My wife, my ex, and I used to read her book together and to Maud. Back then when we were going to be together forever."

"I'm sorry."

"Maudie growing up without me, without a father."

"Tough. But seems you do see her, no? And this summer, she'll be with you. That counts for something. For a lot, actually. I never knew my father. And I turned out just fine," Maggie said, chuckling. "As you can plainly see."

Jackson hesitated. "Wait. I thought you were taking care of your dad. You told me on the phone."

"Wasn't true. I never knew him. Have no idea where that taking-care-of-him story came from."

"How 'bout we do something way out. How 'bout we come clean," Jackson said. "Maybe it could do us both some good."

"What a novel idea," Maggie said.

"You begin. About your dad, or lack thereof."

"Are you sure you're up for this?" Maggie asked.

"Try me."

"Here goes. When it gets boring, just say. Okay, so, growing up, my mom would shut me down whenever I asked about him. I never knew anything about him. After she died, I got up the courage to go into her bedroom. Part of me hoped she'd left me a note or a piece of jewelry, something special just for me. I opened her top dresser drawer. Still interested?"

"Totally."

"I was psyched when I saw this beautiful velvet pouch. I knew there had to be something in there especially for me. First thing I saw was my birth certificate. I'd never seen it before. It read 'Father Unknown.' Then I opened an envelope addressed to Ms. Hazel Moore. 'Congratulations!' it said. 'We are pleased to offer you a spot at the Hartlett School of Music.' Should I keep going?"

"Yup."

"You've got to understand," Maggie said, "that I had no idea my mother had any musical talent at all. Or even any interest. I never remembered her listening to music or playing an instrument. Okay, I thought, this is interesting, but totally in keeping with her silence on anything personal. I looked at the third item and prayed this would be the one that was especially for me. It was a news article. 'A freshman co-ed at the Hartlett School of Music reported that she'd been raped last night behind Butler Hall. The college is investigating.' Then I looked at the date and year."

"And?"

Tears filled Maggie's eyes.

"Oh," Jackson said. "That's a tough one."

"Yeah, well, we've all got a story. Once I found that out, it explained a lot. Like why she and I had the relationship—make that *non-relationship*—we had. Okay, your turn."

"Wow. Can we take a moment to talk about—"

"No. Your turn. Come on."

"Only if we can revisit yours again. I want to know more. Okay?"

"Sure."

"Well, since my ex and daughter are already out there on the table, I'll fill in the details. Tammy had been complaining for years about the endless hours I spent on the job. I tried to cut back, but, you know, once I'm on something, I get one hundred percent into it. Even when I was home, I'd be spending most of the time going over stuff about this case or that. Guess you could say I wasn't such a great husband."

"I think I see what's coming."

"Bet not," he said.

"So, I was lead detective in Madison, population a million. There was more stuff to deal with than any of us had time for. Every day, multiple knifings, shootings, gang shit, you get the picture. I'd been disciplined a few times. Lieutenant kept trying to get me fired. Look at me. Can you tell why? Brought me up for what he said was unwarranted surveillance, unwarranted seizures, going into places without backup. Some folks felt the evidence was kinda convincing. Pretty ugly disciplinary hearings."

Jackson grimaced. He looked down and fidgeted with the paper he had in his hands.

"Fast forward," he said quickly recovering. "I come home one day to a note. She'd had it. Said she'd filed for divorce. Was taking Maud and going to her folks'. About two hundred miles away."

"They upped and left, just like that?"

"Yup. So I quickly took some vacation days and followed her. Here comes the real awful part. I barged into the house. How'd that end, you might ask? I nearly got arrested. She got a restraining order."

"Oh lord."

"That's not the worst."

"After I got back home, I started drinking and, well, after a haze of six months, I was let go. That's a whole other story."

"How'd you end up here?"

"Chief here helped me out. He was buddies with the sheriff in Madison, who gave me high marks, but said I'd run into some hard times. Don't think he ever gave the chief the details. Murray became a friend. I owe him a helluva lot. During these past eight—"

Before Jackson could finish, his phone dinged. Looking at the screen, Jackson said, "Text from the chief. Listen to this: Get to Banyan Way Number Seven. Now. It's Cedric's place. Bombshell.

TWENTY-SEVEN

Jackson swerved in and out of highway traffic, slamming on the brakes, accelerating, braking. Maggie gripped the seat. "Chief won't rest till he solves this one. Wants to go out with a bang. Legacy matters to him. Keeps counting down till retirement. If he cracks this, he's a hero. Plus, a higher paygrade and retirement will be sweeter."

"Something I don't understand," Maggie said trying to keep her voice steady despite the fact that she could be dead any minute. "Why hasn't he called in the FBI? I mean, a missing kid. Don't they always work these cases?"

"Early on, Chief said he would, but only after we'd worked it for a month. Only then would he admit defeat. Locals don't have to involve the FBI if missing kid is over twelve. We're at day twenty-one. I think he's wrong, he should've gotten 'em on it, but it's not my call. Wants to own it. Prove his worth to the mayor and the commissioner. And to you. But damn."

As they drove, Maggie repeated the words in the newest note. "Lust. Whack. Writhing. Cruel. Dum as dirt y'all ain't got know clue."

"Those words," Jackson said, "sound real familiar."

"Of course they do. You've said them a hundred times since we got in the truck and I've no idea how often you repeat them to yourself.

Earworm's never far away. Hey, you know how the chief got a warrant?" Maggie asked. "I mean, what do you think they've got on Cedric?"

"We're gonna find out."

When they got to Cedric's, a neat trailer among dozens of others in a secluded trailer park off CR 93, the chief was standing outside. "You?" he said to Maggie. "What're you doing here?"

"Long story, Chief. Tell you later. She doesn't have to come in or anything."

"Course she does now she's here. We can talk about this later."

The chief was holding up a piece of paper. "Looky here," he said. "This is what I'm talking about. The old nail in the coffin. Found it tossed in the trash. Date, location, and time right here in black and white. *Exact* date, *exact* location, and *exact* time of Heidi's disappearance. Seems it's a diary entry ripped out of the book. Mr. Teacher is not as slick as he thinks."

"Hold still," Jackson said and started reading it from yards away. "'It's a slow easy ride cruising down CR 111 and going past Hyacinth Park and Collins till I get to H and then the fun begins round about 4 and we won't stop till I've got nothing left in me and that may never come.'"

"I'm gonna grill the bastard till he gives it up if it's the last thing I do," the chief said. "Wanna know what I'm thinking? I don't believe that Heidi's dead. Just a hunch. Smith doesn't seem like a killer. More of a tickler. He's keeping her somewhere and doing some shit to her and I'm getting to the bottom of it."

"If you're right—" Jackson began.

"If? If?" the chief yelled. "Come on, Jackson. Stay here as long as you want, but as far as I'm concerned, this is case closed. I'm heading back. Got all I need. Wanted you to give it a once-over. With your eyes, you might find something I didn't see. Get going!"

"Mind if I take a pic of the note before you go?" Jackson asked.

"Course not. Cogitate on it. He's our guy." The chief bagged the note. "Meet me at the shop when you're done."

After the chief left, Maggie said, "Hearing that, looks like I was dead wrong."

"Kinda does. As long as we're here, let's see what else he's got."

"Can I see your phone?" Maggie asked.

Jackson handed Maggie his cell. "He can't shut up, can he?" Maggie said. "The guy simply can't zip his fucking trap. The chief thinks that H refers to Heidi. 'Till I get to H.' Makes sense."

"Yup. And the place and time fit, too." Jackson paused. "However, on the far-fetched scale, one might consider this: Maybe Cedric's got himself a girlfriend who lives along that stretch of road."

"Now wouldn't that be some kind of out-of-this-fucking world co-inky-dink," Maggie said. "We can easily check out who lives there."

"Let's take us a look around."

For the next hour, Jackson turned out every drawer and cupboard, rifled under every cushion, stripped the bed—looking for something, anything, that might show Cedric was the guy. Maggie checked out his books, sorted through his papers, examined his calendar. She found plenty of poetry books, plenty of classic novels—and plenty of smutty magazines. All that, along with meticulously laid-out lesson plans, grocery lists, and even a sweet letter to his mother. While Maggie was poking her nose in every corner of his trailer, she kept repeating the note and diagramming the sentence. It was almost as long as Proust's.

Jackson finally slumped in a chair. "Gotta hand it to the chief. Reluctantly."

"But I still can't put together the guy who wrote the notes and Cedric. Let me see your phone again," Maggie said. "Looks like it was done by a righty, like everything else in Cedric's house. Remember the note in the spokes? Clearly done by a lefty."

"Ya know, thinking about it, Cedric drank with his right hand in the interview," Jackson added. "And gestured, too."

Maggie closed her eyes and let all the notes she'd read pass along the inside of her eyelids. "Okay," she finally said. "Hard to believe it's Cedric. Not only 'cause of the handwriting, but because of how different the notes are from how he speaks and how he writes. He never says just *milk,* for example. It's *two percent and if not then one percent but add on light cream for balance. Other choice is almond milk, but only in glass bottle.* I mean, the guy thinks and writes in paragraphs."

"But, like I said, he could change his style depending on who his words are for, you know?"

"Could."

"On a scale of one to a hundred, how convinced are you it's not Cedric?" Jackson asked.

"From a linguistics POV, ninety-nine-point-eight. You? From a detective POV?"

"Based on his lying about his whereabouts, all the teen porn, this last note stating place and time, I've gotta go with the facts. Ninety-nine-point-eight in the other direction."

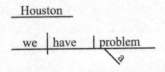

Maggie said the words as she mentally diagrammed the sentence, which was among the simplest diagrammable sentences in English: An apostrophe, not the punctuation mark but the thing being addressed, i.e., *Houston;* subject, *we;* irregular verb, *have;* direct object, *problem;* indefinite article, *a.*

If only life were as formularized and unsurprising as diagramming the parts of speech of a sentence.

TWENTY-EIGHT

"Lemme drop you home before I go back to the chief," Jackson said. "If he already got Cedric to come clean, game over and he'll be breaking out the beer."

"Part of me wouldn't mind being wrong. I still like the chief a lot," Maggie said, "even though I seem to have been dismissed."

"Same. Love the guy. But, I'm also rooting for you."

"You know Jackson, that might qualify as the most positive thing you ever said to me."

Ignoring her, he repeated, "Lusty. Cruel. Violence. Kill."

"Are you ever going to stop?"

"Seems I can't," Jackson said.

"I suggest you go for something more benign especially when you're out in public, or someone's gonna call the cops on you."

"Ha, that's a good one." He smiled.

Maggie asked, "So none of the names I gave you panned out?"

"We checked 'em all. I did it personally. All scum, but their alibis are tight. You have some real degenerate friends."

"Hard to avoid them. You know what Carl Hiaasen said in one of his novels? 'The Florida in my novels is not as seedy as the real Florida. It's hard to stay ahead of the curve.'"

"But you stay."

Maggie shook her head. "Love has no logic."

"Ain't it the truth."

"Some things you just can't let go of," she said.

Maggie began again. "Violence. Kill. Violence. Kill. Something about those words. Familiar in a weird way."

"If you'd stop hanging out with those dudes."

"If you'd stop repeating them."

Maggie kept saying the words softly over and over. Finally she said, "Oh my god."

"Yeah?"

"Oh my fucking god."

"What? What is it?"

"Pull over."

"Huh? What's—"

"Pull over!" She grabbed the steering wheel.

"Hey!" Jackson's truck jerked and nearly skidded off the road.

"Pull the fuck over!"

"Don't kill us."

Jackson checked his rearview mirror and made it to the side of the road. "We could be dead right now," he said as he cut the engine and put on his emergency lights. "That's damn crazy! I take back anything nice I ever said. What's going on?"

"I think I've got something."

"Fine, but we don't have to die with it," Jackson said.

"A mighty *lusty* yell," she said. "You hear?"

"I've been sayin' that—"

"Pounds with *cruel violence*."

"Give me a sec." He started tapping his hand on the steering wheel and mumbling.

"Excuse me, but you're making no sense," she said.

"*Kill* him," he said softly. "*Kill* the umpire!" he said louder.

"My fucking god!" Maggie yelled. "You got it!"

"Somewhere men are *laughing*," Jackson said slowly.

"But not at us! Nobody's gonna be laughing at us!"

"This is crazy," Jackson said. "All those are words from Casey. But what do they have to do with anything?"

"Here it is. Here is what I'm thinking. The person we're looking for, for sure, he knows Casey real well."

"Fine. That's what you almost got us killed for? How many millions of people know the damn poem?"

"Do me a favor. Say the poem and I'm going to recite the note at the same time. Stay with me here. Ready? Go."

As Jackson said, "The SCORE stood FOUR to TWO with BUT one INNing LEFT to PLAY," Maggie said, "I POKE her HARD with MY big DICK she SCREAM and PURR and SPIN."

Jackson continued, "And THEN when COOney DIED at FIRST" . . . as Maggie said, "So LOVE the SINner, HATE the SIN. Did you hear that?" Maggie asked.

"Yeah."

"We're in sync. And I might point out this could be the very first time."

"Not sure where you're going with this."

"To write in meter isn't easy. But writing in iambic heptameter? Nearly impossible." Maggie lit up. "Sorry. I gotta. Don't go pulling any healthy shit on me now." She held in the smoke, then blew out seven perfect big, then seven perfect small rings. "That may be a record," she said.

"Why'd we risk our lives just now? Would you tell me that."

"Who knows that poem well enough to have the beat ingrained in their brain? In every fiber of their body? I'll answer that. The guys on your squad," Maggie said. "Chief said it was part of the job description. Memorize it or else."

"So?"

"Suspend disbelief for a sec," Maggie said. "Hear me out."

Maggie inhaled deeply and let out a long stream of smoke.

"Hold on," Jackson said. "If you're going where I think you're going, you're walking the rest of the way."

"Just saying—"

Jackson roared. "That's a good one. A really good one. Let me think. The guys in the Olemeda PD. Right. Evans. Yup it's Evans. Family man. Worked with him for eight years. Twin girls. About as clean and straight as they come. Or Gutierrez. That's it. The man's been voted captain and has more positive reviews than—"

"Maybe you don't know them as well as you think," Maggie said as Luna Rainbow's words echoed.

"And maybe you lost your mind. Besides, what would they be doing going out to Birchbrook when there's plenty of choices right here?"

"You don't shit where you eat, Jackson. It's a commandment."

"Oh come on! A cop?"

"A dirty one. They exist, you know. In Florida alone," she said, "Remember Gabriel Albala, Boynton Beach cop, arrested for distributing child porn. Florida sheriff's deputy Steven O'Leary, charged with fifty-two counts stemming from planting drugs or fake drugs on unsuspecting motorists. Zachary Wester, nine counts of false imprisonment among other charges. German Bosque, terminated for the seventh time. Misconduct and criminal behavior. Florida's finest, all right."

"But you're talking about the guys I work with. My brothers."

"Do you have any emails from them? Do you write to one another?"

"Stop! This is insane."

"I'll grant you, it's highly unlikely."

"Hey, you on some shit? Have you been—"

"No!"

"Weed? Tequila? Pills."

"I'm stone-cold sober, sad to say."

"If you're lying, you're—"

"Stay focused. Are the emails on your phone?"

"Not doing it."

"Okay, then how about I tell the chief you found a stash in my place and took the pills for your own purposes. Or maybe how you didn't arrest me for obviously being a dealer."

"Oh come on."

"Or that you've got pics of young girls you take with you in your backpack? Pics that—"

"What? How'd you . . . shut up!"

"Fine. Then send me the emails."

Jackson started up the truck and gunned it. He kept his eyes on the road, never glancing at Maggie. Neither said a word for the next twenty minutes.

Once at Maggie's, she said, "Come on. I'm calling a truce. Let's at least eat something. Drink. Cool our jets. Take some time to think about things. Okay?"

Maggie went inside, grabbed two beers, and handed one to Jackson. He stood in the doorway, focused on his phone. After a few seconds, emails started pinging on Maggie's computer.

"You got anything to eat?" he asked.

"The place is yours. I mean it. I have Moon Pies. Peanut butter. Jelly. Make yourself a sandwich. While you're at it, I wouldn't mind one."

Jackson went to the kitchen, while Maggie consulted a book on the coffee table. It was called *Idiolect: How We Say What We Say*. While looking through it, Jackson's phone buzzed. Maggie glanced at it and saw . . . a girl battered, bloodied, and nude, lying in a wooded area. Dead?

"Two sandwiches coming right up," Jackson said.

Quickly, Maggie grabbed the book and went back to her computer. She printed out the emails and brought them to the couch.

"Thanks," she said taking a bite. She focused on the emails and on putting what she just saw in a sealed compartment. For now. To be revisited later. After a few minutes, she said, "Based on these, fuck it. None of them fit the linguistic profile."

"I'm saying it. Told you so!"

"I'm eliminating your buddies."

"If you'd listened to me—"

"However, that still leaves two people." Maggie devoured a Moon Pie. "When's the last time I ate?" she said. "I'm famished." She washed it down with the Bud.

"Two people what?" Jackson said.

"You and the chief."

"Me and the chief what?" Jackson asked.

"Casey. You know . . ."

Jackson grinned. "Brilliant! It's me! Busted!"

"Send me some of the chief's texts and emails."

"You shittin' me."

"Please. This is my last request. Maybe second to last."

"You're going too far."

"Think outside the box," Maggie said, grabbing another Bud. "Pretend the chief's just some dude on the street."

"You drink too much."

"Let's stay focused. Chief's just some dude—"

"You OD'd on pills. I'm not saving you again."

"Stay with me here."

"You smoke like a goddamn chimney."

"Can we deal with my shortcomings later? And if I may say, I bet when we open that can of worms, you have your own share. You really want to go down that road?"

Maggie cocked her head and stared at him.

Jackson turned away. "Getting back to the chief," he said.

"Let's pretend he's someone you know but have no attachment to. Can you do that?"

"No."

"For Chrissake. Fine, fine, fine. Let's switch gears then. How about we start with you," Maggie said.

"Right. Come on, Maggie. You're making a fool of yourself."

"It's you and the chief I need to eliminate. My choice where to begin. I think I'll start with the chief. Is there anything at all that could link him to Heidi's disappearance? Something you saw or heard but maybe didn't register as important? Something about the missing kids on his wall. Something about his obsession with them. Something, anything?"

"The chief. Let me think. What would show me that he kidnapped Heidi? Now that's an easy one," he said smirking. "He's known her since she's a kid. He's good buds with the mayor. There you have it. He kidnapped her! Makes perfect sense."

"What'd the chief do before he came to Olemeda?" Maggie asked.

"For Chrissake."

"Just tell me."

"Fine. Far as I know, he moved around a lot. He told me he'd been restless, never wanted to settle down. Not till he got here. The other places he worked at? Way too much stress, he said. Had to fight for recognition and didn't want that anymore. Wanted to enjoy life. Felt he deserved it. Said that he finally found home. Been honored for almost every kind of award possible. And now, adding to his happiness of being here, he recently got himself a steady lady. She moved in last month, he said. A whole different bounce to his step."

"Hmm. Maybe there's another way to look at it. Maybe he went from one precinct to another because he was forced to leave each place. Not unheard of, you know."

"For Chrissake."

"I'm just asking if anyone ever checked out his past."

"Listen, I've had about enough. I'm spent," Jackson said. "No idea when the last time was I slept. Let's pick this up in the morning."

"I'm serious, Jackson. Please. Just give it some thought. If I'm wrong, you get to peacock. If I'm right—"

Jackson was out the door.

Alone now, Maggie thought of the quote from Twain that she diagrammed yesterday:

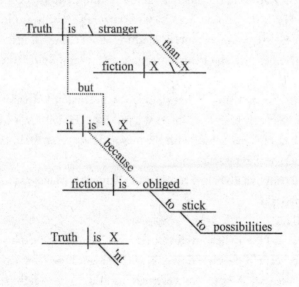

TWENTY-NINE

Early the next morning, Jackson knocked on Maggie's door, opened it, and walked right in. "Come on. We've somewhere to go," he said to the sleeping figure on the couch. "And why the hell don't you lock your door?"

Maggie willed her eyes open. "No. You're not here. It's not morning. I'm having a nightmare."

"I brought you coffee. Drink it. I'm telling you to get up. I'm in my truck. Be there in ten or I'll go to the chief's place alone."

Maggie sat up. "The chief's?"

"Decided for the hell of it to go along with you," Jackson said, "despite knowing it's the stupidest thing I'll ever do. Leave no stone unturned has always been my motto. But this, I swear, is the last damn stone I'm turning over for you. Chief said he's taking his lady to Miami for a special lunch. A little R&R, he said with a twinkle in his eye. Said they'd be checking out the Miami Beach Boardwalk. The ocean. Swim. Snorkel. Lay out in the sun. Stuff we don't do much here."

"Sounds like a lovely day. You're really doing this?"

"If anything's gonna satisfy you, and eliminate him as a suspect, for sure we'll find out. If his home's squeaky clean, we're done. We look around, see if we find anything, then put everything back exactly where it was. Then we leave. Will you be satisfied then?"

"You're serious?"

"Yup. If no porn, no kiddie clothes, no computer smut, no nothing, we can put this shit to rest and move on."

"To the one other cop I haven't checked out," Maggie said softly.

"I'm not dignifying that."

Maggie threw the cover off. "I'm ready." She was dressed in the same clothes as yesterday. "Never understood pj's," she said as they got into the truck.

"I'm breaking every damn rule in the book," Jackson said. "Could mean I lose my job, or worse. I figure we're gonna eliminate him one, two, three and then you'll be one hundred percent in Cedric's court. Don't ask me why I'm doing this."

"I won't. But it means the world to me."

Maggie drank the coffee as they drove down CR 404. Long narrow canals framed the side of the road. Beyond the canals were grasses and reeds growing along the marshes. Maggie had ridden Annabelle down this road dozens of times but had no idea the chief lived out here in the boonies. Soon, the asphalt turned to dirt and the road became bumpier, the piney woods thicker. Jackson stayed under twenty. If he went any faster, he'd lose a muffler, so they bounced along one deep rut after the next. When Maggie banged her head on the window, she gasped. "One piece. I'd like to get there in one piece. You know, Jackson, I've been thinking."

"Uh-oh."

"The chief's exhibiting a classic example of stuck song syndrome, or in this case, stuck poem, like you. It's an involuntary thing. No one has control over it. Stats say ninety-eight percent of people have experienced earworm. I have. For a while it was 'Bohemian Rhapsody.' Then it was 'Bad Romance.' The one that's stuck the longest? 'The Gambler.' And that's the point."

"Glad you're getting to the point. I was wondering where this was going."

"'The Gambler' is a musical memory I cherish from one of the best days of my life. My point is, earworms can be triggered by musical memories or even poetry memories that meant something huge in a person's past. Something good or something bad."

"I know you're going somewhere with this."

"The chief's memory of 'Casey at the Bat' is linked to his childhood dream of being a major league ball player. He never got over *not* being able to pursue that dream. He told me he'd read the poem over and over after he struck out in a crucial game. Most humiliating day of his life, he told me. He empathized with Casey."

"Keep talking. Takes my mind off what we're doing."

"The harder a person tries to suppress the memory," Maggie continued, "the harder the brain latches on to it, forcing it to the surface. Sometimes the constant repetition annoys the hell out of the person experiencing it. In the chief's case, I think it soothes him. I know 'The Gambler' soothes me."

"If we had more time," Jackson said, "I'm sure you could explain more—like, so what? That doesn't make him a pedophile or a kiddie snatcher. But we're here. See this mailbox? It's his." Jackson turned down a narrow road. "Looks like the chief's driveway ought to be in Guinness's as the longest in the world. Says he likes isolation. Doesn't want to annoy neighbors with his target practice."

"You've never been here?"

"Nah. Mostly if we socialize at all, it's for a beer after work. Local bar." Jackson cut the engine. "I'm not a religious man but start praying, because if the chief's not our guy and he somehow finds out that I or we were here, there'll be more than hell to pay. Listen carefully to me, partner."

"I'm moving up in the world. Call me Smiley."

"You're lookout, Smiley. It's *the* most important job. If you see or hear anything coming down the drive, race inside. You've got speed. Use it. Understand?"

"Roger that."

"Seems there's another way out of here, around back. We can hightail it out if we need to. Don't be a disappointment. Be a good partner."

Maggie watched Jackson as he tried the front door. Locked. He opened a window and hoisted himself in. For a big guy, he was agile. A few seconds later, he appeared at the door and gave a thumbs up.

Maggie kept her eyes peeled on the driveway, but after several minutes, she figured that no one would be coming down it except for the chief and his girlfriend, and it was way too early for them to be back. Nevertheless, keeping in mind she was tasked to be a good partner, she forced herself to stay in the truck. She challenged herself to come up with as many new words as she could by taking the last letter of a five-letter word, making it the first letter of a new word, and using only the letters in the original. After she came up with *acres* and *scare, pines* and *snipe, nails* and *slain,* she got bored and decided to go for a stroll down the driveway. It didn't take long for the lure of the house to beckon her. No way she'd come all this way and sit like a disinterested party in some stupid pickup.

"What the hell!" Jackson said seeing her in the living room.

"I couldn't keep doing nothing," she said.

"Partners listen to their partners," Jackson barked.

"Promise, my eyes and ears are tuned to the road."

"I give you one damn thing to do, and you can't even do it."

"I've gotta ask you something," Maggie said. "Something's bothering me."

"Can I tell you how much right now you are bothering me?"

"Why do you have a battered and possibly dead girl on your phone? And pics of girls in your backpack? I checked you out, you know. Only thing I found was that you were a top detective, had an off-the-chart solve rate, but that you'd had a kind of nervous breakdown and resigned. No other details online. You did tell me you'd been drinking too much and said that's a whole—"

"Stop! Stop right there." He came close to her face and with clenched jaw said, "Don't say another word. Listen, I'm here 'cause you want to check out the chief. I'm doing that for you, damn it. So stay the hell outta my goddamn business."

Jackson walked away and with his back to her said, "Here's what I did *not* find so far, Madame Genius. Slutty magazines. Child porn. Pics of teen girls. Girls' clothes. Sex toys."

"Okay, okay."

"You're totally off base here. Why'd I listen—"

"Because maybe somewhere deep—"

"Stop!"

"Fine." Maggie took her time walking around the living room. "Hey, this here's a real pretty Bible," she said picking up the book from a side table. "Listen to what's highlighted: 'It is a trustworthy statement, deserving full acceptance, that Christ Jesus came into the world to save sinners, among whom I am foremost of all.' 1 Timothy 1:15."

"So what!?"

"Jackson, I'm sorry about . . . can we move on? So, Murray's a religious guy?"

"Never said anything about that," Jackson said. "Kinda made fun of Bible-thumping folk. Yet, this here Bible, all marked up. Good to know he's a God-fearing man. Makes it even less likely he's the one."

Maggie picked up a book of St. Augustine's letters on the coffee table. "Who reads St. Augustine? Look at what's highlighted," she said thumbing through. *"Cum dilectione hominum et odio vitiorum."*

"You speak Latin?" Jackson asked.

"Translation's on the side," Maggie said. "'With love for mankind and hatred of sins.' Chief's obsessed with sins. Listen to this. It's written on a Post-it right here on the cover: *Hate the sin; not the sinner.* Then, *Love the sinner; hate the sin.*"

"And?"

"Almost word for word from the first note. Remember? 'Love the sinner' it said, then there was a semicolon before 'hate the sin.' I call this Post-it plagiarism," Maggie declared. "Unless, of course, he's got a photographic memory."

"Oh, I see where you're going. 'Cause he reads the Bible, is most likely religious, likes St. Augustine, is obsessed with sinning, and uses a semicolon—that's it! That's our guy! No worries. That'll stand up in court."

"Nobody uses semicolons. Or at least nobody uses them correctly. And you know what's front and center on the chief's desk at the precinct?" Maggie asked.

"Of course. Like I don't see it every day. Photos," Jackson said. "Shots of big fish."

Picking up a picture frame, Maggie said, "This is the exact same one as on his desk. And I quote: 'With a smile of Christian charity great Casey's visage shone;' semicolon there. 'He stilled the rising tumult;' another semicolon. 'He bade the game go on.' Not one but two semicolons. And in the second line, do you know what separates the two independent clauses?"

"I don't even know what a goddamn independent clause is."

"A semicolon," Maggie said. "In forensic linguistics, that's what we look for. Clues in punctuation, word choice, spelling, syntactic structure, and so on. Remember Berkowitz? Jimmy Breslin called out his correct use of the semicolon. Was startled that the guy used it correctly. Little clues can have a big meaning. I'm saying very few people in the world know how to use that punctuation mark, let alone actually employ it in their writing. But it seems the chief does. Your note-writer does. It's another little bit of the kind of thing I look for."

"Because two people use the same stupid punctuation mark, you're ready to point a finger?"

"I could cite a case in which a murderer was snagged in part because a forensic linguist linked his consistent incorrect use of the apostrophe in contractions—*cant', wont', wouldn't'*—in both a ransom note and in the guy's everyday writing. It pointed the cops toward one of their suspects. That's what I'm all about. Just pointing a finger in the right direction. Another murderer was snared because of his use of commas and unique spacing in sentences. He tried to assume the identity of the woman he killed by writing hoax texts from her phone. But she never used punctuation the way he did."

"Evidence, Maggie. Hard evidence."

"That punctuation. Those clues helped nab the guys. They were presented in court. Don't discount it. And, now that I've seen his notes in the book and these Post-its, I see the writing style changes. Sometimes, it looks like a righty wrote them. Others, a lefty. You wanna know what that tells me? He's equally at home writing with either hand. Now going back, the bike note? Lefty. This last note? Righty. Am I making sense here?"

"Could. Don't know a thing about that."

"I do. Truly ambi people make up only about one percent. Chief's as close to ambi as I've ever seen. Like when he bats. Or throws."

"Yeah, well, not sure that proves anything."

Jackson picked up a pair of glasses laying on the table. "These are his," Jackson said. "Look."

Maggie held them. "The arm's connected with a straight pin. I'm thinking about that screw you found in the field. I know it's a long shot, but maybe some forensic examiner could link these glasses with the screw. You still have it?"

"Bagged. In evidence. But in the chief's defense, he said he'd never gone to where Heidi's bike was. He said it would be too traumatic."

"That's what he *said*."

"Right. Okay, let's keep moving. I'm checking out the bedroom," Jackson said.

Maggie stared at her phone, waiting for results of how many people use semicolons in their documents. "Only one in five thousand seventy-eight documents included one or more examples of semicolons," Maggie yelled. "The documents were randomly plucked from the internet."

"Good to know," Jackson said as Maggie joined him. "Chief talks about his girlfriend. Says he's working on getting her to meet us. She's real shy, he says."

Maggie checked the closet. "No women's clothes in here. No shoes, jeans, or sweaters. No dresses or blouses."

"Maybe she's a nudist," Jackson said.

"I'm thinking she's a phantom."

Maggie checked out the bathroom. "If his girlfriend lives here, she'd have a toothbrush, make-up, maybe a comb and brush. But . . . nada. You find his computer?"

"Haven't seen it. Maybe he uses an iPad and he took it with him."

As Maggie was looking at the books on his nightstand, she saw a thin computer lodged among them. "Found it," she said carefully taking note which book was on top and which below. It was sandwiched between *Helter Skelter* and *The Stranger Beside Me*. "Okay, let's see if this gets us anywhere."

"Don't know his password," Jackson said.

"If we're lucky, he left it on."

The screen saver was a blue sky and a calm ocean. Maggie clicked a file on the desktop and it opened. "No password needed," she said. "Let's take it to the living room."

After checking out a few files, Maggie said, "Nothing the least bit interesting. Fuck! Fuck! Fuck!"

"Don't ever want to say I told you so 'cause I think that's cruel, but . . ."

"Uh oh, almost no battery left."

Jackson looked for an outlet. "Odd, this thing's wonky," he said as he tried to plug in the computer. "Not an actual outlet."

"Whattaya mean?"

"It's not aligning right. Can't plug in anything."

Jackson easily pulled it from the wall. "Well, well, well. Looks like we got us something." He easily removed a shiplap board from around the fake outlet and reached in. "Jesus Christ," he said taking out a large plastic bag. "Whattaya suppose this is?"

Maggie opened it. Dozens of photos fell out. "What the hell. Why would he be collecting . . . Heidi!" Maggie screamed, pointing to one of the photos. "That's Heidi."

"Heidi?" Jackson said, his voice barely audible.

"This girl!" Maggie said, pointing. "I swear that's Heidi. I've stared at her picture in the newspaper hundreds of times a day. Crazy me, but I kept thinking maybe I'd see her on the street. Remember how they found Elizabeth Smart? Several people told police they thought they saw Elizabeth's kidnapper, whose photo had been all over the news, out in the public with a girl—who turned out to be Elizabeth—and a woman. Elizabeth had been missing for nine months at the time."

"There's gotta be an explanation for this," Jackson said.

"Right. He's into child porn and doesn't want anyone to come across the pics, if anyone actually ever comes here," Maggie said. "Besides us."

"Look, just because—"

"Fuck your damn one hundred percent. I'm telling you that's Heidi. These are porn. What's the chief doing with a picture of Heidi nude? And these others? Is being a damn pervert part of a male requirement of living in this great state of ours? Is it? What's up with you guys?" Maggie stared intently at Jackson. "Wanna answer that?"

"Look, you don't know . . . now's not the time, I'll tell you this and then you'll shut the hell up. The pics in my backpack? One's of Maud, of course. The other? She's the one that got away. You know what that means? I was lead detective. This young girl was raped, killed. On my watch. We never found who did it. I've been obsessed. All day, every day. Why my marriage broke up. Why I was kicked off the force. Satisfied? So drop it. We're on Heidi now so keep your shit together."

"Jeez. So what's the pic on your—"

"On my phone? Is that what you're asking? Don't you ever, ever, ever look at my things again. Never! That's a picture of when we found her. The end."

"Oh Jackson, I'm—"

"Focus, damn it!" Jackson banged his fist into the wall. "We're here to see if the chief had anything to do with Heidi. Heidi. Heidi."

"Yes, right, I know—"

"You're fucking impossible," he said.

"I know that, too," Maggie said softly.

"Okay, so the chief knows Heidi, that's a fact. But right now, I can't think of a good reason why he'd have that particular picture. Actually I can't think straight at all."

"And all the other photos? A reasonable explanation for these, too? Look. Guns are lining the wall in every picture. Where were these taken?"

"No idea. Chief's into guns. Says he does target practice every night. That's why he chose this place. But where the hell does he keep them? Not a single one in the house."

Maggie went into the kitchen. "I'm checking the fridge. The stove. Maybe he stores 'em in there." Jackson followed her, peered into the cupboards, and then looked out the back window.

"Whattaya suppose that is?" he asked, pointing to a structure back in the woods.

Deep between dense trees, Maggie could barely make out something. "Maybe a neighbor's place?"

"Says he's got no neighbors," Jackson said. "Okay, new plan. I'm going to check it out. You're heading to the truck. Eyes and ears peeled. If you see someone coming, drive around back. I'll hear you, and we'll bomb out that way."

"Roger that, partner."

"This time, listen to me. I'm dead serious."

Maggie watched Jackson as he went toward the heavily wooded area. For a quick minute, she contemplated listening to him and getting back in the truck.

"Abandoned?" Maggie asked softly.

"Oh for Chrissake. You're the worst."

"We'll clear the place quicker this way," Maggie said.

"You make me sick."

Maggie eyed the empty walls. "No guns here."

"Shut the hell up. I'm begging you, go to the truck."

Jackson shined his flashlight along the walls. "Where's the damn light switch? No electricity? Not a goddamn thing here," he said as he scanned the room. "No guns. No nothing. Seems totally abandoned. Looks like we struck out. Maybe there's a shed somewhere else on the property."

As Maggie walked across the room, she tripped. "Fucking boards."

"For Chrissake. Can't you even—"

"Come here," Maggie said kneeling. "Something strange, no?"

Jackson knelt and easily pried the loose board up. Then he yanked up a few boards around it.

"The place is old. The boards are warped," Jackson said. "But there's a handle here. What the hell?"

Jackson pulled the handle hard, and several boards popped off all in one piece. Shining his light down, he saw a set of steep stairs. "Probably just an old trap door. Leading to an abandoned cellar."

"Makes sense," Maggie said.

"But I'm going down. Maybe this is where he keeps his guns."

"But why's he hiding them?"

"No idea. Look, if you're not going back to the truck, at least stay outside and keep watch. If you see someone coming, we can still get outta here before anyone makes it down the driveway." He walked close to Maggie. "This is not negotiable."

"Got it. I'm on it."

Jackson started down the stairs as Maggie went to the door.

"Found 'em!" he yelled. "Must be a hundred guns lining the walls."

"Well, at least that's settled."

Maggie stayed put upstairs, eyes peeled on the driveway. After a few minutes, she yelled, "You coming up or what?"

"Oh my god," Jackson said. "Oh my god."

"What? What is it?"

"Come down. Now! This second. I think I—"

"Wait!" Maggie yelled. "I hear someone coming."

"Get down here. Now!"

Using her cell to see the way, she quickly went down. Jackson was standing at the foot of the stairs. He leaned close and whispered, "Go to the far corner. I heard something. Murmurs. Crying. Something."

"Not a rat? Don't tell me. I'm deathly afraid of rats. I can't do this."

"Go! It's not a rat. It's not an animal. I'm going back up. Pray it's not Murray."

THIRTY

Maggie shined the light along the walls, the ceiling, the floors. Guns and more guns. The place stunk of . . . Maggie wasn't sure of exactly what, but it was more than a combo of must and mold. Something really rotten. A rat's nest?

She took tiny steps to the corner that Jackson had pointed to, her legs wobbly with fear. She absolutely hated rats. Inching closer, she thought she saw something move—and backed up.

"Noooo," she heard. "Please, no."

Maggie froze. "No," she heard again.

Maggie got down on her hands and knees and crawled closer.

two figures
hugging
cuffed
shackled

She inched closer. "Oh my god. Oh. Oh." She crawled closer, tried to catch her breath, and got a good look. Two girls. "Heidi?" Maggie said softly. "Is that you?" Maggie recognized Heidi's huge brown eyes, thick eyebrows, high cheekbones, thin lips, and a deep cleft in her chin from the newspaper clippings.

Neither girl moved or said anything. Their eyes widened.

"I'm a friend of your daddy's. Mayor Hemphill. Is that your father?"
After a few seconds, Heidi nodded.

"You don't need to be afraid. I'm here to help you. I'm going to take you home." Maggie was speaking as calmly as she could, but her body was shaking. "We're going to get you out of here, okay?"

The girls continued to stare at her, silent and wide-eyed.

"I'm Maggie. Don't be afraid. Who's your friend? She's coming with us, too."

The girls leaned in closer to each other. "Ella," Heidi whispered.

"Hello, Ella," Maggie said. She wanted to embrace them both but was afraid that might frighten them.

Maggie had no idea what Ella once looked like, but now she resembled a drowning rat. She was filthy with matted hair. Her body was covered in dirt from the floor. For sure she hadn't bathed in weeks. Maybe months. And Heidi. Her once wavy blond hair was brown. Her "I Heart Florida" T-shirt had been replaced with a man's enormous undershirt. And she, too, was filthy.

"Your daddy can't wait to see you," Maggie said as she tried to figure out how to undo their cuffs. "My friend's upstairs. He knows exactly how we all get out of here. Do you want these things off, so we can go upstairs and then head home? I'll get him to give me a key and I'll be right back."

"Don't go," Heidi whispered. "Don't leave us."

"You're such a brave girl," Maggie said, touching her leg. "You daddy's going to be so proud of you!"

"The policeman," Ella said. "He said . . . he said . . . if I make a sound . . . he's gonna do that thing to me again. You know . . . get on top of me and—"

"Oh Ella, I promise he's never doing that again," Maggie said and felt she was going to throw up.

"He fed us from this." Heidi pointed to a dog bowl. "He took me here. It was Chief Murray. He was Daddy's friend. I was riding my bike and he said he'd get me to my lessons quicker if I went with him."

Heidi started crying.

"I left my bike. Got in the car."

"I'm so sorry," Maggie said. "But I'm going to get you out of here. Promise. We'll go upstairs and get in a truck and you'll be on your way home in no time. Trust me. Please. I'm going to yell to my friend, but I don't want to scare you, so get ready to hear a really loud voice. Okay?"

They looked at each other and nodded.

"Here goes. Jackson!" Maggie screamed. "Come. Here. Now."

"Can't."

"Heidi. She's here. And Ella. Her friend. Jackson! We need to get their cuffs off."

"Cuffs?" Jackson yelled down the stairs.

"Yes!"

"Jesus." Jackson threw down a set of keys. "These should work. Stay nice and quiet and don't come up till I say. Someone's on the road."

Maggie could hear him talking on the phone. ". . . your guys now, Breakwater . . . found . . . Hurry!"

The girls started crying.

"I'm going to get you out of these," Maggie said, fiddling with the key. "Hold on. Here goes." Maggie undid each of their handcuffs. The girls shook their wrists. Then she undid their shackles. "Don't get up yet. Just shake your hands and feet." The girls rubbed their wrists and ankles and tried to stand. Heidi was able to. Ella sank to her knees. Heidi sat back down with her.

"You're going to be okay," Maggie said. "Can I give you a hug?"

The girls clung to Maggie.

"Promise we're going home?" asked Heidi.

"Promise," Maggie said. "Where do you live, Ella?"

"I don't know," she said softly.

"We'll figure it out. Don't you worry."

"Ella's my best friend," Heidi said. "She's sixteen."

"I think I am," Ella said.

"We'll figure that out, too," Maggie said holding back tears.

"I'm coming down." Jackson came bounding down the steps. Seeing Maggie and the girls, he said softly, "I'm so glad we found you. My name's Jackson and I'm a detective so I can—"

"Don't let him come." Ella held on tight to Heidi.

"Oh, honey. He's a good man. I promise."

"Is he like the policeman?" Ella asked.

"No, sweetie, he's going to get you out of here."

"I've got a plan to get you both safely home, but you've got to do exactly as I say," Jackson said, gently.

"I have an idea," Maggie said. "Let's play a game. It'll get us all back outside and on our way home in no time. It's called Backwards, Forwards."

"I don't know that," Heidi said.

"That's okay. It goes like this. I say the words in a sentence backwards. You figure out what it means by saying it out loud the forwards way—the right way—and then do exactly what it says. Like for instance, if I say, 'upstairs go let's,' you say 'Let's go upstairs'—and off we go!"

"My daughter would love that game," Jackson said. "Her name's Maud. She's about your age."

"Is she here?" Ella asked.

"No. But maybe you'll meet her one day."

"Okay, listen carefully," Maggie said. "Up stand all let's."

"Let's all stand up!" Ella yelled.

"Perfect!"

Maggie and Heidi helped Ella stand.

"This one's going to take some concentration. 'Steps small twenty take.'"

"Take twenty small steps," Heidi said proudly. "Easy."

"Okay, but in which direction? Listen again. 'Stairs the of foot the to.'"

"To the foot," Ella began.

"Of the stairs," Heidi finished. "We're going to take twenty small steps to the foot of the stairs. This is fun."

"Together go let's," Maggie said as she stood between them, holding them steady with her arms under their shoulders.

"I love this," Heidi said.

"Go we stairs the up. All in steps fifteen," Maggie said.

"Up the stairs we go. Fifteen steps in all!" cried Ella.

"Go let's," said Maggie.

Jackson raced up and the girls followed more slowly. As they got closer to the top, Heidi said, "The light! My eyes!"

"You'll get used to it in a minute," Jackson said. "It's a bright and sunny day. Perfect for a drive home. Shield your eyes till you feel more comfortable. Now, I'm gonna give the game a try. Listen. Door front the to go."

"Go to the front door," the girls cried.

When they got to the door, Maggie said, "Okay, from now on, I'm going to say exactly what we do. No more backwards, forwards. It'll be easier—for me, anyway. So, let's wait here until—"

"I tell you when we run to my truck," Jackson said.

Jackson whispered to Maggie. "It's Murray's pickup. He's hanging halfway down the driveway, probably trying to figure out why my truck's in front of his house."

"What'll we do?" Maggie asked.

He turned to the girls and spoke softly, but forcefully. "In a minute, it'll be time to run. My truck's only a few feet away. I know you can do it. You are strong. Once you get inside, get down on the floor. Don't pick up your head—no matter what. Stay as still as you can, and I'll drive us away!"

"I can't run," Ella said.

"Maggie'll help you. No worries."

"Stomp your feet a few times," Maggie said to Ella. "Get the blood flowing. It'll make it easier when it's our time to run run run."

Ella stomped and took a few marching steps.

Heidi said, "I'm stomping, too."

"Good job," Maggie said. "Now you hold onto me," Maggie told Ella.

"Truck's moving slowly," Jackson said. "I'm going out to open the truck's back door. Then I'm going to say, run, and that's when you race inside and lie down on the floor. Can you do that?"

"I can," Heidi said.

"Me too," Ella said. The girls held hands.

After a minute, Jackson said, "Run, run, run!"

All three piled on top of one another on the floor of Jackson's truck.

Jackson was already in the driver's seat and had turned the engine on. "Hold on tight. This is gonna be one helluva wild ride!"

Before the truck moved, Maggie heard a pop. Then another. She felt the front of the truck lowering. She lifted her head enough to see a black pickup coming toward them. It had a crushed passenger side door and tinted windows. "Son of a fucking bitch," she said.

"Cover them, Maggie," Jackson said. "Backup oughta be here soon."

Maggie saw Jackson draw his gun, open the door, and get out.

She whispered a line from *High Noon*:

In her mind, she substituted "us" for "me." She knew Jackson would want to be a hero for them.

THIRTY-ONE

The next morning, after the FBI had been alerted about what had gone down, they called a meeting. The cops from Olemeda, all of Breakwater's guys, Maggie, and several members of the press were invited, and all showed up before the 8 a.m. start.

When everyone was settled, FBI director Amos Addison of the central Florida region said, "As you know, we are now a part of the investigation with continuing input from the Olemeda and Wellingford PDs, as well as from one Maggie Moore. Before I go any further, Ms. Moore, I'd like to personally thank you and acknowledge the huge role you played in this unbelievable story of evil. Pure evil perpetrated by one of our supposed finest is nearly incomprehensible. Ms. Moore spent several hours with our team filling us in on exactly what went down. I'll go over the details with you now because Detective Jackson, unfortunately, cannot speak for himself at this time."

Addison reported how Jackson had found the girls, how Maggie had comforted them and got them to the truck by playing a game of Backwards, Forwards.

"Before Jackson could start up the pickup," Addison said, "according to Maggie's precise statement of events, several shots had been fired and the truck was slowly sinking. Jackson got out, gun drawn, and many more shots were fired. At that point in time, Maggie didn't know exactly what was happening. She was covering the girls in the back of the truck. Then, everything went quiet. Maggie said she wondered if Jackson was dead. Or the chief. Or both. Or she thought maybe the chief would be coming for her and the girls."

Addison paused to drink some water.

"And then?" Pickens asked. "What happened?"

"Then, Breakwater's guys showed."

Stopping to look around the room, Addison said, "A huge shout-out to you guys. Job well done. As it happened, both men were on the ground, bleeding profusely. They were immediately taken to the hospital."

"How's Jackson? The girls?" asked Pickens. "And the chief?"

"I'll start with the girls. They were checked out and treated and, after a long discussion, it was decided that it was best for them to go to the mayor's house with two social workers specially assigned."

"Thank Jesus," Evans said, crossing himself.

"Sad to have to report, however, Jackson's in a coma," Addison said.

"Will he, you know?" asked Evans.

"The doctors are hopeful. He was shot three times. Touch and go. I'll conclude by saying the chief has been arrested and is being treated for his wounds. Jackson managed some perfect shots, placed precisely where they would take the chief down, but not out. Okay, I'd like to thank you for your attention. We've all got to get back to work."

"Back here at three," Gutierrez said. "We have tons to do." Then he looked at Maggie. "Thank you again," he said. "We all owe you so much."

The entire room stood up and clapped.

For the first time in days, Maggie managed a small smile. "All in the line of duty," she said.

THIRTY-TWO

"It's nothing short of a miracle," the mayor said when Gutierrez dropped Maggie off at the mayor's house. "What you went through. How you and Jackson got the girls out of there. I wasn't a religious man before this, but now I'm on my knees thanking the good Lord every hour of the day. For Heidi to be safe. A true miracle. And her friend Ella. Ohmygosh. What that girl has been through. What both girls have been through. But they are alive!"

Maggie and the mayor hugged for a long time. "I can't even find the words," he said. "I'd almost lost hope. The days Heidi was gone were the darkest ones of my life."

"But she's here now. Safe with you," Maggie said.

"I've never been happier. Oh, this is Jenny. And that's Viv. They've been just wonderful."

"Hi, nice to meet you," Maggie said.

"We made a bunch of sandwiches," Jenny said holding a large tray. She handed the girls a plate and sat with them at the table. Heidi and Ella moved close to each other.

"I think you're going to like these," Viv said. "Everyone loves peanut butter and jelly, right?" she asked.

"The girls've been talking to Jenny and Viv," the mayor said. "Child psychologists will join the team tomorrow. They're getting the very best help possible. I'll do anything."

"They're in good hands," Maggie said.

"They were evaluated at the hospital, and they suffered a lot. A program is being set up to deal with both their physical and psychological issues."

"Please tell me, Maggie, how is Jackson? I'm praying for him as hard as I ever prayed in my life. What's the latest?"

"As of this morning," Maggie said, "the doctors are guardedly optimistic. All his vitals are good. There's been no swelling in his brain. They're hopeful he'll come out of the coma. But you never know."

"Is there anything I can do for you?" the mayor asked.

"Knowing the girls are safe is more than enough."

"I'm not letting them out of my sight," the mayor said.

"You saved us," Heidi said to Maggie.

"I love you," Ella said.

Maggie hugged the girls. When they broke apart, Maggie saw that Ella's shirt sleeve had ridden up, revealing a tattoo on her lower arm. Maggie took a long look. "Ella, honey, what's that on your arm? It's . . . it's beautiful."

"I got that a long time ago," she said.

Maggie read the ink on Ella's arm, *Know when to fold 'em.*

Know when to fold 'em.

"Hey, how'd you do that?" Ella asked. "No one can read it. Unless they've got a mirror."

"Where . . . honey, where'd you get it?" Maggie asked, trying to keep her voice steady.

"Me and my girlfriend, we got the same one. She said it was from her favorite song. We'd sing it a lot together. The leader would never have let us get a tattoo. He never even let us go outside the compound."

"Leader?" Maggie asked, rubbing her lip where she'd bitten it hard.

"He saw us writing that way. Said it was evil."

"What leader?" asked Maggie.

"Mr. Kennon. But when we escaped, we got it done," Ella said. "One of the older kids we hung out with took us to this tattoo place. It was a fun day."

"Escaped?" Maggie looked at the mayor. "Do you know about this?"

"They told me last night. I can fill you in," he said. "Why don't you girls go out with Jenny and Viv. Your bikes are in the driveway. Get some nice fresh air."

"Yay," cried Heidi, "bike ride!"

THIRTY-THREE

Three days after the shootout, Maggie was still sitting beside Jackson in his hospital room, having left him only twice—once for the meeting at the precinct and the other time to see the girls at the mayor's. Meanwhile, she'd been taking only aspirin for her splitting headache and aching body. She swore she'd stay sober, without pills of the wrong kind and without booze, for a full month. A concession to Jackson.

"Of course, you want to know how Heidi is," Maggie said to Jackson's unresponsive face as he lay perfectly still. "And Ella." She'd already told him the story but hoped that this time he'd have a response—a tightening of his lips, rapid eye blinking, anything to signal he could hear her.

"So," she began as she sat at the foot of his bed, "I'll start with Ella. She told me that she and Sky had been planning their escape for weeks. They'd figured out the best time to slip out was while everyone was working in the gardens. When the day came, they made their way out with no one seeing them.

"You with me, Jackson? I'll take that as a yes. They ran and ran until they felt they couldn't go any farther. Then they started looking around and saw this town they'd never seen before. They found a place under a bridge where other kids were sleeping. No mamas or papas. They were on their own. Boy did it feel good. Ella said it was the most fun they'd had for a long time. But then, the worst thing happened. Sky got caught. While Ella was out getting food for the other kids, some guys came, grabbed Sky—and that was the last Ella saw of her. From the description the kids gave Ella when she got back, she knew they were Kennon's guys, from the compound."

Maggie walked around the bed and touched Jackson's cheek. "Here's the really sad part. Ella kept hoping Sky would come back. That somehow, she'd find a way. Ella stayed under the bridge with the other kids, hoping and praying. But day after day, she said, no Sky.

"Then one day, Ella told me, a real friendly older guy, a cop, showed up. At first, everyone was scared to death of him. They thought he'd arrest them. But he was so nice. He brought them food, cola, candy. After spending some time with them, he pointed to Ella and said he'd come to take her home."

Maggie sat back down. "You know who the cop turned out to be of course. So happens that for years, the chief had been trolling the area on his fishing trips to Aunt Bertha's. This one time, he had picked out Ella. He told her it was his mission to save as many girls as he could, one at a time. He said that's what policemen do. He asked her what her favorite food was and said he'd buy it for her. Ella figured she'd go with him—why not—especially since her best friend, Sky, was gone. But instead of taking her home, this quote, unquote kind and friendly cop took her to his house and down to that disgusting cellar. He's kept her for over a year, the girls figured, because he took her one day right before Christmas, and another Christmas has already passed.

"Okay," Maggie continued, "there's more. You're not going to believe this part. You're still listening, right? So, when Ella hugged me at the mayor's I saw it. What did I see, you might ask? Well, I'll tell you. I saw a tattoo running along her forearm. No big deal, you might say, yes? Well, it was a very big deal. A huge deal. The ink was in mirror image. I know at this point, if you were sitting across from me at the diner, you'd be breaking into my story and reminding me that I told you I can write in mirror image. My one and only trick. Remember? Of course you do. But did I tell you that I taught mirror-image writing to Lucy? I think I did. It was our secret code. When I read Ella's ink without pausing, Ella was dumbfounded. She said nobody but Sky knew how to read that. Sky? I asked. Who's Sky? Ella said that Mr. Kennon gave them all new names. Sky used to be Lucy. Are you still with me here?"

Maggie looked for a sign that Jackson was hearing her.

"Now here's the kicker. Did you know that the chief had been asked to leave two previous jobs in other states? One was because he was caught watching kiddie porn at his desk after he'd been caught before multiple times. And the other because he'd acted *inappropriately* with several girls on the lacrosse team he'd been coaching. Parents had complained. Neither police department had pressed charges. That great blue wall of silence. They simply let him go, like they do in the Catholic Church. Jackson?

"So I know you've been waiting to hear about Heidi. Here goes. Seems the chief must've been stalking her 'cause for sure he knew her schedule. He must've pulled up beside her as she was biking to martial arts. Of course, she recognized him. Daddy's friend. He told her he could get her to her lesson faster than her bike. She popped right in his car. He said he'd get her bike after he dropped her off. And, well, you know where he took her."

Maggie put a washcloth under the water and placed it on his forehead.

"Making sure you stay cool. It's important. Okay, so you might be wondering about the chief. He's recovering. Seems you managed some perfectly placed shots—down but not dead—so now he'll have to face the music. And I bet you want to know why in God's name he put me on Heidi's case when *he* was the goddamn perp. Here's my theory. He thinks he's smarter than anyone else—and he needs to prove it. Once I helped solved the Louisiana case using linguistics, he needed to prove to himself that he could outsmart me. So he left that note on Heidi's bike. Of course, he didn't have to. He could've just taken her, but he was pitting his brain against mine. Plus, he was staying close to me so he'd know what kinds of clues I was getting from his writings, and then hoping to stay one step ahead. Kinda like what Michael Corleone said in *The Godfather Part II*:

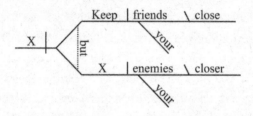

Not that I was the enemy, exactly, but you know what I'm getting at, right?

"Okay, moving on, we're going to switch topics now, okay? I've been speaking with Ginny a lot. Your lawyer is now my lawyer, too. After she'd done some research and interviewed Brittany and Ashley, she set up a meeting with President O'Malley. She laid out all the facts she'd assembled and told him she'd be bringing a case against Professor Ditmire. And what do you think happened? First, O'Malley put Ditmire on leave till all this gets resolved. A trial is set for September. Now I know exactly why you think Ginny's your guardian angel. Ditshit is in deep shit. Do you like that repetition of *shit*? Has a nice ring to it. Almost poetic."

Maggie looked at Jackson's expressionless face.

"Oh, and O'Malley offered me a teaching position after I graduate. Or, if I want, they'll help me find a PhD program that fits my needs. What do you think? Which would you advise me to do? So happens, I decided against both. Want to know what I'm going to do?"

Maggie sat back down on his bed and leaned in very close. "As soon as you're up and operating, I figure we're going to solve another missing person case together. We make a pretty good team. You hear? And I bet you know who we're going to be looking for. Of course you do. You started all this in motion. You found where Lucy had been, where Luna is, and where we both believe Lucy still is. I'm thinking we need to investigate that little concrete thing you saw with your amazing eyesight in the back of the compound.

"Now listen carefully. I've turned over a new leaf. I will follow orders from now on. I'll do exactly as you say, like a good partner. I promise. Will you take me on?" Maggie looked for a sign. None. "I'll take that as a yes. Which brings me to this."

Maggie brought out Jackson's clothes from a narrow locker in the hospital room. She took out his hat, straightened it out, placed a deep crease in the brim, and turned up the sides. Then she put it on.

"Kinda like Smiley's, wouldn't you say?"

No response.

"You can tell me later what you think."

Maggie brushed his cheek with her lips.

"Can you hear me?" she whispered. "Can you wiggle a finger? Or blink?"

Nothing.

"Later is okay."

Maggie cupped his cheeks in her hands and said quietly, "Maudie is coming to visit as soon as school's out. I'm thinking we could bake her a Lane cake. We've been emailing each other, thanks to Ginny."

Maggie stared at Mr. Commanding Presence and remembered the last sentence in *To Kill a Mockingbird*. "Listen to this," she said. "I took a little poetic license and changed a few words, but for sure you'll know where it's from":

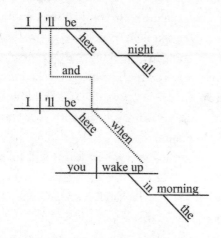

AUTHOR'S NOTE

I am grateful to the authors of the lines Maggie so expertly quoted and/ or diagrammed. Where would we be without Proust's *Remembrance of Things Past: Swann's Way* or "The Gambler," or, for that matter, "Casey at the Bat"? I dare not think about it.

Further thanks go to Elia Kazan (*On the Waterfront*); Zora Neale Hurston (*Their Eyes Were Watching God*); Quentin Tarantino (*Pulp Fiction*); Gertrude Stein ("Poetry and Grammar"); Yip Harburg ("Over the Rainbow"); Gabriel Garcia Márquez (*Love in the Time of Cholera*); Bob Dylan ("Things Have Changed" and "Buckets of Rain"); Ernest Thayer ("Casey at the Bat"); Robert Browning ("The Faultless Painter"); Joel and Ethan Coen (*Fargo*); Bram Stoker (*Dracula*); Toni Morrison (*Sula*); Joan Didion (*The Year of Magical Thinking*); Michael Ondaatje (*The English Patient*); Jodi Picoult (*Nineteen Minutes*); Don Schlitz ("The Gambler"); Margaret Mitchell (*Gone with the Wind*); C. S. Lewis (*A Grief Observed*); Sally Field (1985 Academy Award Best Actress acceptance speech); Harper Lee (*To Kill a Mockingbird*); David Allan Coe ("Jack Daniel's, If You Please"); Hunter S. Thompson (*Fear and Loathing in Las Vegas*); L. Frank Baum (*The Wizard of Oz*); Jane Austin (*Pride and Prejudice*); Tim Dorsey (*Pineapple Brigade*); Joseph Heller (*Catch-22*); William Broyles (*Apollo 13*); Mark Twain (*Pudd'nhead*

Wilson); Carl Foreman (*High Noon*); Francis Ford Coppola and Mario Puzo (*The Godfather Part II*); and Kurt Vonnegut (*Slaughterhouse-Five*).

If Maggie were the summing-up type, she'd probably be diagramming this line from Kurt Vonnegut's *Slaughterhouse-Five*:

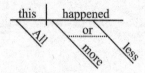

ACKNOWLEDGMENTS

Flash nonfiction:

Kim purchased a puppy but while walking the rambunctious pooch, Kim broke her ankle. Knowing she wouldn't be able to care for the pup for months, she called around to find someone who might adopt her.

Enter Susan, who had lost her beloved dog Sasha a few months earlier. Back and forth, back and forth—and Susan adopted Ellie!

In the course of the back and forth, Susan asked Kim what she did for a living. "I'm an agent, basically of crime novels."

Susan said: "My friend just completed a crime novel."

I am the friend who sent the novel to Kim, who thought it was a fit for their agency, who sent it to Anne-Lise, president of the Philip G. Spitzer Literary Agency, who took me on as a client, who sent it to the extraordinary and legendary Sara Nelson, Vice President and Executive Editor at HarperCollins, who acquired it.

And that's the true story of how *Wordhunter* came to be published. If not for Ellie . . .

Deepest thanks to Anne-Lise Spitzer, Kim Lombardini, and Sara Nelson, all of whom believed in this book from the get-go. Their enthusiasm, support, and suggestions made my sole abiding dream since I was thirteen come true.

I'm indebted to my friends who encouraged me through the years as I wrote and rewrote and rewrote: Susan Reed, Patty McCormick, Dale Grant, Kathleen Boyes, Louise Reiner, Lois Markham. And a very special thank you to Andrea Chapin for her always insightful comments.

For asking the perfect questions and offering expert advice, my thanks to Alexander Grabie, MA in Forensic Linguistics; Heidi Scovel, expert at sentence diagramming; and for the incredible work done by the dedicated people at HarperCollins: Edie Astley, assistant editor; Stacey Fischkelta, production editorial manager; and Kim Daly, copyeditor.

Finally and without adequate words to express my thanks . . .

Jess and Alex,

Quite simply, this book would never have been written without you. Full stop. End of story.

Love you beyond.

ABOUT THE AUTHOR

Stella Sands is the bestselling author of six true crime books: *Baby-Faced Butchers*, *The Dating Game Killer*, *Behind the Mask*, *Murder at Yale*, *Wealthy Men Only*, and *The Good Son*, and has appeared on many television shows, including *People Magazine Investigates*, ABC's *20/20*, and several *Investigation Discovery* shows. She is also the author of a children's book, *Odyssea*, as well as many educational books. She served as the editor in chief of the award-winning magazine *Kids Discover* for nineteen years. She lives in Sag Harbor, New York.